Comanche Moon

Plainsman Series

Book 3

Simon Fairfax

Comanche Moon

Also by Simon Fairfax

Also by Simon Fairfax

The Deal Series

A Deadly Deal

A Deal too far

A Deal with the Devil

A Deal on ice

A Knight and a Spy -road to Agincourt Series

A Knight and a Spy 1410

A Knight and a Spy 1411

A Knight and a Spy 1412

A Knight and a Spy 1413

A Knight and a Spy 1414

A Knight and a Spy 1415

The Plainsman Series

Law of the Gun

Making of a Lawman

Comanche Moon

Published by Corinium Associates Ltd.

A CIP catalogue of this book is available from the British Library

ISBN: 978-1-7391470-8-2

simonfairfaxauthor@gmail.com

www.simonfairfax.com

Chapter One

The day started early for Nate. He had bedded down in his suggan by a stream and risen early. Throughout the morning he brush popped the new valley that he had bought from one of his neighbors who had given up after four hard years of fighting the west Texas weather – a climate that was one of the roughest known to man. It was a harsh environment and not everyone was built to cope with all it could throw at them. It was harder too when the steader had a young family and a wife who had been used to the more civilized environment further east. The war had brought many such families west in search of a new life away from the horrors of the last few years, all of them keen to make a new start until the realities set in.

The mare he rode was a great cutting horse, a tobiano paint with good lines and short coupled. She wasn't much more than 14 3" he estimated, but she floated across the terrain and moved with exceptional grace, so much so that his crew had nicknamed her Dancer in honor of her abilities.

Sometimes he thought she had more cow in her than horse, as even now she spotted one of the small gather of ten steers make an attempt to break away while Nate was herding them into the wash he had been using as a makeshift corral. Before he had time to even nudge his spurred boot to her side she shot off from a gentle walk to a full lope, coming into the errant animal just behind its shoulder, barging and biting it at the poll.

The steer snorted in disgust, trying to bring its wide spread of needlepointed horns to bear, but the cutting pony was far too savvy and closed in tightly, giving no leeway for the animal to turn its massive shoulders and swing the lethal armament in Nate's direction. The steer got the message and turned away snorting to join the others who were about to enter the entrance to the wash. It was about a mile long and five hundred yards wide and was fed by a small stream that splashed down off the granite mesa to disappear into an underground gulley after creating a natural pond that ensured good grass, even in the dry of late fall.

The last of the stragglers went in, kicking high with their hind legs as Nate larruped and hollered at them, slapping his lariat down on his chaps and on the quarters of the final steer. He put Dancer at the entrance and pulled the thorn scrub back to close off their escape. Remounting inside the thorn fence he rode the short distance to the second line of barricade, a rough line of raw pine rails, still seeping resin from where he'd cut them a day ago. Throwing out a loop he pulled one of the rails back, not daring to be afoot among the wild cattle, and dallied it around the horn as Dancer pulled back, opening the gap for the new arrivals to join the others that were already cropping the rich grass within. Only when they were all through did he dismount, replace the rails and tie them with pigging thong. He stepped back and raised his hat to wipe his brow, brushing back the sun-streaked blond hair, a smile upon his face to show that he was pleased with his efforts.

"We're getting there, girl. We'll have a herd to be proud of soon," he said, patting the horse's neck and reaching to lift his canteen and take a long drink of water. He knew he was not the best cowboy on the plains, but he was getting better. There were some who were just naturals with cattle and a rope, and he knew he was not one of them, but his skill lay in organizing a drive and understanding all the qualities needed in a trail boss.

Nate pulled the thorn fence back in place, remounted Dancer and set off west. He had ridden this newly acquired piece of range only a few times, but he remembered a creek bed due west of where he was that offered shade and a shale crossing. Like most men out here, he'd developed an inbuilt memory for terrain and landscape at a time when few formal maps existed. His days as a soldier had told him that such knowledge could often be the difference between life and death, and he had already started making rough sketches of the land, mountains, rivers, creeks, and mesas that covered the extent of his land – Carson Valley, he'd named it, after the young family he had bought it from.

He moved steadily westward, noting the country and looking for any sign of cattle that may have grouped and moved through to seek shelter in the scrub brush, making them difficult to round up and brand. He was dressed in thick chaps against the thorns and scrub, and although he disliked them he had attached tapaderos to his stirrups to offer greater protection against the vicious thorns and wildlife. He had seen a foot turn infected by thorns and wanted no part of it. Doctors were a rare commodity out here.

The trail meandered along the line of an old riverbed before opening out into a small valley of rich lush pasture divided by a creek about twenty feet wide. The banks were laid out in steps where the water had eroded the soil with the passage of time. Mexican buckeye lined the banks, fighting for space between willows and huge live oaks that spread their great canopies outwards giving shade and protection to all beneath. The ford that Nate sought was half a mile away and would be a good place to brew some coffee and seek shade from the midday sun that was throwing some fierce heat even in the fall.

But even as he was thinking of resting through the heat of the day, the pastoral scene was shattered by the sound of war cries coming from around the next oxbow out of sight. Whoops and cries of anger and anguish cut through the air, along with the occasional bark of gunshots. Nate pulled his Spencer .56 from the leather boot and pushed Dancer into a fast lope, jacking the lever as he did so and pulling the hammer to half cock.

The little mare leapt at the chance for speed, bunching her hindquarters as she changed pace, her rider's excitement telegraphing to her through seat and reins. They covered the few hundred yards quickly as the shouts of war became clearer. Nate sat down deeply and thrust his legs forward, and the mare skidded to halt just out of sight of the conflict that was taking place around the next break in the brush. He was expecting to see settlers being set upon by Indians and did not wish to rush in and turn himself from rescuer to victim without first sizing up the situation. He was glad that he'd done so, because the sight before him was something he had never witnessed before: there were two distinct groups of Indians and they were fighting each other. Shielded by a thick clump of black cherry he watched, unsure of what to do – if indeed anything, other than get away fast.

The smaller group on his side of the creek were being attacked by a larger group who were painted for war, whooping as they ran forward on foot, armed largely with lances and bows, each jumping from cover to cover, looking to overwhelm the smaller party who were clearly taken by surprise. He saw that the smaller group had squaws with them, shielded by the warriors who were struggling to defend the position where they had been ambushed at the crossing. Above them, under the shelter of a wooded copse, more of the raiding party were catching them in a crossfire of arrows and single shot Springfields, poorly aimed but nevertheless taking their toll upon the defenders.

Even as he watched and made to move away and leave the Indians to settle their own war, Nate saw two young bucks, deep set and strong, spring forward over shallow boulders to close in upon two of the squaws. Rightly or wrongly, this decided it for him by appealing to his sense of honor. The younger woman drew a knife, promising to sell her life dearly, her left hand outstretched in a claw as she raked down with the knife in her right to fend off the grasping hand of the attacking warrior. The point grazed his arm, at which he slapped her hard across the face in anger and pain. Driving the hilt of his knife into her jaw, she reeled back stunned and dropped, legs buckling. That did it.

I can't let this happen, whether they be Indian or White, Nate thought.

He raised the Spencer to his shoulder in a flowing movement of long practice, pulled the hammer to full cock, and sighted on the Indian grabbing the squaw. In the periphery of his vision he saw the other warrior being attacked by the older squaw. They clearly wanted them alive, he thought, and it was pretty obvious why. More attackers appeared, spurred on by the success of their braves.

You're a fool, Nate, this will get you killed, he thought as he lined up and fired, knowing with the instinct of any marksman that it was a hit. The brave's head exploded as the heavy .56 caliber bullet struck home with devastating effect. His brother in arms looked around surprised, as none of the defending party had firearms. Nate halfcocked quickly, worked the lever, ejected the shell and sent another bullet flying outwards, dropping the second brave. The others halted in surprise, looking to where the telltale pall of black powder smoke gave away his position. Dancer stood stock still, well trained, inured to the sound of gunfire. Nate worked the lever and hammer as fast as he could, judging distance and time as attackers turned to face the new threat and began to run swiftly toward him. Twice more he fired, hitting his target each time at such short range. Then an arrow flew past his head as he moved to reload, partially obscured in the black cloud of gun smoke that surrounded him. He span Dancer on her quarters, seeking the shelter of rocks away from the stream which would offer him a good vantage point. She responded at once, spinning away like the cutting horse she was, driving upwards to the rocky outcrop behind which Nate dropped from the saddle, now mostly hidden from view.

Again he chose a target, this time in the woods behind the defending tribe as the warrior with the cumbersome Springfield had managed to get it reloaded and was about to fire. The man flew backwards, his face a shattered mask of red. Then more whoops came from below, where two more men had targeted the young squaw. One of the defending braves ran up, thrusting his war lance to catch the attacker full in the chest. As he twisted to withdraw it, an arrow flew from the copse to skewer his shoulder. Two more braves now appeared, running to the aid of the warrior holding the girl.

Nate did not hesitate. He bounded back onto Dancer, thrust the Spencer into the boot, slipped the thong off his Colt and charged down the hill towards the squaw without thought or reason, crying his own rebel yell of the Confederacy. Three braves turned in unison, the one holding the stunned girl by her arm reacting first, drawing back his arm and whipping it forward to let his tomahawk fly as Nate was but twenty feet away. Nate's right hand was a blur, and the Navy Colt appeared as if by magic, spitting fire as the chest of the brave flowered red. Twice more Nate aimed, killing two more, spinning Dancer on a dime as she skidded in over the scree. The remaining brave ran, his eyes wide with fear, leaving the squaw dazed. Then as suddenly as it had started, it went eerily quiet as the attackers melted away, leaving their dead behind.

Nate looked around, his eyes wide in anger, seeking new targets, especially any who might be still hidden in the copse above. He dropped down from Dancer at the squaw's side, at which she ran away in fear toward her own people, of which just six braves remained alive, including the one struck by the arrow. Then there was a sudden tension, with no one knowing how to react.

To the Indians, any white man was the enemy – especially in Texas, where they had been betrayed time after time over the decades, with treaties broken and massacres perpetrated under a flag of truce. He saw the warriors draw the strings of their bows, unsure of whether he was friend or foe. Then on the ridge above the bank leading down to them, horses appeared as another band of Indians became visible through the dust raised by their mounts. Each carried a lance decorated with feathers as they rode down the incline to shouts of joy from the men in front of Nate. Seeing the scene in front of them, they surrounded Nate, their lances levelled. Seeing no way out he holstered his Colt and tried to relax, saying nothing and remaining calm.

The newcomers were gesticulating loudly and pointing in his direction as Nate began to silently curse himself for a chivalrous fool. He could easily get himself killed in this tense situation. Then the squaw ran forward to the head of the new arrivals. He was a young brave with scalps hanging from his lance, sitting his horse as though part of it and staring impassively at Nate, neither anger nor sympathy showing upon his stoic features. He looked down at the squaw who now stood beside him as she rattled off a fast flurry of words, pointing and nodding at Nate.

The leader of the new band looked down and asked a question which she answered quickly and without hesitation. He looked again at Nate and grunted a command to the two braves either side of him. One beckoned Nate to ride forward to the leader. He nodded and nudged Dancer forward. As he closed with the leader he took in the high cheekbones and the slightly slanted eyes. The man's black hair was loose and flowed to his shoulders, held by a band with two eagle feathers at the back. His torso was bare, save for a vest of porcupine quills, and his skin gleamed. Nate smelled the sickly rancid smell of antelope fat. His legs were clad in traditional leggings and breechclout, a broad belt at his waist supporting a knife and tomahawk. He held his lance with the end resting upon the top of one moccasined foot.

Nate said nothing but made the universal sign for friend that he'd learned from Cherokee scouts in the war. He motioned that he wanted peace and came as a friend, not an enemy.

The chief, if that was what he was, nodded, pleased with the response. Then struggling with the words, he spoke in English, his tone guttural. "How are you called?"

"Nate Carlton."

"Why you help *Numunuu,* a white man, Texas ride plenty?"

Nate recognized the Indian name for the Comanche nation. He knew that the language of the Comanches was the *lingua franca* of all the plains tribes, yet like most white men he had little knowledge of it, so he responded in slow English, phrasing his words in a way that he thought the Indians would understand.

"It was my honor. The squaw was to be taken, I could not let that happen," he said simply.

The chief gave him a hard stare, then said: "You come now, with us."

At this the two mounted braves crowded in behind him. It was a command, not an invitation, he realised. A cold chill ran through him despite the outward sign of friendship. He did not know what fate awaited him at the Indian camp. The dead were loaded onto horses and the braves bounded upon their mounts.

On the ground they had appeared less than impressive, not as big or well-muscled as their attackers, yet once mounted they took on an identity all of their own, becoming as one with their horses. Nate, ever an admirer of good horseflesh, noted that they were nearly all Paint Tobianos with a wide variety of markings. The leader's mount was no different, a short coupled mare with a handsome head that was on the 'right way'. They moved off at an easy pace, the two squaws mounted in the middle of the line with Nate riding just behind the chief.

Chapter Two

Cresting a rise in an area Nate had never traveled to before, a secluded valley with a small river running through it appeared before them. They passed a herd of buffalo along the way, which caused much excitement amongst the Comanches as they rode by.

The camp was laid out along the river in lines of tipis, with hundreds of horses grazing around it, looked after by the young *tivitsi* horse herders who all looked up with great interest at the new arrivals. Along the river on wooden racks hides of buffalo were drying and large fires were smoking the meat that would be stored and saved against the forthcoming winter. It was a sight that had a certain majesty about it, Nate decided, up there with a large herd of cattle moving across the prairie on a trail drive; a glory all of its own that could rarely be matched.

Camp dogs barked and many of the tribe stopped what they were doing to watch the procession enter the village. A few warriors came forward, throwing questions at the men and glances of mixed concern and anger at the dead braves on the backs of the horses. Nate was confused and nervous, uncertain of the outcome, but he knew that he had acted with the best of intentions in defending the Indian girl.

The young squaw was treated as an honored guest, it seemed, and was led away to a main tipi. Nate watched her go as he was beckoned to dismount, his horse taken away and tied to a picket line. Hostile glances surrounded him, yet he was determined to show no fear, and if he was to die here he would go out in blaze of glory and not allow himself to be tortured to death. He was motioned to the main fire in front of one of the largest wikiups.

"We eat," the leading brave who had spoken to him at the ford commanded.

They sat cross-legged around the fire as other squaws brought some kind of stew, and with nods of encouragement he was urged to eat along with all the others around the fire. More glances came his way, and the men all began to talk at once. Nate understood none of it, but the invitation to eat made him relax a little. If the Indians were willing to share food with him, he might stay alive a little longer. Finally the young squaw reappeared, accompanied by the older woman who had been with her on the trail. She came and knelt before the leading brave, who nodded to her before turning to Nate again.

"I am chief Eagle Feather of the Penateka Comanches. Raven Wing will speak for me as I have little of your tongue."

Then began for Nate one of the strangest situations in which he could ever have imagined himself. Here he was, sat amongst the Comanches, the most ferocious tribe ever to roam the plains, feared and hated by most others save the Kiowa, if the books he had read were correct. The Comanches were the lords of all before them, second only to the white man in dominance, yet comparatively little was known of them, and until the 1850s the settlers and indeed the cavalry had had little contact or interaction with them except in battle.

The girl began slowly at first, in the unfamiliar tongue as though she had not spoken English for a long time and had forgotten some words.

"I am Raven Wing of the Quahadis, Antelope band; Eagle Feather is head of the Penateka, the Honey Eaters, and I am to be his bride," she began, pronouncing the name of her band proudly. "We were traveling from the lands of my father in Northwest Texas at the head of the Red River to marry here, sealing a bond between us as one nation of the *Numunahkahni*." She said the word with a sense of formality, giving the full name of the Comanches. "Ask your questions, as I know that you will have many," she offered.

Nate considered where to start: "Why were the other Indians attacking you, and who were they? Did they want to take you captive?" he said eventually.

"They were Lipan Apaches, a raiding party, out for scalps and captives. The *Numunuu* have always been at war with the Apaches, as we are with most of the tribes. We are in your language the People, enemies to all save the Kiowa. We rule the plains and all run before us," she finished, her head held high and proud, her sharply defined cheekbones showing her breeding and lineage. Nate realized that he found her extremely attractive, despite the difference in their circumstances. As though realizing this, she lowered her gaze once more, casting her huge almond eyes upon him. "They wanted to take me captive and punish the *Numunuu*. They hate us and would have taken me to Mexico or into their heartlands. I am in your debt, for they would surely have captured me if you had not arrived."

"It was nothing," Nate said modestly. "I was pleased to help. Where did you learn your English? You speak well."

She shrugged. "A mission school and from white captives. The elders wanted me to learn so as to understand the white man and be able to talk with him as an equal, not through interpreters with their twisted words."

"What do your tribe and Eagle Feather want of me? Why was I brought here?"

Raven Wing smiled: "They wish to thank you. You saved me, and Eagle Feather wanted your face to be known to all so that you are to be saved in battle. You are to stay here for a feast in your honor."

Nate looked around askance, now more unsure than ever, seeing a circle of stoic brown faces as all the warriors looked at him from around the fire, strong, sure proud men, faces that he would never forget as long as he lived.

* * *

The following morning he made his way back to his ranch house in the Uvalde Valley, his mind still unsettled turning over what he had heard the evening before. He stopped to brew coffee along the way and to eat some of the pemmican given to him by Raven Wing for his journey. It was like nothing he had tasted before, and was a great deal better than any of the supposed pemmican sold by stores in town. The rich dough biscuits had been cooked to perfection, with added saskatoon berries and cranberries.

He knew from experience that if you came into an Indian camp as an invited guest, you were safe from harm for as long as you were there; it was their way and they were people of honor. Yet those same tribesmen would be just as likely to paint for war as peace if they saw you upon the trail the following day. It was an odd way of life to his mind, but no worse than the white man, he reasoned, thinking back to the war. It was just different. For all that, he had an itch at the back of his neck the whole way home, as though he were being watched or followed. He saw no sign, yet that did not mean that the Indians were not there. He had been escorted two miles from the camp and shown the trail he must travel to go east to his homeland.

His thoughts changed as he crested a familiar rise, breaking through a gap in the granite wall to see the basin below him, fringed by pecan trees and prickly pear with cat's claw spread in abundance across the granite mesa, offering a green wall of fauna to the one side of the escarpment. His ranch was laid out before him, the main house in the center near a small pond, with a collection of buildings, barns and corrals around it in a loose semicircle. Poplars stood like a line of sentinels, offering shade but leaving a free line of fire from the buildings that were arranged to provide cross-fire from slits in the shutters. This was Texas, on the farthest edge of the frontier, and every man built his home as a fortress with defense in mind as much as comfort.

Satisfied that all was well, he pushed Dancer down the gentle slope toward the buildings that were now the center of his universe. He had built the spread up from nothing, with money taken from his parents' burning house in South Carolina on a terrible night just after the war. The memory seemed an age ago now, yet he would never forget Craw Gillet and would one day settle that particular score. His business had grown thanks to good friends and the skills he'd learned on the trail drives north to Kansas and Dodge City. Gradually he had expanded his spread, adding two more smallholdings to it with nearly 800 acres to his name. Not large by Texas standards, but it was growing, and he was making his way with more than a gun and a saddle.

He watched as the ranch worked before his eyes. Three hands were watching Morg Newly work the kinks out of a green horse in the corral, the other hands calling out in good natured banter. Hailing from the north in Montana, Morg had followed him south and had been joined by Lily and her mother, and the older woman now ran a café in Flat Creek, the nearest town. Morg and Lily had married and Nate had built a small cabin on the ranch for them away from the bunkhouse. Morg was a gentle rider and easily sat the occasional bucks and corkscrews that the green horse threw in as he worked her around the corral. The hands were so engrossed in the performance that no one noticed Nate's presence until he was quite close.

"So, with the boss away, all you chaps do is loaf around

the place watching the side show," Nate mocked, exaggerating his English accent for effect.

The watching hands all whirled around at the sound of his voice, hands dropping instinctively to pistols in holsters before they saw that it was the boss. Morg stopped the show, dropping from a slow lope and walking the sweating mare over to the edge of the corral.

"Why, boss, we were just watching Montana fall asleep on that horse," Saul Henkman hailed him back.

"I don't know, I go away working my butt off and all I find is the hands asleep on the job. Makes a man very sad indeed," Nate said shaking his head in mock disgust.

"Well, boss, you're gonna love us to bits," Saul replied. "We found ourselves another three hundred head or more roaming free over on the south section. We've been brush popping and made a good gather and shut 'em in a pen, and they're grazing ready to be branded. Thought we oughta come back when Montana got worried as you didn't come home yesterday."

"I had an interesting time myself, which I'll tell you all about later. I've got another hundred or so over to the west and I'll need help bringing them in. Three hundred more? Damn that's good. How's that mare doing, Montana? Think she'll work?" he said, addressing Morg.

"Sure she will. Got some spirit and learns fast. Won't be long afore she's ready to push some steers along, an' she'll likely learn faster that way," Morg replied, his accent a more clipped delivery than the local Texan drawl.

"Good, we are getting ourselves quite a nice remuda together."

"Yeah, ol' Billy Jo, he took off into that plain to the southwest. Mind he reckoned he'd seen some tracks of wild horses out that way?" Nate nodded, remembering the comment. "Waal, he's been gone a day or so an' he'll likely come back with some more. You know what a coon hound he is where horses are concerned," Morg prophesied with a grin.

"He certainly has the knack," Nate agreed with a nod and a smile. He had met Billy Jo a few years back just after the war and they had become firm friends, and it was he who had encouraged Nate to try his hand at being a cowpuncher in the first place. How far he'd come in that time, with a little help from some good people, he thought briefly. Just then a figure came onto the porch of the bunkhouse, raised her eyes to squint against the midday sun and called out to Nate. "Hi, Nate, good to see you back, we were getting kinda worried. Wash up now, it's nearly chow time and I'll be bangin' the triangle soon enough!" she warned.

Lily, Morg's pretty wife, had settled well to ranch life, cooking for the hands and mixing in where she could. Originally from Texas, she had been happy to return after the trouble in Langtonville had soured the town for her and her mother. Yes, he considered, everything was working out well and coming along nicely.

With them all sat around the bunkhouse table and the food finished, Nate started asking about the gathers, numbers and locations, slowly building a better mental picture of his spread. Satisfied, he was about to tell them all that had happened to him over the last two days when Lily called out in alarm from the window overlooking the trail to the ranch. "Nate, there's a whole bunch of Indians coming up the trail towards the house!"

The hands jumped up from the table, their chairs scraping back as they lunged for their gunbelts hanging on the pegs by the door.

"Hold it, boys!" Nate shouted. "Calm down. This won't be trouble, trust me. No guns, just be calm and all will be well."

"Nate, they're Comanches! Know 'em anywhere. Lean devils, tougher'n hell," Saul started.

"I know, but leave it be, Saul, trust me. Buckle your guns on, but leave them in the holsters and don't start anything, you all hear me?" The hands nodded in nervous agreement.

So I was followed. I knew it, Nate thought. He buckled on his own guns and went onto the porch. There before him was a party of twelve braves led by Eagle Feather with Raven Wing at his side. They sat their horses majestically, two of the men holding old Springfield rifles, clearly taken from the dead Apaches after yesterday's fight at the ford. The others carried the traditional Comanche war lances along with other weapons.

"Nate Carlton!" called out Eagle Feather. The chief looked as magnificent as ever, proud and indomitable. He was not as tall or broad as Nate, who stood a little over 6 feet, but he met Nate's slate grey eyes without flinching, despite having ridden into the other man's home territory.

Nate made the sign for peace and friend. "How, Chief Eagle Feather, you are welcome to my home." The chief nodded slowly and looked to Raven Wing. The girl slid from her horse, and Nate saw that she was wearing a doeskin dress decorated with beads and symbols, her hair floating free and ornate moccasins upon her feet. She moved with a lithe grace as she came forward towards Nate as he stepped off the porch, her black hair shining in the sunlight, a shy smile upon her face.

Nate closed the distance, looking down at the seamless skin of her beautiful face. "Today we come to honor you with this gift. It is a rifle boot, and carries big medicine. All *Numunuu* will recognize the markings and none shall attack you when they see it."

Nate looked down at what she was carrying in her arms. It was an ornate rifle boot made of buffalo hide with porcupine quills for stiffness, covered in doeskin, fringed and beaded with intricate patterns that he could neither fathom nor understand. The fringing would shake off water and gave it a unique quality, showing fine workmanship like nothing he had ever seen before.

"I am most grateful for your gift, and shall treasure it always," Nate said solemnly, understanding the symbolism behind the gesture. "Thank you. It is more than I deserve."

She shook her head slowly. "You are now known as..." She spoke a few guttural words he did not understand. "It means 'he who shoots fast'. In honor of your skill with a gun."

"Thank you. I am indeed honored," Nate said. "Will you and the others stay and eat? We have finished but there is food left."

"I thank you but no, for there are too many of us," she answered with a smile. Nate looked puzzled as she turned and spoke to Eagle Feather. He looked toward the granite ridge behind him, where over a hundred mounted warriors, their lance tips glistening in the sun, had suddenly appeared as if by unbidden command.

Nate looked up and gulped. If his hands had attacked the small party when it arrived, they would all be facing certain death by now. He smiled down at Raven Wing. "You are right, there are too many."

She nodded, turned, walked back to her pony and in one lithe bound was mounted.

She smiled back at him and Nate raised his hand, watching them depart in silence, looking down finally at the gift in his hands and wondering at his good fortune. He let his breath out in a long exhale, allowing the tension to drain from his body.

Morg's voice came from behind: "Nate, I swear I could lead you to a desert island without a soul on it and you'd still get into trouble. What the hell happened up there in the hills? What are those Comanches to you?"

Nate grinned sheepishly. "I was just about to tell you when they arrived. Let's get a cup of coffee and all will become clear," he said, walking back up the steps to the bunkhouse.

Nate sat down and explained all that had happened since he left the ranch to the amazement of all who heard him.

"Well I'll be doggone, if that don't beat all, You go out for cows and come back with Comanches!" Saul started, shaking his head in disbelief and holding back a laugh. "But there's one thing worries me, boss. You said that they would know you in war and wouldn't kill you, but what war are they talkin' about? I mean, I know we are always on the edge here, and raids an' such happen from one tribe or another, but you think they're gonna paint for war and start attacking us in force?"

"I know, Saul, and that gave me pause for thought. They've enough men, and if the Comanches join with the Antelopes, the bravest and most aggressive of them all, it could mean trouble. We've broken just about every treaty along the way, from the big treaty of 1840 to the one at San Antonio when we massacred them at the peace talks at the Council House Fight. Half the trouble is the white man can't understand the Comanches' values and one chief doesn't speak for all the tribes, like Sitting Bull for the Sioux or Cochise for the Apaches. All the accounts I've read from Colonel Richard Dodge to Catlin say the same, including Randolph Marcy, who wrote fifteen years or so ago. Now he explored the head lands of the Red River where Raven Wing's people come from. It was pretty isolated and dangerous then, probably still is now."

Nate was pleased with the library he was building in the main house. He only had a few shelves on the walls, but one day he promised himself his own study when he added to the house.

"I must confess, I don't know much about the Comanches, ceptin' they're fierce and they're about the only Indians that fight at night. Why, everyone in Texas calls it the Comanche Moon, and for a good reason," Saul said.

There was silence. Everyone in the bunkhouse knew the legends behind the name.

Chapter Three

The town of Flat Creek was bustling when Nate, Morg and Lily went there in the wagon three days later to fetch supplies. It had grown in size since Nate had started to ranch here three years earlier. The creek had been dammed higher up the valley and a lumber mill now supplied much of the county with timber. Local ranchers spent their hard earned dollars here and a couple of small mines eked out a living in the hills. For all that, cattle were the main source of the economy. Everyone knew it would be years before the railroad arrived in San Antonio to the east, so all travel was by horse or river where the depth of water allowed.

As Nate pulled the wagon to a stop, he saw crowds milling on the sidewalks, with a large cross section of ranchers and townspeople rubbing shoulders with each other.

"Nate, I'm going to see Ma," Lily said. "Morg, I'll see you in the General Store later, should be some special orders comin' in." She smiled and jumped down from the wagon to visit her mother's café.

"You've done well there, Montana, she's a good woman and you'll thrive out here."

"I know I'm a lucky man," Morg said with a grin, "'cause she keeps tellin' me."

"Come on now, let's grab a beer before we set to with the hard work of ordering," Nate suggested.

"Never been known to refuse," Morg answered cheerfully as they moved off to the Boot and Spur saloon.

They pushed open the swing doors and Nate from long force of habit, even though it was his hometown, stood just inside for a few seconds letting his eyes get accustomed to the dimmer light. Sam's words always came back to him: *"Man never died from being careful."*

"What'll it be, Montana?"

"Stand me a cold beer and I'll be a happy man," Morg responded.

Nate ordered the beers and the two men stood enjoying the cold frothing liquid. The saloon was half full, and a few cowhands played poker or stood at the bar flirting with the saloon girls. Nate noticed some faces he recognized, including a couple of small-time ranchers who were all part of the local Cattlemen's Association, which met once a month in a room at the back of the saloon and was always dominated by Buck Durrant, the biggest landowner around. He had built up a herd from the early days and had fought Comanches and Apaches to keep it, and his spread now covered thousands of acres.

Nate started to chat to two of the local ranchers among

the hubbub of convivial conversation and familiarity that was now home to him. His reputation as a gunfighter had been played down in the area despite news traveling across the prairie telegraph of his exploits as a tough trail boss and a marshal in Langtonville, and he avoided trouble where he could. Yet a man's reputation sometimes had a way of following him, whatever steps he took to avoid it.

"Hey, mister, you Nate Carlton, the South Carolina gunman?" a voice came from the bar.

Nate looked over to see two cowpunchers, one a younger man with a mean streak in his face and a tied down gun on his thigh. A young would-be gunman out to make a name for himself, Nate knew the type. He'd seen it before and usually managed to avoid it. The young man's companion was holding his shoulder, trying to pull him back. "Jimmy, you've had enough, leave it!"

"Get off me!" The younger man snarled, shrugging his shoulder free and standing away from the bar into an open space. Nate looked at him, avoiding the challenge in his stare, and turned back to the ranchers with whom he was talking.

"Mister, I'm talkin' to you. Don't turn your back on me. Are you Nate Carlton the gunfighter?" the young man shouted. The saloon went quiet, everyone tense. No one in Flat Creek had seen Nate draw or fight. They had heard rumors, but they knew him as a good man who got on with everybody and minded his own business and had a growing reputation as a trail boss of the first water.

Nate turned back again, sighed and said calmly: "No, I am Nate Carlton the trail boss and rancher, and I'm enjoying a peaceful beer with my friends. Now, drink your own beer and leave me in peace, I want no trouble." Yet for all that he transferred his beer to his left hand and slipped the thong off his Navy Colt out of sight of the cowhand.

Jimmy looked puzzled. This was not what he'd expected. He thought it would be a flash of hands and powder smoke and his target would go down in a hail of lead. Then he came back at Nate again. "Carlton, I say you're a gunfighter, and I aim to prove I'm faster with a gun. I've killed many men, let's see how good you are."

"No," Nate said flatly.

Again the lack of aggression threw Jimmy, who was flummoxed by the reaction. He saw smiles in the crowd and heard a few catcalls. He became angry. The man was mocking him, as was the crowd.

"You'd better fill your hand, Carlton, and prove you're better, 'cause you're dead either way."

Nate's eyes narrowed as he focused. He didn't want this, but it was obvious that the young gunman meant every word. He would have no choice, and after this someone else would come looking for revenge or a reputation to build. It had happened to others. He'd heard that Clay Alison, whom he had met in the war and was now a rancher in Pecos, suffered from the same trouble. Some young hothead or other was always turning up determined to try his hand. Though Clay was less restrained, and you drew on him at your peril. Wes Hardin was another boy up from Texas, sent down the wrong road by the war and fate. But Nate didn't want it, he wanted to live in peace.

Then in the yawning silence there was the unmistakable click of a pistol coming to full cock as the hammer was drawn back. It sounded louder than a whipcrack in the sudden quiet of the saloon. "Now mister, I'm Marshal Paul Walker and this here pistol is primed, ready and on a hair trigger, and at this range I can't miss, even if you are as fast as you say you are. So raise your hands and keep them away from your gun."

Jimmy froze, surprised at this new intervention. Nate was relieved, he had not wanted to kill the boy who could be no more than 18 years old and on a fast track straight to Hell if he kept going like this. Walker stepped forward and Jimmy saw him for the first time: a man of middle years, a creased face showing age and wisdom with a trimmed moustache framing his upper lip. He was neatly dressed with a slight paunch straining at the cord holding his black leather vest together, and in his hand he held a cocked .38 Remington Rider pistol which he'd drawn from a well-worn holster at his side. His eyes never wavered, and despite his youth, Jimmy knew that one false move would see him dead.

"Good. Now you there, his pardner, you come behind and carefully lift his gun from the holster and bring it here to me. Carefully!" Walker stressed, "I'd rather not shoot you, but I will if needs be."

Jimmy's friend answered, "Marshal, I ain't got no part in this game and I sure as Hell don't want none. So I'm gonna do just like you say, real easy, just don't shoot me." At this he slowly reached and lifted Jimmy's Army Colt from the holster, gripping it between his finger and thumb.

"Good, now bring it over here and keep out of the line of fire," Walker ordered.

Jimmy's pardner did just that, placing the gun on the

table to the right of the marshal. Walker turned to Jimmy. "Now you, sonny, keep your hands high and we'll be off to the jail, give you some time to cool off."

Jimmy turned to the marshal. "On what charge? I ain't done nuthin 'cept challenge this yellow gunny to a gunfight. I'll be back when the marshal ain't around to protect you, Carlton, see if I don't. I'm faster and I'll show you."

Nate ignored him, wondering if this would ever stop as the adrenaline coursed through his veins. It was hard to ignore the challenge. His blood was up and a tiny part of him wanted to prove himself against the other man's speed. It was a devil he kept hidden most of the time, forced to the back of his mind. It wasn't the kill, it was the gunfighter's ego, wanting to pit himself against the other man's split second reaction time, to make something from all the hours of practice that he still did, making him faster than ever. He knew that he would carry on practicing against the day when he needed to protect himself and others that he cared for, but this was not one of those days. So he let it go.

You did well, he told himself, but the devil was still there on his shoulder asking for the itch to be scratched.

"I am sure you are, so we'll leave it at that, shall we? You can boast that you forced Nate Carlton to back out of a fight," Nate responded mildly and turned back to his conversation with Morg and the two ranchers, tipping his hat to Marshal Walker, who nodded and offered a grim smile in return.

"Never seen the like. Why'd he do it?" asked Tom Stanley, one of the ranchers who had a large spread over to the northwest of Nate.

"He's just some young kid, looking to make a reputation," Nate replied. "And one day he'll pick on the wrong person and all it'll get him is a place on Boot Hill, with a cold grave and a wooden marker if he's lucky."

Stanley gave him a searching look. "You showed restraint there, Nate. I've heard a few rumors, mind, but I gave them no thought. A man's business is just that, his own. You stand well as a cattleman and trail boss, which should be enough, but we'll always back you come trouble, just remember that. We ranchers need to stick together for the good of the valley and the town."

"I thank you for that, Tom, it's much appreciated."

"Say, talking of sticking together, have you heard any rumors that a wagon train is headed this way from the east?" Stanley said. "Supposed to be full of settlers looking for a new life out here."

"Nope, not a word. Where would they go?" Nate asked. "There's ranches like yours and mine and the free range, but everyone uses that and no one would want to settle on it. And why here? I mean it's lovely, but it's about as wild and rough as it gets with the constant threat of Indians. Then there's drought, harsh winters and hot summers that'll dust up any crops they'd plant, assuming they're nesters. It'd be hard for easterners to settle here. Hell, there are lot easier places to go if they want to move west."

"I know, I know, and I agree with you. Just a rumor, and I wondered if you'd heard anything on your travels, that's all."

"Not a thing, but if I do I'll be sure to let you know.

Incomers like that always cause trouble, and bring problems like wire, like they have in Ohio and other places."

"I hope not, it'll cause wars amongst the ranchers and that's somethin' we don't want. No good'll come of it," Stanley said, and the others nodded sagely in agreement.

Looking at the time by the clock on the wall, Nate drained his beer and told Morg that they needed to move and get to the store. As they left and pushed through the batwing doors a well of talk rose behind them. "Go on, say it, Montana," Nate said, shaking his head.

"That jumped up little gunny will come looking for you soon as he's out of jail. He ain't the sort to let things lie, and you know it," Morg warned.

"Maybe, maybe not, we'll see. I had to give him a chance to walk away."

"It'll get you killed someday, if'n you're not careful. Now we'll have to look out for him."

"You worry too much, Montana. Let's go to the store before Lily spends all our hard earned money. She had a gleam in her eyes that gives me more concern than any young buck with a gun and an itchy trigger finger," Nate chided him with a good natured smile.

In the store they found Lily already ordering from a long list they had put together. There was a wrapped parcel on the counter along with an ever growing pile of goods from bacon to coffee, flour, sugar, canned peaches and other goods, all ready to be carried out and stacked in the bed of the wagon. Lily set the two of them to work, and ticked the items off the list as they went. Nate carried a sack of flour over his shoulder to drop it onto the wagon, and as he did so an unknown cowboy came up from the sidewalk and said: "Say, are you Nate Carlton?"

Nate dropped the sack of flour and slipped the thong off his Colt. Even though the cowboy had not spoken in an aggressive tone, Sam's words came back to him again. It had not been a good day, he reflected.

"Who's asking?" he said.

"Easy friend," the cowpuncher said raising a placatory hand, "I asked around at the saloon after you left. I'm lookin' for work, and they pointed me in your direction an' said you might be hirin'."

"Sorry, I'm a little touchy today," Nate answered, giving the man a once over. He was lean and wiry, with a hatchet face that had seen trouble and come out the other side of it. The eyes were keen and crinkled like many who had lived under harsh suns, and they didn't give much away. Many a man in the west was running from something and nobody was fond of prying. He was well dressed in the good quality range clothes of a top hand and carried a new model Smith and Wesson Russian that Nate had heard about. The holster had a thong hanging but was not tied down. "Where have you worked?"

The cowpuncher reeled off a few names of the spreads that he had ridden for, and Nate looked at his hands that bore the callouses of rope, gun and leather ingrained into the skin. "What's your name?"

"Jim Smith, from Wyoming," he answered.

"Smith?" Nate asked with an arched eyebrow.

"Well, someone has to be called Smith, and I surely can't help it," he answered good naturedly.

"No, you can't, that's fair enough. All right, it's thirty a month and found. Get your horse and throw your bedroll in the wagon. Your first job is to help me load it before we head out to the ranch," Nate answered.

Nate went in, introducing Jim as a new hand, and the loading continued unabated. Once outside, Nate looked surreptitiously under the skirt of the cowhand's saddle, never a trusting man. He saw the branded marks burnt into the leather to make a crude 'JS'.

You're getting old and cynical, Nate old lad, old and cynical, he thought, shaking his head.

Once done, Lily grabbed her mail-order dresses and headed outside with a skip to her step. She had been waiting for these to arrive in time to attend the latest barn dance at the Rocking D spread this Saturday. Everyone was going and she wanted to look her best.

The ride back took longer as the wagon was full and no one wanted a broken axle caused by pushing too hard over the rough trail. It gave Nate a chance to talk to his new hand and get to know him better as he rode beside the wagon. He seemed easy enough to Nate's mind, another drifter looking for work as the mood took him. He'd fought in the war, he said, for the North, but that was a while ago now and everyone was trying to forget the past. The ranch came in sight framed by snowcapped peaks in the distance, and the view took Nate's breath away like the sight of a pretty woman. He loved this valley and the peace that it brought.

Chapter Four

The barn dance at the Rocking D was the event of the year, celebrated by everyone in the fall at the end of a hard season of roundups and trail drives. The elegant ranch house, set on two stories, lay at the end of a sweeping drive, newly laid with a turning circle outside it for buggies and carriages, such as they were. The recently built house was of perfect proportions, with a gently sloping roof over stuccoed whitewashed walls and a long, shaded veranda running along two sides. Two pillars supported the porch area with steps rising to a solid front door.

"Lordy me, I have been told about this new house by the DB boys but I couldn't imagine it until now," Morg said. "I hear tell it even has two bathrooms *inside* the house, if you believe it. Some improvement on the old one that stood the old man in good stead all those years."

"It sure is," Nate said, looking across to the single story dwelling that was the old ranch house, used now for the hands and visiting guests. It paled in comparison. "His new wife Anthea ordered it built, apparently, though how it sits with her stepsons I don't know. It is certainly very grand. Reminds me of the mansions back in South Carolina. Solid though," he added, studying the property. "Good thick stone walls for stopping bullets."

"Say, look at the walls with the ditch, what's that for?" Morg asked as they got closer.

"That, Montana, is a ha-ha. We have them in England. It means no fences, so you get an uninterrupted view, and the cattle can't get up to trample your garden. It's *très élégant*!"

"Nate, you sure do talk fancy sometimes, what in the Hell does that mean?" Morg asked.

Nate smiled, suddenly thinking back to his parents, reminded of the education they had given him and missing them in the moment. "It was invented by a French chap, Dezallier d'Argenville his name was, and we adopted it in England. And what I said means 'very elegant' in French."

"Do you speak French, Nate?" Lily asked from the rear seat of the buckboard.

"I do, Lily, but I'm a little rusty."

"Would you teach me sometime? I would love to learn all those fancy words, they sound so romantic," she said gripping her husband's arm tighter.

"Of course, Lily, any time."

Then they were at the house, circling the buckboard. Nate brought the wagon to a stop and Morg helped Lily down from her seat. The other hands all rode in behind them, dressed in their best clothes with boots shined and ready to enjoy themselves.

The evening was still warm, and tables and chairs had

been arranged outside around the edges of a wooden platform that would be used as a dance floor. Beside the platform, two firepits had pork and beef turning on slow spits. Tables were laden with food and a four piece band of two fiddles, a piano and a banjo were warming up to get the evening flying once the food had been eaten. It was a gay collection of people, Nate decided, looking around at the flirting and cow's eyes directed by the girls of the valley and the town at the newly arrived hands, all keen to dance and romance.

A large figure broke away from a throng and came forward, followed by an elegant lady in a shimmering ball gown that to Nate's eyes must have cost damn nearly as much as the new house.

"Nate, good to see you, pleased that you could come along," Buck Durrant said, extending a thick, dry and calloused palm to shake Nate's hand.

The man didn't change, Nate considered. His large, bulky frame had gotten a little thicker with age, and his bull neck and almost white hair framed a brown face with high cheek bones that showed a strength of character that had helped him forge this ranch from nothing. His clothes, though well cut, struggled to contain the broad deep chest of a man who was a force of nature.

"It's a pleasure, Buck. Delighted to attend, and I don't think I could have kept my hands away, they've been talking about it for weeks."

"Now I don't think that you've met my wife Anthea. My dear, this is Nate Carlton who owns the NC Connected over in the next valley."

The elegant lady in the shimmering gown came forward, a smile of welcome upon her lips but a hint of disdain about her eyes. She was about ten years younger than Buck, tall and poised, with a classic beauty that was borne of good genes, with porcelain skin and a fine bone structure. Her blonde hair was piled upon her head in a French Twist like Nate's mother used to adopt. A graceful hand was extended, and Nate wasn't sure whether to kiss it in a formal manner or shake it. He chose the former, taking her hand and bending forward in a bow. "How do you do, ma'am?"

"How do you do Mister Carlton?" she answered, surprised. "Why, Buck, I didn't know good manners like these existed west of Boston," she praised, her eyebrows raised and her voice deep and cultured.

"Ah, my dear, Nate is the exception. He is actually English, but he doesn't hold your Tea Party against us," Buck joked. "His parents came over years ago and settled in South Carolina."

"Ah," she said, and that one word encapsulated more feeling than a whole string of words to Nate's ears. Rumor had it that she spent as much time back east with 'her people' as she did at the ranch roughing it in the west.

"I do admire the new house, ma'am, it's beautiful, and..." Here he admitted to playing up to what he felt was an errant snob of a woman. "The ha-ha is *très élégant*," he finished with a smile.

"My, my, educated *and* well-mannered. You're a rare man in this part of the world, Mister Carlton. You and your wife must come and have supper with us one evening," she offered. Nate was surprised. Having been exiled from Isobel's mother's circle, he was now being invited into the lion's den. It was something of a novelty.

He replied before he gave thought to his actions: "I should love to, ma'am, but I have no wife."

A knowing smile crossed her lips. Her arm engaged his and led him forward: "Well, I'm sure if we put our minds to it we could find you one. Now let me introduce you to some people, for we have friends visiting from Boston."

Nate suspected a trap, but he was too late, it was sprung in an instant. A well-dressed group of people were gathered together away from the westerners, and the circle opened as Anthea approached. She began the introductions, leaving two young people until last. "This is our son, Timothy, recently returned from Harvard law school. He has plans to set up in Flat Creek."

Nate shook hands with the young man, who was as pale as his mother, with little of Buck's genes in evidence to Nate's eyes. He was tall and slim, and his handshake seemed limp and boneless. He had white hair and strangely colorless eyes that were difficult to define. He came across as quite diffident, with a genial manner and a ready smile, charmingly pleasant. This was the half-brother to Buck's other three sons by his first wife, who had been the daughter of a Mexican Don, a family of great lineage, and who had died of Smallpox years before. By all accounts it had been a marriage of convenience that had turned into a love match. The two wives could not be more different, he realized.

"Nate, how do you do? Please call me Tim, although my mother insists on Timothy." He was softly spoken, with a curious mix of Boston and Texas accents. His manner was one of nervous energy, controlled but somehow eager to expand and find an outlet.

Nate was not left to ponder, as Anthea was on a social mission. She introduced him to the young woman at his side: "And this is my niece, Susannah, fresh from Boston. This is her first time out west."

So the trap closes, he thought. She was tall and slim, like her aunt, but her figure filled out the ball gown she wore with aplomb. Her skin was almost translucent, a shock against the red hair and crystal green eyes. If that didn't betray Irish ancestry then nothing did, Nate decided. He offered her his best smile, exaggerated his English accent and was charm personified. A harmless flirtation would do him no harm, he considered.

"Susannah was saying how she would like to ride out on the range. Maybe you would be good enough to show her around?" Anthea's question was framed as an order. Nate had experienced many a senior martinet officer do the same thing to him in the war.

"It would be my pleasure, ma'am," Nate offered gallantly as she released his hand with more than just a gentle squeeze. Her gaze was as challenging as her aunt's was predatory. *Careful with this one, Nate, you may get a tiger by the tail,* he told himself.

Later that evening, with the food finished, Tom Stanley sought him out, a glass of whisky in his hand: "Nate, you mind our conversation the other day in town about a wagon train headin' this way?"

"Of course, but all I've heard about is a load of mule skinners bringing in supply wagons to Rocksprings to the north. Could that be it?" Nate answered. "Big trail of wagons from what I've heard, heading on to Fort Stockton."

"Can't say I've heard anything about that. Could be, but the word is this is a proper wagon train full of settlers. Say, talking of Fort Stockton, are you bidding for the contracts they have out for beef and horses? The new fort needs both," Tom asked.

"I heard about the contracts. We certainly can't do the full contract on the horses' remounts, as we haven't enough stock of our own for the ranch remuda. So if it gets filled by someone else – which it almost certainly will," he said, nodding in Buck Durrant's direction with a knowing look, "we will bow out. The cattle, now, that's another story. We'll certainly tender for them."

"In that case, may the best man win," Tom offered. "It'll be tough, though. Most folks in the valley would love to thin their stock for the winter and have the money in the bank, saving the feed and grass."

"I'll drink to that," Nate said. What he did not say was that his silent business partner, Paul Tranter, was already at Fort Stockton trying to negotiate a deal with the officers and agents in charge of procurement. With no telegraph in Flat Creek, it was difficult to get an immediate update, but knew how persuasive Paul could be and how well connected he was throughout the states and the cattle industry, from politicians to generals. Tranter had a reputation for honesty and for always delivering on any bargain struck in his name, as well as for the quality of the beef that he promised, which was more than the spavined racks of bones some delivered, skimming the army in the process.

"I'll see you later, Nate. I promised my wife I'd dance with her and this is her tune." Tom strode off in search of his wife and Nate was left alone with his thoughts. His gaze drifted over the crowd and saw the other three Durrant boys, half-brothers to Timothy, talking amongst themselves. In looks they were nothing like him, dark skinned with their mother's heritage, taller and more well-muscled versions of their father. The mother, Consuela, had apparently been very beautiful, and she had clearly passed on her looks to the boys, who were all darkly handsome.

But they looked furtive to Nate's eyes, and whatever was being said it was not with smiles or goodwill. Nate decided to drift over to say hello. They saw him and broke the conversation. "Good evening, boys, enjoying the dance?" Nate said.

"Nate, good to see you," Ricardo replied, offering his hand.

"And you, Rick, Benny, Dan. You boys setting plans – to catch a girl maybe?"

"Ha, you guessed it," Benny responded a little too quickly, looking cautious, as Nate had hesitated slightly before adding the last of his question. "And there are certainly some pretty *señoritas* here tonight," Benny offered a little too quickly.

Dan was the middle son, built like his father with big shoulders and heavy features. "Don't you worry, Nate, we'll save some for you," he joked, easing the slight tension.

"Well, that's very kind of you and I thank you most warmly," Nate mocked. They laughed and joked over who was to get whom until Nate broke it off. "Well I see my date has already been chosen by your stepmother." He nodded towards Anthea who was beckoning him over to join her and Susannah.

Rick grinned in understanding. "Good luck there, Nate. She's a spirited filly, that one."

"Thank you for the warning." He raised a finger to his temple in a mock salute and walked over to meet his fate.

Nate asked Susannah to dance and led her adroitly around the room. He was an excellent dancer, having been taught well, and he was light on his feet despite being a strong partner.

"My, but you are a good dancer, Nate," she breathed in his ear.

"Thank you, Susannah. I had a good teacher."

"Who?"

"My mother."

"Your mother? Tell me about her."

The dance continued and they talked easily in each other's company, taking two more dances until they heard raised voices from the other side of the floor. Turning, Nate saw his new hand, Jim Smith, arguing with one of Tom Stanley's Circle T hands over a girl. It often happened at barn dances. Too much booze, too few pretty girls and too many tough men who'd been working hard all day and needed to let off steam. As he watched, he saw a big bully of a man from the Circle T pushing Jim. Nate had seen him before. Bull Hind, his name was, and he was aggressive and reckoned he was the 'bull of the woods', always looking for trouble. The poking in the chest came from him, and the situation was about to explode when a whip cracked the air, and all became silent.

Buck stood there, holding a whip in his hand. He had anticipated this, knowing the way of cowhands and wanting to stop it before it started. "I won't have gunplay, and I won't have fights breaking up the dance," he said. "If you two want to fight, take it out onto the grass over there. Any more trouble in here and I'll use this on you." He raised the whip and they all saw that he meant every word.

Bull gave Jim an evil grin. "Come on then, shrimp, let's go if you're man enough."

The talk welled up, with some wagering on the outcome. There were few takers on Jim to win.

"Will you excuse me, Susannah? That's one of my hands and I need to see what happens. I'll come back and take the next dance as soon as the fighting's done."

But she stayed, her arm clamped to his. "Nonsense, Nate. I'm no shrinking violet and I have attended sporting clubs with my cousin in Boston and seen boxing matches before on open nights. There is even a club for women now, teaching shooting, riding and fencing, I'll have you know."

Nate was surprised and impressed, yet he doubted that the display to come would be set according to the Marquess of Queensbury rules. It would be a brutal, knuckle head and knock 'em down brawl if he didn't miss his guess. "Sure, if you insist, but if it gets too much I will return you to the safety of the dance floor and your aunt."

She tutted, as if to say that such a thing would not be necessary and pressured him to lead the way. The two protagonists stripped their jackets and squared off, Bull bringing up his hands in huge ham-like fists to chest height, ready to pulverize the smaller man.

Jim for his part kept his hands open, only part clenched, as much to grab as punch. Nate was a keen student of the pugilistic arts, having been taught to box by his father, trained in Savate by the husband of the French Creole cook and given some lessons in dirty fighting as well. He had wrestled a bit along the way, always learning, and now he thought Jim might be fixing to do just that.

The big man closed, left up ready to jab and the right to follow. The move was telegraphed to Nate's eyes. He took a brief look at Susannah's face to ensure that she was still all right and saw that her eyes were wide in anticipation, an almost gleeful look in them at the prospect of the fight that was to come. Her arms gripped his in excitement, and he felt the warmth of her body as she leaned in against him. He was surprised and puzzled in that fleeting instant, yet had no more time to ponder it, turning back to the fight.

As he had thought, Bull jabbed with the left once, twice and then brought a huge overhand right in to level Jim. The smaller man seemed to almost take his time to Nate's tutored eyes. Relaxed and still in balance, he just danced back as the haymaker flew forward to miss him. Angry at the miss, Bull twisted from the hips to bring round the left in a hook. Jim causally flipped up his right hand still unclenched to brush it away as man would a fly.

The man has good reactions, Nate thought, *I wonder how he is with a gun.*

Bull was mad now. "Come back and fight, shrimp! I am gonna crush you." He snarled. He rolled his shoulders, hunched and came forward, his palms now open. He knew he could take punishment and had been hit by far bigger men than Jim. He would close, Nate thought, grab Jim by the throat or head butt him first and then crush the life out of him. It would get nasty from here. Jim was still relaxed and danced lightly from one foot to the other, keeping Bull on the attack and offering no defense as yet. Then, as Nate suspected, Bull came in fast, his neck jutting forward in pure aggression and his eyes wide with hate and anger. Jim let him come, and the crowd bayed for blood, cheering the two fighters on as Bull lunged for the neck with grabbing hands to crush it. Jim stood there, apparently immobile, his feet apart, front to back, in what Nate saw was a dangerous fighting stance, his right hand lower. Just as Bull was about to close, Jim twisted from the hip and his right hand flew upwards, fingers bent at the second knuckle, smashing into Bull's throat and crushing his larynx. He did no more but stood back, watching as his opponent's eyes bulged in disbelief and pain, his hand going to his damaged windpipe through which he was gasping for air that would not come.

The cheering stopped, glasses slipping from hands in disbelief to bounce upon the grass. Silence reigned, except for Bull's impersonation of a beached fish that was desperate for air. Jim just looked on, his harsh hatchet face dispassionate, not at all surprised at the outcome, not turning his back until he was certain. It was the action of a fighter who knew what he was capable of doing in any confrontation. A dangerous man, Nate thought, and one who would bear watching. The fight was over almost as soon as it started. Two punchers from the Rocking S bent down to help Bull get his breath while Jim still watched from a distance as the big man massaged his throat.

Gradually getting his wind back, Bull sat up scowling at Jim, who shrugged, his face showing no emotion as he turned to a girl who had been watching. "My dance then, I guess?" he said. There were cheers from the crowd as he took the hand of the girl in dispute and led her back toward the dance floor.

Bull stood up still wheezing and looked at two of the fallen glasses lying on the grass. He grabbed them and cracked one against the other to a tinkle of glass that was lost in the noise, leaving him with two jagged daggers of glass, one in each hand. He ran to attack Jim from behind and Jim was unaware of his danger until Nate intervened.

"No, Bull!" Nate shouted. Halting his assault, Bull turned. "Oh, you wanna try me now huh, after your little hand punched me? Come on then, boss man, let's see how you do."

Nate disengaged himself from Susannah, knowing that there was no reasoning with this sort of murderous blind rage. He quickly slipped his jacket off, holding it by the collar, letting his hand fall to his side. Bull lunged, the lethal jagged edges of glass flashing forwards to slice into Nate's flesh. Nate brought his jacket straight up into Bull's eyes, causing him to flinch and rear back. It was all the time Nate needed. He hopped on one foot, closing the distance, and launched a roundhouse Savate kick straight to the back of Bull's leg, his pointed cowboy boot digging straight into the man's sciatic nerve. Bull howled in pain as his leg collapsed beneath him, just as Nate withdrew his foot and flipped a *parade du coup de pied de figure,* a kick straight across Bull's jaw that dropped him unconscious to the grass.

Once more that evening there was stunned silence, no one had seen fighting like it before and looked from Bull's prostrate form to Nate standing balanced and ready.

"Guess he couldn't take his liquor," Buck said, breaking the tension. "Come on, everyone, show's over. Let's get back to the dancing." The two hands made to help Bull again as everyone started to drift back to the dance.

Susannah clapped, her eyes sparkling. "My, but you are full of surprises," she said. "Do tell how me you did that."

"I was just lucky, I suppose," Nate answered modestly, a sheepish grin on his face.

Jim came over to thank him.

"Not at all Jim. When a hand works for me he's part of the crew and we all look out for each other."

"Thank you, anyway, and one day I'd admire for you to show me what you did back there."

Nate brushed it off and said: "Another time. Let's get back to having some fun."

The talk welled up again, but the dance had continued unabated, and everyone went back to it, most people forgetting the ugly incident. As the evening drew to a close, Nate took Susannah back to her aunt, bade her good night and went to fetch the buggy from the area near the barns where they had all been left. Shadows thrown from oil lamps cast a pale light guiding the revelers to the buggies and wagons. Nate was moving cautiously, not wishing to trip over in the semi darkness, when he saw off to the left a bulky figure mounted upon a buckboard, who from his build could only be Bull, now seemingly recovered from his early injuries.

He was clearly having an argument with someone whose identity was hidden by the shadows of the nearest barn and was no more than a silhouette to Nate's eyes.

"Look, I did what you told me, and now I want my money," Bull demanded.

"I told you to make trouble between the spreads, in particular the NC Bar, not get beaten to a pulp. All you did was get everyone on Carlton's side." The voice was audible but hard for Nate to recognize.

"Yeah, well how'd you like me to beat you to a pulp instead?" Bull snarled in anger.

There was no response save for a pistol coming to full cock, the sound made more sinister in the darkness. "I don't think that would be a good idea, Bull. You just mind your manners and do what you're told and you'll get paid in full," came the softly spoken yet menacing reply.

Whoever had drawn the gun was quick, Nate realized by the lapse of time from Bull talking to the hammer being drawn back. Someone had a gun hidden here, when all guns were traditionally left outside on barn dance nights, which were about the only time that cowhands went anywhere without being 'dressed'. Nate heard the crack of a whip and stepped back from the trail just in time to see Bull driving the buggy home in anger. He stepped forward quickly, hoping to see who it was that had been speaking with Bull. But no one was there, and all he was left with was the faint taint of cologne and cigar smoke. Whoever it was, he moves mighty softly, Nate mused, tucking away the information for the future.

Chapter Five

Two days later, a lone rider came along the trail heading up to the NC Connected. Dusty and travel worn, he still sat the saddle with an almost military precision, Nate noticed, shading his eyes against the low-hanging sun.

"Who's that ridin' in, Nate?" Lily asked as she came onto the porch.

"Rides like Paul Tranter, and if it is him, we shall have some news either way. Put the coffee on, Lily, and set another place for supper. He'll be tired and hungry," Nate said, stepping down off the porch to meet the rider. As he got closer he saw that his guess was right: "Paul! Good to see you," he called. "I'd almost given up, thought you'd hightailed it back to civilization!"

Tranter took off his planter's hat, waved it and set his horse into a lazy lope to cover the ground a little quicker. When the two met he reached down to shake Nate's hand in a dry, calloused grip. To Nate's eyes he looked as spry and dapper as ever, despite the covering of travel dust. His face was browned by the sun and framed by a longer but well-styled mane of grey hair, his shrewd eyes missing nothing.

"Nate, why it's good to see you. Damned if I don't know whether it's me getting older, but journeys seem to take a whole lot longer these days," he joked.

"Well you're here now and most welcome. I've been looking out for you for a few days, hoping against hope that you might bring some news."

"Yes, there's lots to tell, but first I need a cup of coffee and a slug of whisky to kill the trail dust. Or maybe..." He eyed Nate hopefully. "...some of that fine cognac to which you are partial."

Nate smiled in reply, reminded as always of his late father whenever he met Paul. "Of course, ride up and we'll get the coffee and cognac ready for you." They talked in general terms, neither wanting to raise the subject of the army contract until Nate had allowed Paul time to wash off the dust of his long journey and prepare himself.

"You've done a lot of work here, Nate. You're building right well."

"Yes, it's all coming together. We added another few hundred acres in the summer after the Carsons sold up and left. It's a start at least, and it feels like the heart of a good spread that I can call home. One day, God willing, it will be bigger and better, and I may even build a house like the one I had in South Carolina."

Paul looked at his young friend and nodded, saying nothing, knowing how much the past still weighed on Nate's mind. A while later they sat on the porch, coffee and cognac before them, Paul puffing gently on one of the long slim cheroots that Nate occasionally smoked. He held it close, admiring the dribble of smoke as it lazed its way upwards. "Good tobacco, Nate. You were always an excellent judge of the finer things in life. And now it's going to get better," he pronounced with a smile. "We lost the horse contract, which is more lucrative on the hoof, but we won the beef contract," he said with a note of pride in his voice he could no longer contain.

"Really? Well I'll be, you did it."

"*We* did it. Your reputation as a trail boss and purveyor of good cattle is spreading. That and greasing a few palms along with my contacts, either way we have it tied up if I do say so myself."

"How many?" Nate asked with bated breath.

"Initially five hundred head at sixteen dollars on the hoof."

"Think of all that winter feed we'll save. Why we'll be under grazed and away next year, and we keep finding them, hundreds of unbranded cattle. I reckon this calls for a celebration. I'll buy you the best meal in town if you're up to it. Damn it though, won't old man Durrant be hacked off?" Nate said with a sneaking sense of elation.

"Well, he's got some consolation. At least he got the remount contract, and good luck to him with that one. All those broncs to bust and get ready," Paul commented.

"Mmmh. So we need to get our own stock ready. When do they want them?"

"Just as soon as you can drive 'em up, and obviously before winter sets in hard. They have some Indians on the nearby reservation, and they need to feed them as well from the allocation."

"Talking of which, I had a bit of a run in with the Comanches down here."

"Really? I mean, I know the peace such as it is, is fragile, but tell me what happened. Was it a raid?" Paul asked.

"No, it was the darndest thing." Nate told Paul the whole story as the other man listened without comment, raising his eyebrows occasionally.

"That rifle boot is big medicine, Nate. You keep it to hand, it might save your life one day. The Comanches are always raiding, usually for food and rifles. Most times they kill a few folks and then move on. That's the way it is right now, with this supposed peace. But it's interesting what you say about the two lodges forging stronger ties. The Quahadi from what little I know are the most dangerous and warlike. If they paint for war for whatever reason, they could cause big trouble, Fort Stockton or no."

Their thoughts were interrupted at that point as the whoops of Nate's hands came across the evening air, pushing in a small herd of another three hundred or so head.

"Come and meet the rest of the boys, they'll certainly be pleased to hear your news."

Paul stayed for two days before beginning his return ride to Fort Stockton, wanting to ensure that their interests were looked after and no shenanigans were taking place to usurp their contract.

After he had gone, Nate, Billy Jo and the new hand Jim went out riding some of the new land to the southwest, where Billy Jo had found the herd of wild mustangs that had been circled and herded back to the ranch to provide another twenty or so head to add to its remuda. The wild stallion that ran the herd was wily and managed to escape with some of his mares, yet it was still a good haul, giving them a few young stallions that they could cross breed with.

Before them a tall outcrop of rock rose to form a natural wall across the landscape some fifty feet high. It seemed to taper off into the distance as far as the eye could see, dotted with isolated buttes and rising mounds where the rock had been eroded over the millennia. The wall led toward far mountain peaks that even now showed white tops of high altitude snow.

The outcrop was topped by a craggy ridge, and no one had yet figured out how to get past it, or indeed around it, not knowing if it was a mesa or the gateway to a hidden valley, as Nate had hoped when first he saw it. They hazed some loose cattle into a shallow arroyo, boxed them in and went to explore the rock face before them. Although the ground was churned up and dusty, making tracking hard, Nate spotted a few trails leading off into small arroyos directly below the rock face. Always curious, he followed one that had more hoof marks than the others, and found that it led to a craggy rock face eroded into weird shapes by time and weather. A seamed split appeared to rise up about twenty feet, getting wider as it went. At ground level it was only two or three feet wide, and it meandered off in a curve, preventing anyone from seeing further. No cow could get through there, especially one with a wide spread of horns, but smaller tracks showed that grey fox or rabbits and hares had made the passage.

"Sure is odd, the way the trail just stops like that," Jim commented when Nate returned. "Is there a way in?"

"Not that I can see. It comes to an end just before the rock face, where a tall split in the rock rises up, but it's way too small for horse or steer. One day I'll take a better look and see whether I can find a way in. I'm curious to see what's behind it."

They moved the rest of the steers into the arroyo and secured the entrance, then made camp for the day, planning to stay the night before herding the steers back to the ranch. With the camp settled, Nate went off to practice by himself away from the others, easing tired muscles from the day's hard riding, relaxing and warming himself up. He worked on his gunplay for half an hour, sensing someone's eyes on him as he practiced all the different angles with both left and right hands. He did not fire any rounds for fear of spooking the cattle, but it was enough. As Sam would have said, a tool that's rusty and blunt is no good to anyone, and there was that kid in town who would be out of jail and looking for trouble right now. Then, as was his way, he turned back to camp and span, his gun magically appearing in his hand with a will of its own. Nate smiled to himself, pirouetting and returning the Colt to its holster in one smooth move.

"The boss do that every day?" Jim asked, jerking his thumb over his shoulder. It was the first time he had been out riding with Nate, and he was unaware of his habit.

"Yep," Billy Jo answered quietly, wanting the conversation closed. A man didn't ask too any questions of another in the west, and as long as it didn't hurt you let him alone whatever he did. Especially if he was the boss and a good friend.

"So that gunny in town called it right when he said he was a gunfighter?" Jim asked.

"Nope. He's is a cattleman who knows how to use a gun well. That's all there is to it, and you'd be well to mind that. The boss don't like any reputation spreading."

Jim raised his hands in a placatory manner: "No offense. I just saw how fast he was and was curious. Seems I may have heard his name linked to some gunfighting trouble along the trail, that's all."

"Yep, well we're a family at the NC Connected, and we like to keep it all amongst us," Billy Jo finished curtly. "Now, how's about some more coffee?"

Jim saw the hard gleam in Billy Jo's eyes and went off to brew a fresh pot.

The gather had been hard work, but the herd was finally ready. "How many do you make it, Billy Jo," Nate asked sitting his horse with one leg hooked around the saddle horn, his black Stetson pushed back on his head, wiping his forehead with his bandana. The hat had been a present from Isobel Hart as an apology and a thank you for saving her life. It had a band of silver conchos around the crown that sparkled in the sunlight.

Billy Jo had a string of rawhide in his hand and was counting the knots in it as they came together to compare notes: "Well now, I figure it to be five hundred twenty one head of prime beef."

"I must have missed one, I counted five hundred and twenty all told."

"Yeah, that damned muley ducked out and you probably missed him. He'll be one for the pot afore we're done, I'll tell you."

Nate laughed. No cattleman liked hornless steers, they were always trouble. "Well, it'll give us enough to take some losses, even though it's less than two hundred miles to Fort Stockton."

"I know, but it's far enough out on the plains and heading to injun territory. If it ain't Comanches it'll be 'Paches, Kiowas or Utes," Billy Jo lamented. "Talking of which, you'd better cover up that shiny band on your hat when we get moving along. Nothing like those silver conchos to get an arrow in your back or a bullet in your head."

"Don't you worry, I'll cover it before we set out," Nate assured him. "Now we'll rest 'em here tonight then push the whole herd out early the day after tomorrow. Head directly north then drive 'em out west afterwards up into new territory. It'll be unbroken country until we meet the Goodnight Loving trail, then we pretty much follow that to Fort Stockton," he explained.

The two left the herd that were bedded down on new grazing. Already a bull had staked his claim as lead steer, bellowing into the evening air, challenging all comers to his right to lead the herd.

"Is Lily coming along as cook?" Billy Jo asked.

"Nope, she'll stay here. Her ma's sending out one of her helpers to keep her company and we've got that young boy over from near San Antonio that you recommended. He'll be here in a couple of days to look after the spread while we're away. I've got Mary Lou coming down from the north, she's my good luck mascot on these drives and she's coming in as cook, and I think Sue's joining as cook's louse. Emmett will wrangle for us, so we'll have a full house. Should be enough for just five hundred head."

"Oh, I mind Mary Lou. She surely does make the best biscuits I've ever had on a drive, and I reckon I might have to marry her someday just on the strength of 'em."

Nate laughed. "Well, you better tell her that, you old romantic, and I am sure she'll marry you in a heartbeat."

The two men joked with each other as they headed back to the spread, where Nate saw four horses tethered outside the ranch house, two of which were unsaddled and had clearly been led. As they got closer, Nate recognized the brands as belonging to the Rocking D, and he was puzzled. One, he was sure, was Susannah's little clay bank dun mare that she'd ridden when he had taken her riding to show her around. She'd been good company and had proved to be an excellent horsewoman.

The door to the ranch house opened and Susannah stepped out onto the porch. "Hey, Nate, surprise! We thought we would ride on over before you left for the drive," she called out. Beside her was her cousin Timothy, who nodded and smiled before placing his hat back on his head.

"Nate, good evening, I hope that you don't mind us visiting just as you're about to head off," he said.

"No, not at all, although we've still got lots to do before morning. But I would be a poor host if I didn't offer you a coffee and maybe an early supper." Nate smiled. He hated his plans being changed, and despite the fact that Susannah looked stunning in a white blouse and doe skin divided pants cinched at the waist by a wide belt, he still needed to finalize matters around the ranch with no distractions.

"Well," she said, moving forward to stand before him, the full power of her beautiful eyes engaging him as she slipped her arm through his in a gesture of forced intimacy. Her perfume enveloped his senses and he saw Lily raising an eyebrow in the corner of his vision. "Nate, I have a little more to ask than supper," Susannah continued, "although it is so very kind of you. You see, I was really curious to see what a cattle drive would be like, and my friends back east would be so jealous to hear I'd been on one. A ranch is one thing, but to go on an actual drive, why it would be so exciting!" she gushed.

Nate looked aghast. "Ma'am, a cattle drive is no place for a lady. It's full of dust, danger and death. When you're not being eaten alive by mosquitos or starving from eight straight hours in the saddle, dog tired and ready to drop with your body aching all over, you're wet or frazzled. No ma'am, I'm sorry but no, I would not wish to take on the responsibility. What would your uncle say if something happened to you?"

"Don't you *ma'am* me, Nate Carlton!" she declared stamping a booted foot. "You've seen me ride and you know I can handle a horse. I've even brought two extra as part of my contribution to the remuda. I won't be any trouble, and I might even be able to help. I learn fast and could be a sort of unpaid hand. I'll stay out of trouble and do what I can. What have you got to lose?" she pleaded, offering him her most winning smile.

"Susannah," he declared in exasperation, "a cattle drive is

a lot more than a tour around a ranch on horseback. Does your aunt know about this foolish idea?"

"Of course," she lied, "and she applauds it!" she said defiantly. Nate said nothing. He shook his head and caught Timothy's eye, who shrugged as much to say *women*. Yet he remained silent, his face hard to read.

"Come on, let's eat. Join me in the ranch house. Lily, two more for supper I'm afraid."

Susannah flung her head from side to side, her long mane of wavy red hair bouncing like a chief's war bonnet as she walked back into the house, her eyes on fire with fight and determination.

Over supper he reiterated the reasons not to go, including the danger and finding her a safe place to sleep.

"I have a bedroll, and you will have a cook along – I assume that will be Lily?" Susannah nodded in her direction as Lily brought peach cobbler to the table after the main course had been cleared. "So there will be another woman on the drive that you say we females are not suited for. I would not be all alone and unchaperoned."

"Actually no, Lily is staying here, but there will be Mary Lou and Sue, two rancher's daughters who know their way around a trail drive and have lived this life since they were born. And the kind of chaperone I am worried about has long hair and feathers, and will either scalp you or worse." Nate made a decision that went against the rules of strict propriety: "Do you know what happens to white women who are captured by Indians?"

Susannah blushed to the roots of her red hair and nodded.

"And I guess that isn't something that's discussed much in the smart drawing rooms of Boston society, is it?" Nate continued.

There was a sense of unbending determination in her manner which Nate could not fathom, and he appealed to Timothy who had still kept quiet through the discussions, not adding to either argument. But now he spoke softly to Nate's appealing glance.

"I learned a long time ago that my cousin is a very determined young lady who will brook no argument," he said, holding his hands apart in a shrug.

"Hmmm. Well, before I give any answer I need to speak to Mary Lou and Sue. They'll have their say in this too. They should get here tomorrow."

"Oh, thank you, Nate," she said, placing a proprietorial hand on his arm. Lily looked on, raising an eyebrow once more as she caught Nate's eye. "Then can we stay tonight?"

Nate sighed and explained that the guest room he was building was not finished so she could have his bed. "Tim and I can rough it in the unfinished bedroom."

Tim swore off, saying that he would ride into town where he had some work to do, and would return tomorrow either to wave his cousin off or escort her back to the Rocking D. He was a lawyer and land agent for the town, working in a newly opened office where he was kept very busy.

"Well have care in the dark, although I see you're dressed now." Nate nodded at the Smith and Wesson sitting in a well-designed holster at his hip. "That's the new .44 Russian I've heard so much about, isn't it?"

"Yes, pa bought it for me. It takes the new rimfire cartridge and fits my Yellow Boy too. Means I can carry shells on my belt in these loops." He pointed at the cartridges tucked snugly in the leather loops around the gun belt.

"Interesting idea, I like that. May I have a look?" Nate asked.

Tim hesitated like a dog that was having his bone taken away from him, and drew the revolver almost reluctantly, the seemingly boneless pale hand turning to a blur as he span it around in a practiced move to offer it butt first to Nate in a sort of reverse Road Agent's spin. Nate raised his eyebrows in surprise and reminded himself once again never to judge a book by its cover. The gun had a shorter barrel than his own Navy Colt, he noticed, and the balance was different. Pointing it away from anyone, he pinwheeled the pistol, testing it. As it slapped into his palm he brought it up, instinctively lining on an imaginary target. It had a nicely curved butt, but to his mind did not offer the same wonderful instinctive alignment that the butt his own Colt presented. Even his spare Remington Beals felt better, probably because it was made under license from Colt, and it had almost identical grips and was newly converted to take 44-.40 metallic cartridges. Tim seemed tense; like Nate he didn't like anyone else handling his gun.

"Thank you," Nate said with a smile, passing it back. "Nice gun."

Tim exhaled and some of the tension seemed to go out of him. "I like it, but I need more practice with it," he said. "Pa says there's no point in having a gun unless you can use it properly and hit what you aim at."

"Amen to that."

"Well, I'll be on my way. Susannah, until tomorrow," he said kissing his cousin on the cheek.

After he had ridden off Lily came up. "No need for you to leave your bedroom, Nate. Susannah can sleep in our spare room that ma uses when she visits from town." Nate breathed a sigh of relief, though he didn't know quite why. Susannah was a lovely woman, but he did not want to get entangled with her – especially if she was coming on the drive, which he privately dreaded. It was no place for a lady of her breeding.

Chapter Six

Nate rose early the following day to make the final preparations for the drive. He rode out on Buck to look at the herd, checking it over and making sure that the wrangler, Emmett Hinds, was happy with the remuda. The man had accompanied Nate on two major drives north together and he trusted him implicitly with the horse stock. He and his boy Abe held the herd together well through thick and thin, and knew each hand's mounts as a father knows his children.

"All well, Em?"

"Sure thing, Nate. Nice bunch in the remuda, couple of wild ones but they'll larn soon enough and settle, I'm bound," he said quietly, coiling the lariat in his hands after lassoing one of the new ones and putting it back where it belonged within the rope corral that would serve as a home for the herd on the trail.

Abe smiled shyly at Nate and gave a nod and tug at his hat. "Say, Mr. Carlton, you expectin' some more riders maybe? I see some comin' in from the north now," he said, pointing out the almost invisible figures moving across the landscape to the north, his young sharp eyes picking out the four riders heading their way.

"Sharp eyes you have there, Abe. Well done. Yes, it'll be Mary Lou and Sue, along with their fathers for protection, I guess. Now we're a full house," he said, pleased. Then his mind turned to the decision he had to make on Susannah and whether she could come on the drive.

The riders soon closed the distance, and to Nate's eyes Mary Lou looked as pretty as ever. She would be about eighteen or nineteen years old now, he judged, and the promise of her youth was blossoming into full womanhood, with striking blue eyes and her mass of black curls that was now partly tucked under the Stetson that framed a lovely face. Sue was pretty in a different way, with a touch of the tomboy still about her. Both wore big grins at seeing Nate, and demanded a hug in turn. Nate shook the hands of their fathers who had ridden along and promised to help edge the herd north before setting off back into the Nations and and their respective homes.

"Now, Mary Lou, I need to ask you something and I want an honest answer."

"Why Nate, honey, you gonna marry me after all!" she declared, a big smile on her face – and for a moment Nate was almost tempted. It had been a longstanding joke between the two of them since their first drive together after the war, and although the harmless flirtation had come to nothing, something still bubbled under the surface.

"Ah, if only, Mary Lou, but I could never keep up with you," he responded in kind, carrying on in the usual vein.

"Yeah, you couldn't, 'cause you'd stop to chase every good looking girl from here to Dodge," she mocked him.

Her father looked on with a proud grin at his sassy daughter, who he knew could hold her own in any company and had the local cowhands all in a tizzy competing for her charms.

Nate shook his head with a grin of his own, but then the levity left him. "But seriously, this concerns you and Sue," he said turning to the younger girl who watched their interaction with amusement. They both looked on in interest now as Nate explained about Susannah.

"Nate, mind if I ask you a personal question?" Mary Lou asked.

"Sure, go ahead."

"This here Susannah girl, she sweet on you? 'Cause if'n she is, she sure is in for a surprise when we get on the trail. You change out there, Nate, all you see are steers and fears. You become so damned focused it hurts to watch. I've seen it, I know. And if some young eastern gal thinks she's gonna be taken for some kinda sightseein' romantic ride, she sure is in for one helluva shock."

"I say amen to that, Mary Lou," Sue chipped in. "You don't see nuthin' but the drive, and everythin' else goes to Hell. But that's what makes you so good at what you do. So you take her along you'd better make sure she knows what she's lettin' herself in for and no mistake, 'cause we ain't got no time to mollycoddle her neither."

"No, ladies, don't you cover it in molasses, you just spit it right out." Nate laughed out loud, loving these two fiercely independent women.

"Waal now, honey, you asked, an' we done told you," Sue drawled with a grin.

"That you did, Sue, that you did. Jim, Bob, my heart goes out to you two gents having to cope with these two, it does indeed," he said, turning to their fathers.

"Waal you could always turn Mormon and marry both of us!" Mary Lou retorted.

"OK, OK, I surrender, I'll go and speak with her now before I'm mauled to death by you two mountain lions." He gave in as the two girls laughed.

He mounted and pushed Buck into a canter, laughing to himself at the two firecrackers that he loved and admired so dearly. Arriving at the ranch he saw Susannah sitting on the porch drinking a cool glass of lemonade.

"Nate, good morning!" she heralded him. "Beautiful day isn't it?"

"It is Susannah, it's all that. Did you sleep well?"

"I surely did, like a log."

"Well that's good, because if you do come on this drive – and I'm still not saying you can – then this will be the last lie in you get for a while."

"Nate I understand, I really do," she answered sweetly.

"Do you though, Susannah? This drive will mean long hours in the saddle or riding on a hard wagon seat. It'll mean being dog tired, with no time for the frills and fripperies you've been used to. There are no passengers on this trip. Everyone, especially me, will be concentrating on one thing and one thing only, and that's getting the herd through to Fort Stockton safely. Everyone will be mean and short tempered, with no time for polite conversation and sometimes no time for sleep. And there's the ever present danger of Indians or rustlers attacking us. I lost a good girl on my first drive and I still hate myself for it now, even though I thought I'd covered all the angles," Nate finished.

Susannah sat quietly through his speech and when it was over she said, "Did the two girls say all this, or are these your own words?"

Nate snorted in disbelief. "For what it's worth, they're my own words, but they echo them, and they pointed out what a tyrant I can be on the trail, whether you believe it or not," he answered.

"I hear everything you say and I still want to go along. I'll muck in and learn fast. I really want to go," she said defiantly, "and I promise to get along with ... what are their names? Mary Lou and...?"

"Sue. All right, but on your head be it. But you cause one single problem and I'll tan your hide, hog tie you and throw you in the back of the chuckwagon, I swear I will. I learned under a hard-bitten taskmaster named Randall and I've probably got worse since then. This drive and the sale mean so much to me and the ranch that I will do anything in my power to push it through. Are we clear?"

"Yes, sir, mister trail boss, sir," she replied with a grin and a mocking salute. "Now come and have some lemonade with me and tell me all about what we're doing."

Nate shook his head in disgust at his own perceived weakness, knowing that he would regret it and what the girls would think of him. *Damn it to Hell!* He cursed to himself.

At this point Sue and Mary Lou came up with their fathers, who were curious to see what manner of woman had gotten under Nate's skin so badly. They saw why he was attracted to Susannah as they got closer. Dismounting, the introductions were made and Mary Lou fired the first salvo with no reticence. "Is Nate actually gonna let you come along? If so, I hope he's told you that it will be hard work all the way, and that by the time we finish we will all smell like polecats and look like scarecrows," she warned, taking an obvious dislike to the eastern girl.

"Why, honey, don't you worry none," Susannah replied, mocking Mary Lou's accent. "Nate has told me all about you and Sue. We'll get along just fine, you see if we don't," she purred back at her.

Mary Lou gave her a scathing look and turning away said quietly to Sue, "Oh isn't she though? Still, it's a long drive and we'll see how long she lasts being at odds with us."

Jim and Bob looked on, almost feeling sorry for the eastern girl, knowing how strong willed their daughters could be.

Next to arrive was Timothy, half expecting to be hauling his unhappy cousin back to the DB ranch. He was seemingly surprised at the turn of events and was making to leave as Susannah came down to see him off and have a quiet word in private.

"Now, Tim, you leave it a while before you tell Aunt Anthea anything. We're heading north tomorrow then following the Goodnight Loving trail all the way to Fort Stockton, that's what Nate said."

Tim asked a few more questions then placed a kiss on his cousin's cheek. He nodded to the group on the porch and rode off in the direction of town, delaying his arrival at the Durrant ranch still further.

The next day the herd set off north, all the hands doing their part and Susannah following at the back, watching how they herded the cattle. Choking on the dust and the stench at the rear of the herd, she soon moved away to the side where she was little more than an ineffective but pretty observer. Later she rode with the other two girls. She saw how they wore men's pants, with Mary Lou sporting a pistol in a holster at her waist, which amazed her. Mary Lou followed Susannah's glance. "This is Texas, lady, everything here is out to kill or bite you. I don't want either, so I keep my Colt handy," she said.

Susannah looked surprised but carried on wearing her split doeskin skirt and pristine blouse topped off with a new Stetson that had yet to be shaped and worn to the correct jack deuce angle. She carried a quirt ringed around her wrist as her only defense and watched with awe as the herd continued to move to the whooping and hollering of the hands.

Nate came up to her when the drive was under way and said, "There it is, the start of the drive. There's nothing like it, and it's something I'll never get tired of watching." He smiled at her, but as she was about to reply, a steer made a break to the right and he wheeled Dancer away. "See you later, Susannah," he shouted as Dancer began homing in on the errant steer, ready to force it back to the herd.

* * *

Buck Durrant slammed his hand down on the leather-topped desk, making his wife, Anthea jump. She didn't like her husband when he came out west. He changed somehow, became more aggressive. She preferred the man she knew in the east, and she felt more at home there. But his money and prosperity had helped her blue blood family financially, so she had to put up with it. But at times like this it was a trial – why must he be so loud and offensive? She sighed and walked away to leave him to whatever he was exploding over now.

"You say he's started his herd already? Damn his Limey eyes, how'd he get them together so soon? We only just heard about the contract for the horses ourselves."

"That's what Susannah and I went to find out, and she's riding with him on the pretext of seeing what a trail drive is like," Timothy answered, fearing the dominant father figure before him.

"What? She's going with him? And he agreed to take her?" This time Buck was more amazed than angry.

"She told him Aunt Anthea had given her permission, and she can be very persuasive. You know what she's like, she wraps men round her little finger."

Anthea, who had not quite left the room, heard the conversation and span around: "She's done what? She cannot possibly go. What a reckless and ridiculous idea, out there all alone with those men and no one to chaperone her – even without the dangers and Indians and such like," she cried in disbelief.

"It's OK, Ma, Nate has two women acting as cooks on the drive. He always takes them, apparently, they go on every drive he makes. They'll look after Susannah," Timothy answered.

"Oh, and that makes everything alright, does it? Buck, you will accompany me and we will go over there directly and fetch her back. What in tarnation will my sister say if she gets to hear about this? I swear she'll have an attack of the vapors."

"Anthea, I refuse you very little, but this time I'm saying no. I have a herd of horses to get ready. I have neither the time nor the inclination to help your niece. If that hot headed little madam wants to go on a drive, let her. She won't last a minute once she learns it's not all romance under the stars, with no soft bed or baths, bad food and hard riding. For what it's worth, I think Carlton's a fool to take her, but he'll larn soon enough. She'll be a thorn in his side and if we're lucky she'll slow him down enough so we can beat him to the Goodnight trail and get the best grazing before he does, 'cause it sure as hell won't recover at this time of the year. If they get rain, it'll be mud for breakfast." He laughed harshly.

"Pa, we got ourselves another problem." It was Rick who had spoken as he entered the room, twisting the Stetson by the brim in his hands. His father was one of the few men he was afraid of, and he had felt the belt on him more than once as he was growing up. Buck Durrant was a hard, rugged old man with little give in him.

"Well don't just stand there, Rick, for God's sakes. What is it?"

"Waal, me'n the boys was out this morning and we reckon someone's been rustling our stock down off the west range. Took about fifteen, maybe twenty head, I'd guess, and headed due north across the river."

"Well, what are you doing here then? Get after them, or do I have to do everything?"

"I sent Sim to track them, we'll catch up with his trail, sure we will, Pa."

Buck Durrant shook his large head. "Get me a horse saddled now and tell the rest of the crew to start mustering the horse herd. I want to be on the trail by tomorrow morning."

"Sure, Pa," Rick answered. He and his brothers were relieved to be getting away from the old man's wrath. Then he did what he always did and called them back just as they were making to leave.

"Rick, were the horses of those rustlers shod or unshod, or did you even look?"

Rick frowned briefly. "We looked, sir, and they were shod all right. I'd swear to it."

"Alright, get to it then, I'll be out to my horse in a minute."

The brothers left Timothy and Anthea alone with Buck in the main room of the big ranch house. Buck took the gun belt off the hook and strapped the well-worn leather around his waist.

"I'm sorry my dear, but this is important. Nobody steals from me and lives to talk about it. I gotta get there before they hit the Nueces or there will be hell to pay and we'll lose 'em on the flats." He turned to Timothy. "Son, you want to help your mother get Susannah back you go to it. But I have neither the time nor the inclination to go chasing after some dumb girl when there are rustlers to catch." He kissed his wife briefly on the cheek and then was gone, shoving his hat upon his mane of hair as he went.

"Oh, that man is so darned irritating sometimes," Anthea said, stamping her delicate foot. "Now get a buckboard ready, Timothy, we're going to get Susannah back," she demanded.

"Ma you're wasting your time, they'll be on the trail now. You'll wreck the buggy and strand us out there, and Susannah won't come back anyway, she is one stubborn girl," Timothy replied.

"Oh, that girl! And you're defying your own mother now too, are you?" she raged, clenching her delicate hands and shaking small fists in front of her.

"Ma, calm down. I'll tell you what I'll do. I'll set out on horseback and follow the herd or cut it off as they hit the Goodnight Loving trail. I'll make sure she's OK. I'll easily move faster than a trail herd, why they can only do ten or twelve miles a day. Don't worry, I'll look after her, just you see if I don't."

He hugged his mother and made to leave, his thoughts swirling as he went, thinking about what he planned to do.

Chapter Seven

It had been more than a week now of dust, hard riding and the occasional drama. Susannah had enjoyed the novelty of trail herding at first, and had even tried a couple of times to head a steer back into the constantly moving mass of horns and bellows that made up the herd. She found the work grueling even in the comparative cool of the fall, with no stopping from dawn until dusk, constantly on the lookout for dangers and not getting her horse's leg down a gopher hole or getting caught in the thorns and brush as the cattle made their way steadily northward. Once she had nearly been gored by a steer with a huge rack of horns and only her savvy horse had saved her. She screamed with fright and in a fit of pique had slammed her quirt down hard on the animal's nose.

The hands had laughed, applauding her spunk and telling her that she was getting there. The two girls on the wagons witnessed the event and gave each other a wry smile.

At first Susannah tried to keep up with Nate, hoping to

waylay him in conversation or spend some time with him. She soon realized that it was not to be. He spoke a few words to her now and again, but he was always on the move, riding hard and alternating between drag and point, trying to be everywhere at once, always offering an encouraging word or harsh rebuke if a hand got it wrong.

Jim and Bob were leaving the herd to split off to their own small ranches, and were not surprised at Nate's behavior as they had seen him in action on his first drive when he had saved Jim from a hanging and set him by accident on the trail to become a respected trail boss in his own right. They waved the girls off as they parted company and headed north.

"Whoo-ee, I tell you, did you see that there Susannah's face the first time she tried to get a seat on the chuckwagon? Lordy me did she get a telling from Mary Lou," Bob exclaimed.

"Waal now, she done wanted a firsthand experience and she sure got herself one," Jim replied. "Didn't realize that the cook on a trail drive answers to no one – not even the trail boss. Nate might be the boss, but Mary Lou's word is law round the chuckwagon and no mistake. That there wagon is like a king's palace. She sure larned, an' mighty quick, too. Just you wait 'til I tell Martha when we get home!" He laughed.

"Think she'll make it?" Bob asked.

"If'n she does she'll either be broken or a better person with none o' them airs and graces, that's for sure. Now we best keep our eyes peeled if we don't want our scalps to be decorating some Indian's lodge pole come sundown."

They set their horses northward in the lowering afternoon sun.

Two hours later Jas Box, Nate's half breed scout, came riding back at an easy lope to halt at Nate's side.

"Found anywhere, Jas?"

"Sure have, boss. See that rise yonder? Well she hides a sort of basin just off the trail, the Pecos runs alongside. Good grazing and wood for fires, an' a whole heap of Pecan trees all loaded with ripe nuts. It'll be a happy night for all of us if the girls can rustle up some pecan pie," he said, rubbing his stomach in appreciation.

"Well, I'll tell you what," Nate said. "You go an ask them nicely to bake a big one, because they won't take that from this mean old trail boss."

Jas tipped his hat and smiled, riding off to the girls to inform them of his find.

"Pecans, Jas?" Mary Lou said. "You pick 'em and we'll bake'em. We still got some eggs left from that last steading on the trail and some corn syrup too. Guess it's your lucky day."

"Sure thing, ma'am. I'll get right to it," he said with a whoop and was gone.

Later, as evening faded into darkness, Jas sat with the others around the campfire, his stomach full of pecan pie. "Thank you, ladies, you've made me a very happy man and it sure does beat beef stew every day."

"Well, seeing as you are so happy, you can take second watch," Nate ordered. No one liked second watch. Just as you'd fallen into a deep sleep, you were disturbed to go out on herd duty. Jas moaned something about keeping his big mouth shut in future and went to look for his bed roll.

At around midnight he was gently shaken awake, needing little promoting, for no man – especially one with Kiowa blood in him – slept deeply on the trail. There was always some part of a man's mind that was on alert for any kind of trouble that might be just around the corner. The night was fragrant with sage, smoke from the coals of the campfire and a hundred different scents of the wild drifting in below a cloudy sky, occasionally lit as the half-moon peeked through breaks in the cover.

He rode gently around the herd, singing softly to the lowing cattle, disturbed by the occasional rustle of wild turkeys that perched above in the pecan trees. They were better than guard dogs, he knew, and would alert him to anything that tried to sneak along the treeline into the basin before any man could hear it. A mountain lion howled its mournful lament in the night to the west, high and far away in the rocks, but the sound made Jas pause and pull his rifle from its scabbard, resting it across his knees in readiness. Nobody wanted to shoot unless they had to, for there was no surer way to cause a stampede at night. The herd was strung out along in a long line by the river, seeking the sweeter grass that was fed by the waters.

Jas caught it as he started to sing again, the first bustle and flurry of flapping wings followed by squawking and uproar: something was spooking the birds upstream. He called as loudly as he dared to the other rider, Cal Rodean, who was patrolling the eastern flank. "Cal, y'all hear anything upstream?"

"Yeah, the turkeys are squabblin' somethin' cruel. I'll take a look see," Cal called back. He rode up the line of cows, leaving his position to follow the riverbank. As he emerged from cover, an arrow thudded into a tree near him passing close by his head. "Indians!" he shouted. "All hands and the cook!"

Nate stirred from a light sleep, brought to wakefulness by the shouts. Grabbing his gun belt he strapped it on, feet in moccasins as he slept, he ran to his night mount, Buck, who was loosely tied to the chuckwagon, and vaulted aboard bareback as the other hands were rising and made to follow him. "Mary Lou, look after Susannah and keep her with you. Shoot anything that comes near you. We'll all be out there!" he shouted over his shoulder as Mary Lou pushed her head out from under the wagon, a Winchester in her hands.

"Will do, Nate!" she called as he galloped off.

He could hear war cries, howls in the night like coyotes mixed with gun fire and shouts from Jas and Cal who were trying to locate each other. The cattle had risen in huge clumps of shadow, upset at the noise and excitement, and the cowhands expected them to stampede at any moment, only their full bellies and the natural enclosure of the basin holding them in so far.

"Billy Jo, Montana, stay with the herd, stop them from stampeding. Run them back to the butte there if they try, it'll pen them in. I'll take the fight," Nate called, taking command instinctively as the other hands rushed to obey. They shouted 'Yo!' in the time honored fashion and pulled up reluctantly, knowing what he said made sense. They holstered their guns and took lariats in their hands instead, moving the herd to compress it, not giving them space to run.

There were more shouts and whoops, and sporadic gunfire as Jas and Cal dug into positions of cover and tried to see where the enemy was coming from. As he got closer, Nate saw a few arrows had hit trees nearby and one ricocheted off a clump of rocks as he neared. Diving down off Buck he rolled and came up next to Jas.

"What the hell, Jas? Where are they?"

"Don't know, Nate. Damnedest thing, none of 'em have come close. If they wanted to raid, they'd have been in and out stealin' stock, but either we caught 'em just in time or they're after another target," Jas replied, puzzled. At that moment a Winchester cracked from the chuckwagon, followed by a handgun.

"The girls!" Nate shouted, fearful that something would happen to them as it had to Rusty on his first drive. "Not again," he said, swearing to himself, "never again."

"Go, Nate. We'll hold 'em here. Go see to the girls," Jas said.

Nate ducked down and ran the few steps to where Buck was ground tethered, seeing even as he ran the shadows of steers heading for the river as the hands fought to contain them. He fired two fast shots at a rider silhouetted above the cattle, and thought he heard a groan of pain, hoping that one of his shots had found its mark. The girls were more important than the herd, and he raced forward. He would not lose them to Indians and a fate worse than death.

Buck slid to a halt before the wagon as Nate landed again in a roll. "Mary Lou, you OK?" he asked, his voice hoarse with fear.

"Sure, Nate. Got 'em cowerin' away an' I can barely see a

thing, just bits of movement. Darndest thing, never seen an Indian attack like it. Think they're drawing us out thin? I guess the cattle is what they want. Must be," she answered, never turning to face him as she and Sue kept their eyes focused on the darkness, ready to shoot anything that moved.

A shadow came into sight and three weapons flew to aim and barked their different calibers, flames lancing forth. Hit by three bullets, the figure raised up and flew backwards, pirouetting to fall out of sight behind the cover of the rocks from which he had risen. The two girls cranked the levers of their Winchester Yellowboy rifles, jacking a new round ready into the breech, each capable and calm. Nate caught his Navy on the recoil, cocking the hammer ready for the next assault. There was noise and scuffling, as though whoever was out there was pulling the dead or injured man away in the manner of Indians picking up their dead.

Still tense with expectation, Nate asked: "Where's Susannah?"

"In the wagon lying down low I hope, behind the flour sacks," Sue answered. "You in there, gal?"

"Yes, I'm here. I'm all right," came a timorous voice.

"Good, stay there," Nate commanded harshly. "You girls OK here?" he asked, now anxious about the herd.

"Nate, since when did we'uns need nursemaidin'? Go an' look after your cows afore you lose the herd. This was a ruse, nothin' more. Skedaddle," Mary Lou ordered.

"Damned if I don't know who the boss of this outfit is." Nate sighed, shaking his head. "I think I'm more afraid of you two than the Indians."

He jumped back on Buck and headed back to the herd, which had been tightly corralled by riders. Morg had broken off to cross the river where Nate had hopefully shot the raider earlier.

"Morg, where are you?" Nate called out, not wanting to be shot in the confusion of the night.

"Come ahead, Nate. They done gone, just me and these poor frightened li'l ol' cows," Montana called, the tension evident in his voice even as he laughed off the danger. "Reckon they might've made off with a few, though. Seems like tracks headin' away up the bank but it's difficult to see properly with all this cloud. I caught a quick look when the moon peeked through."

"Good, at least we saved most of the herd. If we fail on a few head I'll buy some and tag them in to replace those we lost. We'll take a head count when we get nearer Fort Stockton." They set to, hazing the cattle back across the shallow river to join their lowing companions on the other side. "Puzzles me why they didn't take more," Nate said, almost to himself as they pushed them through the water.

"Likely you winged one and they were grateful for what they could get. Let's hope the remuda is safe," Morg said.

"I didn't hear any shots from that direction, and Emmett would have sold his remuda dearly. His boy's a dead eye with a rifle, too."

"Everyone here?" Nate asked, and the hands all shouted out their names in the darkness. "OK, we double the guard. I doubt they'll be back, but you never know. I'll stand this watch and get the girls to put some strong coffee on, though I doubt anyone will sleep well now."

There were some red eyes around the campfire the following morning as no one had managed more than a brief catnap for the rest of the night. Jas came in from scouting around as soon as the dawn had given him enough light to track properly. He dropped off his horse carrying one of the arrows that had so narrowly missed Cal in the night.

"Damn it, Nate. I know I'm half injun myself but this don't make sense. This here is a Comanche arrow, from the Quahadi lodge, or I miss my guess. Now those boys're fighters and raiders of the first water. They don't pussyfoot around. Hell, I'd expect to have a lance through my chest right now. Then there's the attack on the wagons. Nothin' 'gainst Mary Lou and Sue but they didn't press home and they musta known they was womenfolk and food an mebbe guns in there.

"They did get some cattle, though. Looks like a few tracks, admittedly all mixed up every which way and pretty hard to tell across the shale. Looks like they pushed back and forth. Some got back and some got away, I haven't looked too far as I wanted to get back and I wanted to keep my hair right where it is. Still, it don' look right. Somethin's odd here."

"We'll move on as soon as we can. They've taken whatever they wanted. We have the herd, we're all alive and we can move on along the trail, thankfully." Nate said. "Let's break camp and head 'em out, get a good start on the day."

Chapter Eight

They pushed along the line of the river then headed out into more open country with buttes and low lying hills to either side and lesser trails crisscrossing the main route. Sage and brush covered the plains, fighting for space with grass. Then Jas pointed off to the south as buzzards circled high, cawing their terrible cries of death across the sky.

"I see it Jas. What do you think?"

"Could be a trap, Nate. I've known times that injuns staked out a hide or a body to draw others in and ambush them as they approached seeking to help the injured or dying man, drawing them in for more scalps," Jas offered.

Nate made a snap decision. He wanted answers, and he was still not happy about the Indian raid the night before. "Billy Jo, you're *segundo,* keep this line and follow the trail. If we're not back and you hear more than three shots leave it. We'll either be beyond help or winning.

"Jim, you and Jas come with me. I'll take the direct route up to the hills. Jas, head north, Jim take the south. Keep your rifles at the ready. And go easy. I'll have the shorter ride so take off now. As soon as you're happy, fire one shot in the air; two means bad news and get the hell out of there. Got it?"

The men nodded. They shucked their rifles from their scabbards and headed off at a steady lope taking a wide circle toward the circling buzzards. Nate gave them a head start, then headed directly to where the circling birds hovered.

Within a few minutes three rifle shots echoed across the landscape, and moments later the three men met at the point roughly under where the buzzards had been circling. There before them in a rocky outcrop was a grisly find, swarming with flies and ants. Three white men lay in a rough circle splayed apart in death. Each had been scalped, bullet wounds were evident and two bodies were punctured by arrows. The smell was rank, and each man gagged at the stench of death before them. They'd seen it before, but it never got any easier.

"Do you two recognize them?" Nate asked doubting that they would.

Jim hawked and spat before answering. "Hell no. They sure made a mess of 'em, though."

Jas came forward. He had spent part of his childhood in the Kiowa tribe and had seen scalpings many times before. "Nope, but somethin' ain't right somehow," he said, rubbing his chin and looking about before setting off to look for tracks. He came back quickly, after getting no further than twenty or thirty feet in a rough circle.

"Only tracks that show are shod horses, Nate. If injuns did this, they would've had to hold off wide an come in on foot, got them and high tailed out with the hosses. Now that's fine, but it don't read right. There's a boot mark here that don't belong to any of 'em."

Nate said nothing as he studied the three dead men. One had been shot three times; another once, high up in the shoulder, and a third gut-shot. The arrow wound was in the throat of the man who had been shot in the shoulder. "Three men here, three men shot or wounded in that attack the other night. I know what's bothering you, Jas, there's not much blood. Look, a man gets hit in the neck with an arrow, he bleeds if he is still alive. There are just spots here and there on the rocks. You'd expect more."

"They took their weapons, tho', just like an injun would; yet y'all are right, there ain't no blood. Don't look right, don't feel right," Jas said, "Somone's made a clumsy attempt to make us think injuns did it."

"Why, though?" Nate asked almost to himself, puzzled. Then he snapped: "The herd! They've drawn us away, and they could be watching ready to raid it right now – whoever *they* are. Damn it to hell, I hope Billy Jo is keeping a good watch."

They remounted quickly and rode back to the herd at full gallop, hoping and praying that the trap, if that was what it was, did not get sprung before they returned.

The herders saw the fast galloping horsemen and drew their rifles from the boots on their saddles, poised for trouble. Skidding to a halt, Nate explained what they had found and that he thought the earlier attack was white men making it look like Indians.

"So you don't think it was injuns, Nate?" Mary Lou offered from the seat of the chuckwagon, which after the previous night's skirmish had kept close to the herd instead of roaming ahead to look for the next camp site.

"No, I don't. In fact I think those three dead fellas are the men we shot in the attack on the herd the other night. One had three bullet holes in him. Does that sound familiar? You, me and Sue.

"But what gives me greater cause for concern is what they were doing. I mean why didn't they scatter the herd? If they were just Indians raiding, then sure, take a few beef, go away and kill them for winter or make up their own herds. So why didn't they press home the attack?

"And if they were white men, why not drive off the herd, kill us in the dark and gain themselves five hundred head of prime beef? If they had pressed home the attack in numbers they'd have needed to mount a raid, they could have done much more harm. They could've spread them all out and taken more than a couple of measly head, which is what we think they did."

Then Nate made a decision: "Jas, scout out ahead, rifle at the ready. Take a wide loop and see what sign you can pick up. I'll take scout for the herd. Any tracks, go easy, I don't want you getting ambushed." Jas nodded and made to turn toward the hills. "Also, look for a spot to do a herd count. You know what I mean, somewhere either just off the trail or on it where we can pinch them in. I need it done before River Flats, which is the next and last town before Fort Stockton."

"Yo, boss," Jas shouted and made off to change his horse before going scouting.

"What you thinkin', boss? You're worried, aren't you?" Morg asked.

"Yes, something's nagging at me but I'm damned if I can figure out what," Nate replied.

Two hours later they came to a bend in the river with large cottonwoods on the bank and a granite mesa protruding from the hillside. Jas had pointed it out to Nate earlier, and they now sat with the wagons reinforcing the treeline so no cattle would try to push three or more abreast through the naturally thinned line between the river and the rocks.

"Right, Montana, I want you and Saul to haul out any cattle we tell you to on the hoof and push them away toward that small arroyo up on the left."

"You want us to cut the herd?"

"I do, and snap to it. We may not have much time," Nate ordered. He now knew what he feared, and if it happened it would be soon.

"Sue, you know all the local brands. Anything you see that's not NC Connected you yell out to Montana or Saul while Billy Jo and I count 'em. You too, Billy Jo. Anything you see, shout it out."

They now realized what Nate was worried about. The cattle bellowed, fighting the tightening of the gap that was thinning the herd down as the cattle slowed to a noisy ragged line two or three deep. Here and there a shout went up as a steer was roped or hazed out of the herd. The process was slow, and once or twice the cattle fought back to be with the rest of the herd, but eventually Morg and Saul had gathered a small breakaway group from the main herd and pushed it into the narrow arroyo, keeping them in place with a thorn bush fence.

"Waal, I'll be," Billy Jo started, "if that don't beat all. I make it five hundred and three head without those other brands."

"Yes, so do I," Nate replied pleased with himself for getting the correct tally. "How many, Montana?" he shouted across to where Morg and Saul were keeping guard on those they had pulled out.

"Thirty five head of mixed brands, Nate. We got some Rocking D, a few Circle T, some of Luke Hemple's Flying H, plus a couple more I don't know. Hell, has there been rustling at home? How in tarnation did they get here? 'Cause they sure as hell weren't in with this bunch when we left home," Morg said.

"I know, and I'm guessing that's what they did the other night. Whoever it was pushed these cattle into our herd under the pretext of raiding. Now we need to move them out, because if I'm right, we're going to have visitors soon, and they won't be very friendly. Morg, ride to River Flats and see if you can rustle up a couple of hands. Get them out here pronto. I need these cattle moved away from our herd, and fast. If there is any law in town, bring them along too. The town might be too small for a full-time lawman, so bring the mayor or an official, hell, bring anyone who stands as a solid citizen," Nate ordered.

"Right, Billy Jo, you and me are going to get these strange cattle moving. Mary Lou and Sue, leave the wagons and help to get them started. I don't want them mixing up with our herd again. Susannah can sit on the bench and hold the mules steady. We'll haze them hard to begin with for the first mile and then ease off and you can come back. The rest of you boys hold the herd back until we are out of sight," he instructed.

"We will, Nate, but Susannah has gone," Billy Jo said.

"Gone! Where?"

"Don't know. She had her horse tied to the back of the wagon and it done disappeared. I followed for a bit while you were up there, but it was met by another horse and they headed north towards the Pecos."

At this point Nate saw Jas returning at a fast canter from the east. He pulled up short and said: "Boss, I found tracks, distant, but around the north. One horse shod, no injun pony, I followed for while, and he was sure bein' careful. I let him go a few miles then the tracks went away headin' north."

"Damn her, I'll have to go after her," Nate muttered.

"What in the Hell for?" Said Mary Lou. "Weren't no sign of struggle and from what Jas says the two horses met easily and went off side by side. Stay with the herd, Nate. That one knows what she's doin', so don't you go all Southern Gen'leman on me," she ordered.

It went against the grain, but Nate finally agreed. "Well, if that's what she wants to do, so be it. She'll hit the Pecos River soon enough with whoever she's met. They'll probably get a boat downriver to Rocksprings and ride from there." He shook his head in exasperation, cursing her under his breath, still worried for her safety. He mounted up with the girls and headed to the arroyo to where the cattle were waiting.

It was hard work. The strange steers wanted to go back

to the herd and the two men and the girls fought and cursed, pushing them on while everyone battled to prevent the main herd from moving forward as the cattle left. Finally, they created a gap of some hundred yards, and it became a little easier to keep the two herds apart. At half a mile they lost sight of the main herd, and the small group of steers became easier to manage. After a mile Nate sent the girls back to the main herd and the wagons, just as Morg returned with two cow punchers. They were old and grizzled and their days of long hours in the saddle were over, but for this sort of drive and distance they were perfect.

"I'm Bill and this is Pete," one of the newcomers said. "We'll hep get 'em in, it'll be nice to do some work instead of winterin' around the stove yarnin' about old times." He laughed. Without being asked, the two old timers set to, shaking out their lariats as they worked, driving the small herd forward to River Flats, falling easily into the work they'd done all their lives. Then Nate saw a man dressed in town clothes coming up from behind, sitting his horse awkwardly.

"Thank you. Billy Jo, you go with them. I'll be along soon."

"Nate this is Phil Whiteman," Morg said. "Runs the local store and is on the town council. He offered to come as witness and to oversee things. They got no official lawman but Mr. Whiteman here'll see all is legal and proper."

"Howdy, Mister Carlton, heard you had a problem and I'll help if I can. Morg here explained what happened and I'm glad to oblige. Seems like you're doing the honest thing and I wouldn't see you hang for it."

Nate was pleased to get an independent view on the situation. "I'm obliged to you, Mr. Whiteman. We were set up, I'm thinking, and I don't want any fuss with my neighbors at home thinking I rustled their cattle to fulfill my contract with the army. Can we take them to town and have a corral ready for them or some safe pasture where they won't stray?"

"Sure," Whiteman replied. "There's a couple of corrals just outside town with enough grass and water nearby to hold 'em there for a few days, so it won't cost much. You figure the owners will be along for 'em soon?"

Nate gave a tight, humorless grin. "I do, and if I've called it right they won't be wanting to drive them all the way back home again."

"Waal I guess we'll see you in town soon enough. Oh, by the way, I brought a tally book with me. We can sign a paper here agreeing to the numbers and brands so's we can hold 'em for you legal like?"

"That will do very well," Nate agreed, and with the brief note signed, Whiteman rode off to catch up with the small herd and Billy Jo.

Nate and Morg rode back to the herd, which was now moving steadily forward along a trail that would give them a wide berth of River Flats. As the day was coming to a close they all saw the dust of riders in the distance.

"Waal now, looks like you called it right after all, Nate," Mary Lou said, handing him a plate of stew and biscuits.

"Mmm-hmm." Nate nodded, thanking her and slipping the thong from his pistol. "All right, boys, no trouble. Don't push them, leave it to me. But if they start shooting, be ready. Morg, slip out to the side there in that copse of pecan trees in the brush. Stay hidden, take your rifle and be ready, but only on my command."

Nate stood casually, watching as the riders got closer. He recognized all of them. In the lead was Buck Durrant, looking mean and formidable. Every face there was unfriendly, especially Luke Hemple. Of all the men in the Uvalde Valley he was the least friendly to Nate, having missed out on the sale of the Carson homestead when it had been sold specifically to Nate. He had wanted to expand, and that land would have given him an opening to more water.

"So, Carlton we caught up with you." Hemple snarled.

"And a good afternoon to you, gentlemen. Buck, Rick, Tom." Nate nodded to the others, completely ignoring Hemple. He was annoyed, and he knew it was not his best trait, but rudeness like this put his back up and he pushed back in his own way – by ignoring him. "You're all a long way from home. You come ahead of your horse herd, Buck? What can I do for you?" he finished mildly. He was now more than ever convinced that whoever had pushed the strange cattle into his herd under the cover of the raid had planned this whole event. He carried on eating his stew, the plate in his left hand, the fork in his right, seemingly at ease. "You'll have to forgive me, it's been a long day and I'm hungry. Set for some coffee if you like."

"See here, Carlton," Hemple started again, "don't you try to bluff–"

"Shut up, Luke, I'll deal with this," Durrant snapped. "It's like this, Nate. We've all lost some stock to rustlers, and the tracks headed this way, and here you are with a herd headin' to market. We think you've got our cows in your herd an' we need to check it."

"You telling or asking?" Nate said mildly, feeling his anger rise. He knew these men and had laughed, drunk and worked with them; he had taken their stock to market without a murmur, and now this. It didn't make sense, he thought.

"I ain't askin', Nate. We've come a long way and we want our cattle back and we want to see the man that stole 'em hung."

"Seems to me that if you won't let us see for ourselves, you got somethin' to hide," Hemple said, snarling again.

"Luke, you have been riding me now since the minute you arrived," Nate said, falling back on his English manners. "So shut up, there's a good chap. Buck, is that your last word? Just like that you want to run roughshod over me and check my herd?" He put another mouthful of stew into his mouth and chewed calmly. He knew that his whole attitude was irritating Hemple and the others. They had come in all highly strung, expecting a fight or an easy victory, and things weren't going to plan.

"Yes it is. Now we're gonna check that goddamn herd with or without you." Durrant made to push his horse forward.

"No!" The friendly man from the neighboring ranch had gone, so had the trail boss they knew well. Nate had dropped his fork and in that movement the Colt had seemed to jump up to meet his hand, ready cocked and aimed straight into Buck Durrant's chest. They'd heard the rumors, but no one had ever seen him draw. Yet here he was, ready armed and cocked in a split second, his face an implacable mask. Everyone froze. "Montana, anyone lets loose you take old Hemple out of the saddle first, I'd surely hate to see him get my ranch."

Montana shouted back that he had him covered from the copse.

At which Hemple hastily drew his hand back from his holstered Colt. To his back and left Mary Lou called out from her position sitting on the chuckwagon seat. "I got Rick and Benny with this shotgun, Nate. Can't miss 'em," said Mary Lou from the wagon. His other hands had all turned their long guns towards the new arrivals.

"Leave it lie, Rick," Nate ordered.

Rick, who Nate really liked, had tried to make what he imagined was a fast draw, but now he held his hand still, barely on the butt of his Colt, not believing what he had just seen.

"Hold hard there, Nate, I'm moving my hand away. Man, you're fast. I'd never have believed it if I'd not just seen it with my own eyes. Lordy, no wonder you keep it quiet."

"I'd as soon you didn't blab it around, Rick. Now, *Mister* Durrant," Nate began talking again to Buck. "You wanted to look at my herd. With my permission you'd be most welcome to, but just keep that hothead Hemple under control. Then once you have done your looking I will explain what has been going on up here. You and Ricky can look, or you and Hemple, seeing as though he is so all-fired keen to look at my cows.

"The rest of you stay here," Nate finished. There were murmurs of dissent from the other ranchers. "What, don't you even trust your own friends now? And whoever goes looking leaves their guns here. Trust goes two ways. Remember you are on my permission to inspect my herd."

They all knew it was a terrible insult to accuse another man of rustling and to ask to inspect his herd. It was something that was rarely done, usually with a lawman doing the asking, and even he'd better have a good reason and a gun handy or a rope ready. Nate pinwheeled his Colt before their eyes and returned it to his holster, holding his hand out for Buck and Rick's gunbelts as they unbuckled them.

Everyone stayed tense while Rick and Buck made their way around the herd accompanied by Billy Jo, the best cattleman of them all. It took about half an hour, and they came back shaking their heads.

"Nary a one. Every one of 'em bears the NC Connected brand – and there's no alterations, Luke, before you say anything to insult Nate further," Buck said sharply in Hemple's direction. The rancher looked angry and then shamefaced.

"Well, where did them dad-blasted cows get to then?" he asked angrily.

"Why don't you get off your horses? Mary Lou there will swap her shotgun for a coffee pot if you ask her nicely, and I can explain."

The tension was broken, and a few sheepish grins appeared as the distinctive sounds of shotgun hammers being lowered were heard. Everyone seemed to breathe a sigh of relief at once.

"Why sure I will, honey, just as soon as Mr. Durrant here says please," she responded with heavy sarcasm, jumping down off the wagon seat to start preparing coffee and grub. Once they squatted down Nate began to explain. There were looks of disbelief around the campfire as he did so.

"So what happened to the cattle you found?" Hemple asked abrasively.

"They're all safely in a pound at River Flats. You'd be most welcome to fetch them from there, or we can take them on to Fort Stockton with our herd and I'll pay you the same price on the hoof that I get for mine. Your choice. And Luke, if you don't believe me there are three men lying rotting in the rocks back thataway, you're welcome to go and check them over."

"You didn't bury them?" Buck asked.

"No, I was too worried about my herd and being ambushed. Besides, I didn't ask them to attack me, and they got what they deserved. It could so easily have stirred up trouble among us all and been the death of the valley back home with no one trusting each other. What put you onto it, Buck?"

Durrant explained about the rustling and how he'd sought out other ranchers. "You seemed to be the only one free from all this rustling, so we checked with your ranch, and no one seemed to be aware of any missing–"

"I hope you were polite to Lily!" Morg snarled.

"We were, son, keep your hair on. I have no truck with upsetting womenfolk, you know me better'n that," Buck assured him. "And talking of upsetting women, my Anthea's in a takin' about her niece, Nate. Where is Susannah? I hear that she went on the drive with you?"

"She did but she went off north, left the camp in the

early hours this morning. And before you start painting for war, she snuck out and went to meet someone. They joined up and their tracks went north towards the Pecos. They'll probably get a shallow keel boat and head downstream 'til they hit the rapids and then go across country or ride until it becomes navigable again."

"What the hell? You let her go and didn't get after her?" Durrant shouted.

"Buck, what would have happened if I hadn't been here today? If I had not seen all this and realized what had happened to the herd and your cattle. What if I'd have just taken off after her? Think on that. Everything, all occurred at just the wrong time – or maybe the right time, like it had been planned."

"What are you saying?" Buck asked defensively.

"Nothing, I'm just making an observation." At this he saw Rick looking across suspiciously, not at him but with thoughts that were obviously occupying his mind.

"Waal, now, I can add somethin' to that," Morg spoke up. "I was chattin' to that fella from town, and he said a man had been there the last two days and was aimin' to come back with someone. They were headin' for Fort Stockton then on up to the railroad. I reckon your niece has high-tailed it back east, maybe had enough of us western folks. Mind, the drive must a been pretty hard on her."

"Why I'll tan her hide, just you see if I don't!" Buck said, exasperated at Susannah's antics.

"I'll tell you what, Buck, I'll send word to you by telegram as soon as I hear, or you're welcome to tag along with us to the Fort, it's only a few days' ride now. We sure do need a wire in Flat Creek, it certainly would make life easier."

"I've been saying that for long time, maybe we should look into it. I'm obliged to you, Nate, and I'm sorry for that business earlier." He held out his hand in friendship and Nate realized how much it would have cost him to apologize for the confusion earlier that evening and how close it had come to shots being fired. Nate knew one thing at least – there weren't many people who got away with pulling a gun on Buck Durrant.

Chapter Nine

The rest of the drive felt like an anticlimax. Rick decided to stay on with Nate and see the drive home, for which Nate was grateful. An extra hand was always welcome. He also wanted to see if there was any news of his cousin. Fort Stockton was a welcome sight after the trials of the trail. It wasn't quite the same as coming to an end of the long drives and the trail end towns of Abilene or Dodge, but it made a change from constant movement and harsh conditions. The newly recommissioned fort stood out, its freshly hewn timber forming the main stockade. The town was set on a broad plain surrounded by low lying hills giving off to a fertile basin of rich farmland riddled with the small streams and watercourses of Comanche Springs.

The grazing was good, although to Nate's eye it was starting to turn a little yellow as the fall took hold and temperatures dropped, and because of its proximity to the Chihuahua desert. Scrub and trees of live and red oak dotted the plains forming clusters of small woods ascending to the hills. In the distance a huge red stone mesa dwarfed the landscape like a natural cathedral overseeing God's creation upon the plains. A whole new town was springing up as Fort Stockton was on the main trading route and the wagon trail through to San Antonio.

Corrals had been erected and a small company of soldiers came out to meet them under the command of a lieutenant.

"Lieutenant Crawford, sir," he said, saluting Nate, who by force of habit returned his salute, smiling inwardly at how some habits die hard. "I assume that you're Mister Carlton?"

"I am, lieutenant, with your beef here as promised."

"We were expecting you, sir. Your business partner Paul Tranter assured us that you would be here on time, and so you are. Major Wade is expecting you inside the post."

"That's perfect. If you'd show us where you'd like the herd we can see to the cattle and count them off for you."

Lieutenant Crawford showed him the way to the designated corrals and offered help from some of the 'Buffalo Soldiers', as the 9th Cavalry was known, being almost entirely populated by black troopers. Nate had heard of their exploits fighting in the Indian wars and knew that the name had been given to them as a term of respect by the Comanches and other tribes who they had fought so well.

With the cattle seen to and the numbers tallied, Nate was introduced to the camp commander in his quarters, which after the deprivations of the trail seemed very luxurious. Nate felt uncomfortable in his dusty trail stained clothes, aware that he had not had a bath in days.

"Mister Carlton, how do you do? I am Major James Wade, commander of the post and the 9th Cavalry. I trust that you had a good journey." Nate saw a youngish man in his late twenties or early thirties, well turned out in a uniform that had seen use, wearing a large mustache and lines about the eyes that spoke of action, not polishing some desk in Washington.

"How do you do, sir? Well, we had our moments, but nothing more than I've experienced on the trail before. It just comes packaged in a different way each time." Nate smiled.

"I can identify with that. It's like fighting Comanches – they still attack, but each time they do it is different just to keep you guessing. Least I can do is offer you something to wash the trail dust away, and I have a very fine bourbon for just such an occasion," Wade offered generously.

They saluted each other with a glass and talk fell to the frontier and inevitably to the recent war, with both men skirting carefully around a subject that was still raw, agreeing that they were glad it was all over. Then Paul Tranter appeared through the doorway, and the company became even more convivial. Nate found the major good company and readily accepted an offer to come to dinner in the officer's mess that evening.

"I understand that you have two young ladies along. I'm sure my men would enjoy their company as a change from their old commanding officer," he said gallantly.

"Well, I'm sure they would be delighted, Major, and I will certainly ask them. Probably cost me two new dresses, though." The men laughed and Nate begged leave to clean up and ready himself for the evening ahead. Once he and Paul were alone he told him all that had occurred on the trail.

"You had a close call, Nate. It could all have ended in bloodshed but for your cool head and cleverness. Not easy to out-think it all. Who do you think was behind it? Someone must've been pulling the strings. Someone who wants you out of the way. Jealous because of the army contract, maybe?" he ventured.

"I guess there are too many pieces missing from the puzzle to put it together right now, and I think I'm only seeing half of it. More questions than answers – and it concerns the Uvalde Valley as much as anything that happened on the drive, of that I'm certain. Now I'm going to have a word with the adjutant because sure as hell there's nothing happens on this post that he doesn't hear about. Then a trip to the saloon is called for, followed by the livery stable. That'll give me a better idea of what's been going on."

An hour later Nate had some of his questions answered, and when he met up with Paul again he was bathed and in clean clothes with Mary Lou and Sue in tow.

"From the description given to me each time I asked, it seems that Susannah was here, so we can calm Buck's fears on that score. They set off north under a cavalry escort to the railhead. Apparently a patrol was heading north anyway, and they joined them for their protection."

"That damned Yankee miss. Why I knew all along that she was no good," claimed Mary Lou.

Nate laughed at her natural prejudice. Then Paul asked: "The six million dollar question is who was she leaving with? I mean, was it anyone that we know from the description you got of him?"

"I'm glad that you asked me that, Paul, because if I was

pushed I would say it sounded like her cousin, Tim Durrant."

"Waal now, nothing too serious about that – after all he brought her to your ranch and vouched for her."

Mary Lou and Sue both snorted together. "Yeah damned easterners comin' out here, just can't hack it," Sue said. "Wonder where he's gonna fetch up, 'cause from what you say he's got hisself a law wrangler business in Flat Creek and he'll need to be back to it."

"We'll see what's going on when we get back, and you can be sure I'll have some questions for Tim when I see him," Nate said.

Later, with everyone dressed up including the two girls – for whom Nate had, in the time honored fashion bought two new store dresses as a thank you for helping them get to the end of the drive – they entered the officer's mess with Sue on Paul's arm and Mary Lou on Nate's. They were the toast of the evening, with the other officer's wives pleased to have some new female company to talk to. It was a memorable time, with some impromptu dancing care of the hastily assembled band of the Company G of the 41st Infantry who were also stationed at the post.

The crew had celebrated off post, and the following morning there were some sore heads as they started the long journey back to Flat Creek at a much quicker pace without the hindrance of the cattle, making faster time despite the wagons.

* * *

They arrived back at Flat Creek a few days later. Mary Lou and Sue had been met by their fathers at a pre-arranged time that was out by just a day and given safe escort back to their homes. Before she left, Mary Lou came up to Nate to say goodbye.

"Ever you come this way again you be sure to call in, Nate. And don't you go losin' your heart to no eastern filly. They just ain't right for you, despite your education an' all. I'm not the young naïve girl I once was, and I won't wait forever. There, I've said too much, but some things've just got to be said." She grinned at him to take the seriousness from her words. "Either way, I'll be here for next year's drive, an' so will Sue. Just holler and we'll be there."

She pecked him on the cheek, left his brief embrace and disappeared toward her father who had a horse ready for her before Nate could form a reply. Mary Lou had grown up and she didn't feel like a young girl anymore when he embraced her. Damn it, why did he feel suddenly empty now she'd gone?

With these thoughts turning in his mind, he arrived at Flat Creek to find that events had overtaken them all. The saloon was their first stop, and Nate stood the crew a round of cold beers after the dusty trail. The saloon was quieter than usual, and the reason why soon became apparent.

A cowpuncher at the bar was knocking back a slug of whiskey, and he was shaking as he did so. "Worst thing I ever done saw. Whole darned family gone in one raid. Parents, two boys and two little girls...all gone," he muttered. "Burned and scalped, all of 'em – 'ceptin' the girls, and there weren't no sign of 'em." They all knew what this meant.

"Who are you talking about?" Nate asked, moving to the man's side, now very concerned, the pleasure at the success of the drive dissipating.

"The Gilmores over on Forest Peak, they got hit by injuns yesterday evenin', look of it. House burned, cattle stolen. We saw smoke as we was herdin' cows over on the edge of Buck's range." The man was still pale and in shock.

"You sure it was Indians?" Nate asked gently.

"Damn it, man, what white man would do a thing like that?" the puncher asked in exasperation, and the crowd around him nodded. "Was I you and I just got back from my ride I'd get back on my spread an' prepare for a raid, 'cause once they start they get a taste for it and they'll come at night like the Comanche always do."

Nate shook his head in sympathy. "Good advice, friend. I'll be on my way." He knew that the Gilmores' spread was little more than a hundred and fifty acre Land Grant Scheme. It was way over on the other side of the valley abutting the far side of Buck Durrant's vast acreage and had been settled on free range under the government scheme a few years ago by the Gilmore family. They'd been good people, he remembered, and the girls were about nine or ten years old. They would have been easy targets for a determined raid and a lone family trying to eke out a living on a rough and hard frontier wouldn't have stood a chance.

He ordered a cold beer for the boys, but as he turned he saw Morg leaving. "Nate, I know they're probably OK but I need to make sure Lily is safe. I'm headin' back now," he said, a worried look on his face.

"Alright, Montana, we'll be just a few minutes behind

you." He gulped the frothy cold liquid, suddenly sad inside at the loss and the change in the valley that he could feel coming, along with the uncertainty of the possible attacks that could affect anyone. With the beers finished the rest of the boys made to leave with Nate following in their wake, hoping that his friendship, such as it was with the Comanches, would prevent his ranch from being attacked, if indeed they were planning to strike anywhere in the valley. Somehow he doubted it. There were questions here that needed answering.

"I'll catch up, boys, I need to see Marshal Walker. I won't be far behind you."

They offered to wait but he ordered them off to get back to Lily with Morg. He pushed open the door to the marshal's office, catching him in the process of cleaning, oiling and reloading one of the Winchester rifles from the rack on the wall.

"Morning, Marshal. Expecting trouble?" Nate asked.

"Hi, Nate. Good to see you back safe and sound. I heard you'd had yourself some trouble on the trail. Bad business, from what I hear. Good that you kept a clear head and avoided gunplay. You're a steady hand, Nate, and no mistake, but then most of the good guns always are. No need to prove anything and avoid trouble where they can."

Nate said nothing.

"Oh, I know, I know, a reputation can get a man killed," Walker continued. "Hell, I saw it my own self couple days 'fore you left, though you do your best to cover it all up. But I heard about what happened out there, and Danny can't get over what he says was the fastest draw he's ever seen. I hope it'll blow over. Talking of which, that Jimmy fella that tried it on with you in the saloon a few weeks ago? Waal he's back around and working for the Rocking D, so be warned. If he hears talk of what occurred – and he will, I'm bound – it'll prob'ly fire him up again."

"Obliged to you, Paul, but that's not why I came to see you. I heard about the terrible events out at the Gilmore place. I didn't know them well, but they seemed nice folks. Are you sure it was Indians who did it?"

"Waal now, that's an interestin' question. Why do you say such a thing?"

Nate explained about the attack on the trail that had been made to look like the work of Indians, yet it was clearly whites. Walker asked Nate how it had been set up, and he was intrigued. "Somebody has a grudge that's for sure," he said. "Anyways, I'll mind it. I'm off to see Buck and take a sweep by his place, then on to the Gilmores afterward."

"You sure that's wise, sheriff? Indian or white, if they're out there hunting trouble and you're alone, the odds aren't good."

"Don't worry I've got a fast horse," he joked. "And Buck will lend me a couple of men. We'll go out together, there's safety in numbers."

"Alright well if ever you need a hand just shout, I've had some experience of being a lawman, and while I don't want any more I'll always back you."

"Yeah, I heard about how you cleared up Langtonville, and I appreciate the offer. I'm due to meet up with my opposite number from across the county line. He's a deputy sheriff, too, so we'll have a chinwag and see how she sets."

Nate made to leave, then two thoughts occurred to him. "Say, is Tim Durrant back? I hear he went north after his cousin."

"I don't know about that, but he was surely missing for a couple of weeks. He's back now tho', saw him this afternoon not half an hour ago as the news reached town. Said he'd been on a trip north and was eager to see what had gone on at the Gilmore's homestead."

"Thank you, Paul. One more thing; have you heard any more about a wagon train heading this way?"

"Now you're about the third person to ask me that question, and yes, I have. A young puncher came in two days ago sayin' he passed them on the trail from San Antone. Didn't know quite where they was headed, but they was comin' in this direction down the main trail from what I gather."

"Thank you, Paul. Good luck at the Gilmore place." Nate tipped his hat and left Walker's office. Part of him wanted to go and speak with Tim Durrant, but he was more worried for the ranch. He mounted Patch, his Appaloosa quarter horse stallion, and set off home.

Chapter Ten

Marshal Walker rode out of town about an hour later, leaving word for his deputy who was out doing the rounds in the county looking into the cattle rustling. It was a big county, and with only two men their time was inevitably spread pretty thin. Walker started out in the early evening, knowing that he would only just make the Durrant ranch by dusk if he was lucky, but that there would be a warm welcome for him and a bed for the night at the very least.

He headed west, looking carefully over the trail and keeping his eyes and ears open. There was trouble brewing, and he did not want his scalp hanging in some Comanche's wikiup. It was still light when he saw the smoke hazing upward some distance from the trail, the fire not in sight but clearly made by a white man, for no Indian would be so obvious as to make smoke like that in the open, not in Comanche territory unless he was part of a larger group that was able to protect themselves with enough firepower.

"Fool," he muttered to himself, "prob'ly some nester or

tenderfoot doesn't realize the danger he's in. Come nightfall he'll be scalped if there's injuns around."

He pulled off the trail, making for the small outcrop of rocks that sheltered the fire that was making the smoke. It was sheltered within an aspen grove, and whoever had set it had clearly used green wood to make the fire. Walker shook his head in disgust, it was just asking for trouble.

He entered the clearing alert and with the loop off the hammer of his Remmington pistol, his nerves a little on edge as no one was in sight. He saw a coffee pot burbling over the large fire that was throwing smoke into the air. "Hello the camp," he called out, stopping his horse just outside the inner ring of trees. He saw a horse hobbled in the grass in the fading light, and the animal lifted its head and nickered a greeting to Walker's own horse. He called again, assuming that the camper must be off gathering wood or water down at the nearby stream. But he was wary now. He dismounted and eased his Remmington out of its holster, unsure of the situation, some sixth sense warning him that not all was well here.

He left the ring of the campfire and began to make his way through the brush to where a stream burbled away. In the shadows and gloom he saw a figure turned away from him, bending and picking up firewood. He called out again to get the man's attention, not wishing to startle him out on the range where any reaction could be dangerous. This time the figure turned and smiled in the fading light. "Oh howdy, marshal," the man said. "Didn't see you there, you sure know how to sneak up on a man." The voice was softly spoken, harmless and unprepossessing.

"Waal I'll be. What are you doing out here–"

Paul Walker's words ended in a gurgle as the point of an arrow suddenly emerged from the front of his neck. His instinctive reaction was to turn, dropping his gun to grasp at the wooden shaft that was even now taking his life away. He uttered a cry of surprise and astonishment, "Whyyyy…?" falling face first to the rocks by the stream, choking on his own blood.

"You took your sweet time," the wood gatherer growled.

"Had to wait, the dry wood made a noise and he was too sharp for that, he'd a shot me," his companion said.

The wood gatherer grunted in what may have been agreement. "Come on, we have work to do. Get my horse out of here an' bring in those two unshod ponies. We made that mistake on the trail north of here from what I heard. Nate Carlton is too clever by half, but not this time. This time it's all gonna look just the way it should."

The two men set to work moving the marshal's body, re-setting tracks around the camp and setting the scene to make it look like an Indian attack. One of them fired Walker's pistol, hitting two tree trunks before returning it to the marshal's dead hand. Satisfied with their efforts, the wood gatherer gave the scene one final look and nodded before parting company with the other killer and riding off.

Three days later, Nate rode into town escorting Lily on one of her regular visits on the wagon as she went to collect more supplies and see her mother. Morg tagged along, keen to watch over Lily with the threat of more Indian attacks. He and Nate should provide enough of an escort to keep her safe, especially with the sheath for Nate's rifle in prominent view, which carried big medicine where the Comanches were concerned. Nate was thinking about the land that was shut off by the escarpment in Carson Valley and was more than ever determined to see what was behind it. With this in mind he had ordered some dynamite, mindful of his experience with the miners outside of Langtonville and how it had sealed off the pass to the pursuing outlaws. The sheer power and destructive force of the explosion had left a big impression on him, so he had investigated further and had a more stable mix of blasting sticks ordered to be delivered to a very nervous Henry Wilkins, the store owner. Wilkins advised him to pack the sticks carefully and on no account to let them overheat if he wanted to live long enough to use them.

"Don't worry, Henry, we have a deep cave in the rocks at the back of the ranch house. They'll be cool and safe in there and it's far enough away from the house."

"Waal I hope so, 'cause if they go off there won't be much of you to bury, Nate, just you mark my words," Henry warned.

Nate laughed it off and loaded the rest of the supplies into the wagon. "You go and see your mother, Lily. I need to go and check if the marshal is back from his trip to the Gilmores."

He left Morg and Lily to gather the rest of the supplies and drive the wagon carefully home. Minutes later he was talking to deputy Macey Green. "No, Nate, he ain't, and tell the truth I'm a bit worried. He should have been back long before now, less'n he stayed over at the Durrant place before headin' back here."

The door opened again at that moment, and Buck Durrant came in. He must have caught the tail end of the conversation, Nate thought. He looked somber and troubled. "If you are talking about Paul, then I'm afraid I have some bad news. He won't be making it back. His body was found by two of my hands out on the back of my range yesterday."

"Where? How?" Macey stuttered.

"Out on the lower range just by the Aspen creek. Boys saw buzzards circling and went to investigate, found him dead with an arrow through his neck by a small camp he had made near the stream."

Macey turned white with shock. "No! I don't believe it. Damned injuns again. We're gonna have a full uprising if this keeps on. First the Gilmores, now Paul. Who's gonna be next? Someone needs to tell the governor, maybe get some troops out from Fort Stockton or closer."

"Sorry to hear that, Buck," Nate said. "Are you sure it was Indians? You know what happened on the Goodnight trail."

"I know, and those were my thoughts too, so I checked on the way in. No bullet holes, just an arrow through the neck. He'd been scalped too." Durrant paused, the memory of the dead marshal still all too clear in his mind. "Tracks of unshod ponies all around the camp site. Not like with the herd, so I don't reckon there's much chance of a mistake here," he finished.

"Mmm, I see. Well, if you don't mind I'll send Jas out to scout for sign. He might be able to tell us more," Nate asked.

Macey was clearly in shock at the loss of a man who had been not only his boss but a good friend and mentor as well. "Sure, Nate, sure," he replied. "Do whatever you can. I'll get a wagon sent out to recover the body."

"No need, Macey," Buck interjected. "I had one of the boys bring him in on a covered wagon, couldn't leave him out there with the buzzards an' all. He's at the back of the doctors now. We brought him back quiet like, so as not to cause a fuss."

"Thank you, Buck, I appreciate it. I'll go over now and see the body," Macey said, his face a sickly color.

Nate followed the deputy out through the back door, as he too had interest in the circumstances of Marshal Walker's death and wanted to see the evidence for himself.

Walker's body was discolored from a couple of days in the open and his head was covered with a cloth and twisted to one side by the arrow that was still in the back of his neck. Deputy Macey was young and had not seen but two dead bodies, and certainly nothing like the violence before him. He excused himself and threw up in the yard at the back of the doctor's rooms. Buck and Nate admitted that it was not a pretty sight by anybody's standards, made worse by the fact that both men had known the marshal well.

Nate left a short while later. He wasn't happy with what he had seen of the body, but he said nothing to Buck or the young deputy. He headed for the ranch, where he found Jas herding cattle in one of the far pastures. Explaining what had happened and how Marshal Walker had met his death, he asked Jas to come to the place where the marshal had been killed. They talked as they rode.

"I've got a naturally suspicious mind, especially having served as a peace officer," Nate said, "and when something happens in the same way and everything looks too obvious, there's usually something more. I get a feeling there's something not right in this valley, and it all started with my impromptu visit to the Comanche camp. It was like they were quietly painting for war, and all this..." He spread his arm. "Was planned."

They found the spot easily enough from the tracks that led off the trail and followed the lines of the wagon to the clearing where Walker's body had been found and dismounted.

"Everything will have been trampled on and the sign mussed up near here," Jas said looking at the ring of stones that supported the long dead campfire. "But it will be further out where the real story is told. You can stay here, Nate, and I'll be back when I'm happy with what I've found, or you can tag along behind me – long as you keep out of the way."

Nate nodded, always keen to learn, and accepted Jas's order, knowing how important it would be not to disturb anything until he had seen all clearly. He kept a few paces back, watching as Jas walked carefully on the balls of his feet, noting everything whenever he stopped as the ground, the trees and the wilderness gave up their secrets to the skilled tracker that he was. Half an hour later, having skirted the camp, he followed a line down to the stream, squatting down in the brush where the marshal had been skewered from behind by the arrow.

He shook his head, a tight and humorless smile on his face. "Waal now, they done think they're really clever, but it won't wash, surely it won't. See here?" He pointed. "The marshal now, he walked out this a way, likely heard somethin' or saw someone at the stream. Anyways, he stopped right here, and my guess is this is where he died, or certainly where he was struck by the arrow, but it came from behind and it sure weren't fired from no bow. Look there, see the outline of a deeper impression? Now I bet a jasper was waiting here, stood forward with all his weight and thrust the arrow by hand straight into the back of his neck. Easier see? Softer, no big bones or large muscle. Still, it would need some heft to get it done right and kill him.

"Then he falls here, sort of collapses and they tried to get rid of all the evidence, but they left some signs. See these marmot droppings? Well, that little critter was after the blood that spilled. Nearly got rid of it all too, but he missed a bit on this chickweed leaf here, see?"

Nate nodded picking out the tiny dark speck that he would never otherwise have noticed, knowing that he was in the presence of a master tracker who would have put his poor skills to shame.

"Now I'll just follow the tracks back and then I'll have the full picture," Jas said confidently.

Minutes later they were back at the campfire and Jas nodded in satisfaction.

"Sure warn't no Comanche did this. Oh, it was dressed

up mighty well to look like it, set up real good in fact, but my ole pappy would have laughed at 'em. Poor old Paul was lured out thataway over by the stream, killed there or near as damn it. Two men carried him back here, dropped him by the fire and shot off a couple rounds from his pistol. Prob'ly find it empty if'n you was to check.

"Then they scalped him and injun'd outta here, made tracks with unshod horses, rode round a bit before makin' a big circle west and back to town, I'd guess, the two fellas splitting up. Nice horse with a big gait one of them was on."

Nate smiled in disbelief. He knew tracking was an art, but he'd never seen it done like this before. "Ha! Would you like to tell me what the chap on the nice horse was wearing and what he looked like as well? You know, seeing as how you are so well acquainted with him." He raised an eyebrow in sarcasm.

"Waal, seein' as how you come to mention it," Jas responded in kind, "he was about a hundred fifty pounds, five-ten, maybe a touch less. He wore a blue wool jacket or shirt and he sure weren't no nester. That do you?" Jas finished with a grin.

"I have absolutely no idea how you know that, but I believe you and I'll bear that in mind. All right, we need to get to town and report what you have found to deputy Green. Come on, if we hurry we'll get there by supper and we should be able to get back from there to the ranch before nightfall."

The two men set off at good pace for town, where they were greeted with skepticism by Macey Green.

"Look, Jas," said the deputy, "I don't mean to call you a liar, but are you sure?" he asked.

"Yep, sure as shootin'. The ground don't lie, and it was all there plain to see if you knew where to look."

"OK, there'll be a coroner's inquiry and I'll be asking you to testify there, but I don't know it'll help us much to find out who killed poor old Paul."

"That's fine, Macey. We'll be around and you know where to find us," Nate said. "Now we need to get some grub, I'm starving, then we'll head back to the ranch tonight. I don't want to leave it light handed just in case."

After treating Jas to a good supper at the saloon they headed back out to the ranch as night was falling.

"You know one thing puzzles me, Nate," Jas said, deep in thought. "Everyone says that Marshal Walker left town late afternoon or early evening, and by all accounts he told a few folks where he was going."

"Yes," Nate responded, certain he knew where Jas was going with this.

"Waal, if'n he left then, and given where he was found, he could easily have made it to the Durrant ranch that night and gotten hisself a warm bed, good food an' all. So why in tarnation did he make camp where he did, and how did whoever killed him know he would be there and get to him?"

Nate nodded his head in agreement. "Both very good questions, Jas, and ones I'd like to know the answers to. And somehow I've got to figure it out, because nice as he is, dear old Macey isn't the man to do it, and someone very clever and very ruthless is behind this and has their own agenda."

"Agenda?" Jas queried.

"Yes, they're planning to stir things up between the Indians and whites – and maybe between the whites themselves."

Chapter Eleven

Two days later rumors spread of another raid, this time against Tom Stanley's Rocking T. The attack happened at night, and this time there was no doubt it was Comanches. Stanley had sent a couple of ranch hands out to pass the word around the valley, and one of them was now standing on the porch of the NC Connected ranch house.

The hand told Nate what happened with horror in his voice: "They hit us after dark on the range and at the ranch house. Ran off some stock, burned a barn, killed two hands and then whooped off, disappearin' into the night like ghosts. It was terrifying, I tell you."

He explained about the attack on the range, telling Nate how the attackers had chosen the time and place, but luckily the crew had their repeaters to hand and ready. They had two men on guard and twice the number of hands in the floating outfit than was necessary, otherwise they would all have been killed.

"The attack at the ranch," Nate asked. "Is Tom sure it was Comanches?"

"Hell, Nate, yes. They even killed a couple of 'em, and though their bodies were taken back they saw feathers and everything. They was well armed, too, with two or three rifles and pistols, not just lances and bows."

"Yes, sorry, I was just making sure."

The hand looked puzzled but answered the other questions thrown at him by Nate's crew.

"Thank Tom from me for the warning," Nate said eventually. "Do you want to bunk down here tonight? It'll be dark soon and you don't want to be out alone at night."

"Obliged, Nate. You know I'll take you up on that."

"Good. We'll get some extra chow for you if you ask Lily nicely." Nate went off by himself to think. He had a nervous energy about him, he knew, and he needed to expend it while he thought things through. Around the back of the ranch house was a small lean-to, and in there he had a punch bag set up and a pair of light leather padded gloves. He eased off his boots, slipped on moccasins, stripped off his shirt and started to stretch as he had been taught by Michele Casseux many years ago. He stretched and warmed up, hitting the bag, slowly increasing power before starting to kick in the style of Savate fighters everywhere, beginning with the *coup de pied au corps*, aimed at the stomach and higher, followed by roundhouse kicks he had trained for, working hard for half an hour and raising a heavy sweat. It was all about footwork and angles, he knew. The knowledge had been drilled into him from the start of his training. Then he warmed down with a more pugilistic style of boxing he'd been taught by his father and finished with a stretching session. When he was done he was exhausted, but his mind was clearer, and things were falling into place.

The warm light of oil lamps flickered about the ranch, and he heard owls start their nightly symphony. The odd mountain lion joined the concert, but the cries sounded genuine, with no hint of a Comanche mimicking the creatures of the night. Satisfied, he ate by himself in the house then read, putting the book down at times to consider matters as they entered his head.

The following day Tom Stanley's puncher left early while Nate took up the chore he had promised himself weeks ago. Today he would try to blow a passage into the Carson Valley Canyon, as he had named it.

He'd managed to find a way up through the outside of the rocky escarpment that had gotten him up on top of a mesa, where he'd had a broken view of the land inside that was restricted by the twists and turns of the rock formation. But to Nate it had looked like a paradise, with grassland interspersed by streams and stands of trees. He had to find a way in, he had promised himself, even if it meant work after blasting at the rock.

As day broke Nate retrieved the dynamite from the cool of the cave at the back of the ranch house.

"That trickling stream certainly kept it cool," he said to Morg and Jim, who were watching with a certain amount of trepidation as he produced the wooden box carrying the explosive. "So we're going to settle this nicely in the back of the wagon wrapped in blankets to cushion it against any bumps and bangs. Hopefully we will arrive in one piece." He smiled at the two nervous looking men.

"You sure about this, Nate?" Morg asked.

"Don't you worry, Montana, you can ride as far from the wagon as you like. I'm the one taking the risks here. I've left half the dynamite in the cave as I'm not sure how much we will need. I'd rather take less and come back again once the explosions are finished and give everything time to settle. Did you bring the blasting caps from the house?"

"Sure, Nate, I got 'em here like you asked, all wrapped up as well."

"Good, we don't want you blowing your fingers off. It'd make Lily very unhappy," he joked.

With the dynamite safely roped in place on the bed of the wagon, Nate secured the blasting caps away from the box under the seat beneath him. This is how the miners in Langtonville had done it, and they had taught him their secrets. It was a useful lesson, and he never knew when he might need it on the ranch, he had thought. Soon he would test the lessons they gave him on how to use it.

He drove off at a steady pace, the two riders keeping up with him but staying at a safe distance, neither totally happy with a potentially bumpy ride despite his assurance that the miners were much more gung-ho about transporting the dynamite even when there was a higher content of nitroglycerine in the mix. They'd told him that it would still take quite a concussion to set it off spontaneously – and then only if it was old and unstable.

By midday they had arrived at the fissure in the rock face

that Nate had partially explored weeks before on the cattle roundup.

"OK, boys, we'll set up here under these trees. I'm going into the crack in the rock there to see how far I can get like before. That's where I'll place the charges, and I'll set a pattern leading outwards."

He unbuckled his gunbelt so it didn't get caught or scratched by the rock, placing it on the seat of the wagon, but not before drawing his smaller Colt Police Model .36 and shoving it in his belt. He had had the gun rechambered for metallic cartridges, and it served him well as a backup gun.

"Just in case I meet a rattler in there. I wouldn't want to be bitten with nowhere to run," he said.

"Rather you than me, I hate tight spaces," Morg said.

"Me too. My older brother used to lock me in a cupboard under the stairs back in England when we were young. Never really got over it, but it has to be done." He briefly turned his thoughts to his brother George, who was either still soldiering in Europe or working in some far flung part of the Empire. Then he dismissed the thoughts, knowing that he had to concentrate if he was to be safe in his endeavors.

He left off his Stetson and leather vest and headed for the fissure, which at first seemed quite wide and was tall enough for him to walk in upright. But like most eroded passages in the red rock, it soon narrowed and he had to pass through it sideways. He'd gone about forty feet before it started to drop, although there were still animal tracks heading inwards on the sandy floor, and here and there some hanging fern clung tenaciously to the walls of the long fissure. It twisted and turned, and Nate lost sight of the entrance. When he looked above his head, he saw a thin sliver of sky a long way above him, where the seam had been split by nature, pushing the rock apart into a devil's chimney that led seemingly all the way to the daylight at the top.

He shivered, not wanting to be stuck here. At least he could now stand upright again as the split widened, but then it came to an abrupt halt, dropping down to where a stream trickled out slowly, eroding the rock until it was too low for a man to pass through. The gap was some two or three feet in height, and Nate saw that smaller mammals had made the onward journey, so it should at least lead somewhere, he reasoned.

Nate had no intention of trying that packrat tunnel. He reached into his pocket, fetched out a box of matches and struck one. The match spluttered and flared to life, but as the flame matured it wobbled and weaved, eventually snuffed out by the draft caused by the air running through the lower tunnel. *So it does go somewhere*. Nate thought with hope. *But I'm damned if I'm going to follow it. Right, Nate, my boy, time to go and get the dynamite.*

With cold sweat pouring off him, Nate edged sideways back the way he had come, the opening widening out and allowing him to breathe easier as his chest expanded after being constricted by the closeness of the rock walls. Pleased and relieved to be out, he breathed deeply, glad of the sun's warmth upon his body.

"Whoo-ee, I sure as hell don't want to get trapped in there," Nate said emphatically. Morg saw his tension and nodded. "Alright, Jim. We need to set up the dynamite. Fetch the blasting caps off the wagon bed," he said.

"So how does this work?" Jim asked, interested.

"A chap called Nobel figured it all out. He discovered that you need a really high heat to set off the main charge with any certainty. These are fulminate of mercury," he said, holding up a blasting cap. "They create a small but very hot charge that sets off the larger stick. Simple really. Each cap gets pushed into a stick with the fuse cord hooked up to it. We set the fuse cords so the spark meets all the charges at the same moment – by which time we will all be well out of the way."

Nate pulled lengths of detonating cord to allow for where he would set all the charges throughout the fissure. Then he laid out the fuse cord for each stick, working backwards into the fissure and allowing the long lengths of fuse to belay as he walked backwards disappearing from sight.

"Montana, move the horses and the wagon around to the next bluff away from the noise and rocks," Nate shouted. "I don't want the horses spooked."

"Will do, Nate," Morg answered. "You be OK, Jim?"

"Sure thing, Morg. You take 'em away an' I'll look after things here."

The two men nodded at each other, but as soon as Morg had taken the horses away, Jim pulled out a stick of dynamite he had secreted about him. Carefully pushing the blasting cap into the end as he had seen Nate do, he ran to the entrance to the fissure, struck a match on the rocks and ignited the fuse cord. Satisfied it was well and truly alight he threw the stick of dynamite between the tight walls of the rock before turning and running as fast as he could. The line of fuse cord was only about twelve inches long and would burn very quickly, he hoped, setting off a major blast as it ignited the other lines Nate had already laid.

Jim was about thirty yards from the entrance when the shockwave hit him, followed by a roar of sound that smashed into his ears. He was thrown forwards and hit the ground face first, just managing to get his arms up before ploughing a groove in the loose shale with his chin.

As he lay there, stunned and barely moving, Morg came riding around the corner.

"What the hell, Jim, you OK?"

Jim didn't hear the words and barely moved. He lay moaning on the floor, some of it for effect but partly because he was genuinely stunned.

"Where's Nate?"

Jim motioned backwards with his arm. "In there..." he croaked. "Musta gone off early, poor devil never stood a chance."

"Oh God, no..." Morg was shocked and at a loss. "Not Nate." He ran to where the line of debris defined where the fissure had once been, calling Nate's name and hoping against hope to hear a response. He began a futile scrabble, trying to pull what rocks he could from the ground to climb up and try to get at the man who lay inside, now dead no doubt, blasted to pieces.

He slumped into a sitting position, his nails shredded and his fingers bleeding from his efforts, still not believing what had just happened, looking up at the solid wall of rock that now blocked the former entrance to the fissure. He smacked his Stetson upon his knee.

"What in hell happened, Jim?" he asked.

"Don't know," Jim replied. "I had my back to the rocks, laying out the lines like he told me ready for him to come back out. He was certainly a ways in when it happened, had to be. He'd of bin crushed or blown up," he finished weakly, seemingly unsure how to go on.

Morg stood unmoving, shocked by the loss of his boss and more importantly his friend, who had been such a force of life. It seemed impossible that he was dead, blown to pieces in an accident. Then he ran back to his horse. "I'm goin' for help," he said. "Do what you can to start moving rocks."

He vaulted aboard his horse and set off for the ranch at a pace.

The air around the valley was now unnaturally quiet, the way it always was after an explosion. The birds had been stilled, and all other animals were frightened off by the event. "Well, Mister Carlton," Jim said. "You sure done me a favor by headin' into there with all that dynamite. I was wonderin' how I was gonna kill you, bein' as how you was so fast with that gun of yours. Now I reckon I'll hang around for a coupla' days then skedaddle outta here and pick up my reward." Jim looked skyward, a humorless grin on his face. He stood, dusted himself off and went to walk around the corner of the escarpment to find where Morg had tethered the horses, pleased that he had not returned too early to see him lob the dynamite into the fissure. "You're a nice young fella and I wouldn't have wanted to kill you for the sake of it.

But I woulda done, if'n you'd got in the way," he muttered to himself.

Morg returned with the other ranch hands just as dusk was falling, seeing Jim sat by a campfire nursing a cup of coffee.

They all sat looking at the tragedy before them, realizing that it would be a miracle if Nate were still alive. Jas asked how it had happened, keen to understand everything. He had no knowledge of dynamite, but he could read a man as well as most civilized men did a book. He said nothing, but he wasn't happy. He wished Billy Jo was here, but he was a good day's ride away finding more wild horses for the ranch.

He wasn't satisfied with Jim's version of events, but he held his peace.

"You say Nate found another way up and in, Montana?" he asked Morg who was comforting his wife.

"Yeah. He found a way, he said, using a rope and such, but he couldn't get over," Morg replied. "Says he found a sort of ledge inside, between two mesas, tole me it gave a view into the valley beyond. But I don't know where, and it was a helluva climb some ways to the south, he said. Even if we could find it, it would take days to get over and in and then how in God's name do we get Nate out? He's bound to be bad hurt, even if...even if he is still alive. He's got no food, no water. Aw hell, you know what I'm sayin'."

Jas nodded. "I'm going to find a way, starting now." He said no more, walked to his horse and vaulted aboard, walking him away south, skirting the wall of rock before him. The other hands looked at the pile of rock and knew in their hearts it was a futile task.

Chapter Twelve

Within the devastated fissure they would have seen a figure, battered and shocked, but at least alive. Nate came round about two hours after the explosion. He had been knocked out by the blast, but the open sky above and the fact that he had been so far into the tunnel around twisting corners and angles had dissipated the force of it. The sticks of dynamite near him had not exploded because he had been cautious and had not planned to insert the caps until his return journey, content at this stage to place the sticks at intervals into the crags and crevices he had noted earlier. The fuse lay on the ground, harmless until it was connected to the dynamite itself. He believed that one of the sticks nearer the entrance had gone off, and this had sealed the fissure forever.

He could barely speak. Little more than a croak came when he tried to clear his throat that was clogged with dust and the stink of nitroglycerin and dope from the exploded dynamite. He spluttered and retched a racking cough from his lungs. His head span and his vison was blurred. He had been sent flying by the blast, and without his hat he'd been thrown bodily into the wall of rock, and the impact had gashed the side of his head. He raised a bloody hand and felt a deep cut under his matted hair.

Well, I'm still alive, he thought, *and by rights I shouldn't be.* His body protested when he tried to push himself upward into a kneeling position. Achieving it despite the pain, he rolled back and leant against the rock, the whole movement taking a tremendous effort. He suddenly realized that the seat of his pants was wet and almost laughed with relief. The rule of threes: three minutes without air, three days without water and three weeks without food were enough to kill a man, and he could survive longer on the first two. He scooped out a hollow into which a trickle of water pooled to form a small basin of liquid. He pulled gently at his silk bandana, soaked it in the water and began to wash away the grime and dust that coated his face. With just that small action, he began to feel better. He let the water clear and then soaked the bandana again before sucking at it to wet his lips and parched throat.

With this done, he took stock of his body and was relieved to find that nothing was broken. He tried to stand and discovered that his muscles ached like he had been breaking in a wild mustang for an hour. He then looked up and saw the last vestiges of daylight above. He estimated that he would be about sixty feet into the tunnel, if not more, so it would be useless to expect help or to call out through dense rock – if indeed anyone was there. No help would be coming. It would take weeks to remove all the rock, even with an army of men who knew what they were doing, and none would dare use dynamite for fear of killing him a second time – that is if anybody thought he might still be alive in the first place. He thought about firing the Colt, but was worried that he might bring down more rock that had been loosened by the blast. His only way out was to try to shimmy up and scale the devil's chimney above him, which seemed to be about two to three feet wide in places. It was not something to be done in the dark, so he would have to wait until daylight once more peeked out from the top, a long way above him. As the darkness enveloped him, he felt the raw fear of claustrophobia as though the walls were closing in as well as the night. He reached into his pocket with shaking hands and drew his matches out, striking one and instantly feeling better when its light showed him that the walls were as far away from him as they had always been. Then he saw the three remaining sticks of dynamite on the floor in a canvas bag with the lines of fuse by their side. "Damn I was lucky," he croaked to himself as he pinched the match out. "Going to be a long cold night, Nate my boy, and no mistake."

He settled down and tried to get as comfortable as possible, having soaked the dynamite in water first to make it as inert as possible. He shivered and slept fitfully through the dark hours of the night, waking before the morning light entered the valley once again to partly illuminate his rocky prison. He wetted his bandana again and sucked the moisture from it, easing his dry throat. Then looking upwards, he plotted a rough route for his climb, looking for places where he could get hand and foot holds. Satisfied, he reached for the first handhold, braced himself with his foot and levered himself upwards, hanging by just one hand and a foot, his boot scrapping against the solid granite. He managed to get about ten feet off the floor of the cave.

The chimney narrowed, and he braced his left foot back against the wall behind him, effectively wedging himself into position. Then he braced his hands back and front and pushed upwards, gaining a precious foot of height with each push. It was exhausting and he was drenched in sweat, his muscles flagging with fatigue as he gradually climbed the chimney toward the light at the top of the rock face that seemed to be getting no closer.

As he gained another few feet, the two sides closed in to no more than two feet apart. He panicked and shivered, the fear of claustrophobia threatening to overcome him once more. He would be wedged here forever, his demons taunted him, causing him to panic as he hung by his fingertips when his feet slipped from their hold. "I won't die, I will not give in," he muttered as he gritted his teeth in anger and pain. His feet scrabbled for a hold, pushing front and back against the opposing faces and gaining traction, easing the terrible strain from his arms and tendons as his sanity returned. Finally, he managed to wedge himself into the narrowed gap, which was so tight that he was able to get one knee into the flat rock to relieve his aching muscles.

Nate reached up and used his bandana to wipe his eyes that were stinging from sweat. He looked up and saw a small ledge that had been eroded into the face, no more than a foot wide. He reached for it and found that it dipped with a worn serrated edge, providing a good handhold. He pulled again, gaining two feet in the draw, and was able to wedge and lever himself until he actually stood on the ledge, leaning back against the opposing face. It was the first relief he had gained since starting the climb.

Nate stood, leaning back as he would against a saloon wall. His back and legs ached, he had scraped the fabric of his shirt away in places, and his scratched back was now bleeding. Gasping as his chest rose and fell, he sucked air into his lungs. He realized that the rock walls were cleaner and less damp, and looking up he saw that he was only about thirty feet from the top. Pushing himself for one last effort, he rose again, not wanting his muscles to atrophy with cold or adrenalin. It seemed a long way, but suddenly the sky opened up above him. He wedged his boots into the rock, sought handholds and pulled hard, flinging himself waist first over the lip of the chimney. He rolled over to lie on his back, looking at the blue sky above him and feeling the warmth of the sun for the first time since the explosion. He found he was almost crying with joy as he realized that he had made it, and was not destined to die in that dark, deep fissure.

Nate edged away from the opening, with no desire to look down into his former prison. He sat upright, leaning back on his straight arms and looking all around. He saw that he was atop a pillar of rock that flattened to a plateau about a hundred feet across that continued along the line of the valley like a huge castle wall, guarding the secrets within.

Now comes the hard bit, he thought. He knew that he

had to get down from the plateau – preferably on the outside, or he would find himself a prisoner in the paradise he had first espied some weeks earlier. He stood, letting the breeze blow his hair and the sunlight work its magic upon his skin. He went as near to the inner edge as possible to look down into the secret valley below. The vista below him showed a rich and fertile cover of green grasses and a few trees that would offer shade to the cattle and horses that he was surprised to see were already there. "That means there has to be another way in," he said to himself.

The valley opened out wider than he had first thought with maybe hundreds of acres of prime unfarmed land, little used save by the small number of cattle and horses. Springs and a stream crisscrossed the pasture, giving life to all things below. "Well I'll be, never would I have dreamt it would be like this," he muttered. He knew he would have to survive – if only to find a proper way to get back in.

Nate moved off, turning to his left down the slope of the plateau, hoping to find a way down as he was still a good hundred feet or more off the ground below. A thought occurred to him, and he went to the other side of the rim and looked down at where the blast had been set. He could make out the remains of a campfire, now dead and cold, but there was no one around to hail and ask for help. Looking over on hands and knees he saw that this was the lowest point, but the sheer rock face dropped down to the talus below, offering no encouragement to try to climb down that lethal precipice.

Disappointed that no one was around, he moved back into the center and make a decision between left or right:

both ways sloped gently upward and there was going to be no easy way to do this. He walked along the top of the ridge, taking his time and searching as he went for a way down either side. Even inside the valley he would have water and some way to get food. Here, he was tired, hungry and desperately thirsty. He had walked about half a mile and found no way down until a series of ledges appeared – not carved by nature but by man. They were like giant steps, but wider, offering a path that twisted and turned, going back into the rock itself.

Nate knew about the ancient peoples who had lived here before the Indians and had been driven out by them. Little was known of these long-dead civilizations, but he had read that they had their own culture and tribes, living primarily as cave dwellers. Drawings were occasionally found on the walls depicting scenes from their way of life. The giant steps led to a cave with symbols upon the walls showing scenes of animal hunts and tribes gathering. They were intricate to Nate's eyes, and showed a culture that was long gone. Smoke marks still lined the walls from years ago, and a few broken pots were strewn across the floor. He struck a match to see better in the darkened cave and saw that there was still an old torch lying on the floor, covered in a pitch-like substance. He struck another match and was rewarded as the old brand flickered into life, throwing ghostly shadows onto the walls. More importantly, the flames blew away from a draft, and Nate followed it, seeing internal steps carved into the rock, worn with age. They led downwards and he followed, hoping against hope that they might lead to a way out.

They brought him down to another level where the

wind howled in from the far side. Here a ledge led to a broken stone bridge, long eroded and weakened with the ages. All that was left was the nub of rock at each side with a gap of some six feet at the center. Nate's mind turned over: take the jump or stay here and go back up to the plateau? He made a decision, put down the brand, walked to the back of the cave and ran. He launched himself into the air, preparing to land on the ledge on the other side of the sheer drop. He landed on the other nub of rock, but it crumbled away, leaving him desperate for balance, grasping at air. After a second in which Nate felt the yawning chasm beneath him he fell forward, his hands madly scrabbling at the red rock at the opening of the cave. Fear clawed at his stomach until he finally got a solid grip and pulled himself bodily inwards, his feet still dangling over the drop. He lay there panting, letting the realization that he was safe sink in. Bruised, he got up and saw that he was standing in another cave in which steps led down again, his progress helped by holes that gave light from outside.

He slipped a few times, but covered in by the tunnel he was able to grasp the walls until he came out on a ledge that turned in on itself. It was invisible from the outside and some ten feet above the ground with a gently sloping talus leading to the plain below.

I've made it! He thought with relief.

There were marks where a wooden ladder had once been lodged and small cut outs that offered footholds. He slipped over the edge hanging onto a rocky outcrop and dropped the final four feet to the talus, toppling over in an ungainly fashion and rolling to a stop as he hit the grass below it, relieved to be out in the open at last and on the right side of the mesa. He stood, brushed himself off and made for the small stream that trickled through the valley, where he drank his fill and washed off the dirt and grime, cleaning his head wound with his bandana.

Although he felt better, he knew that he was not out of the woods yet. All he had was a small caliber pistol, five shots, no canteen and no food or hat. He faced a walk of some twenty miles back to his ranch, with Comanches on the loose and someone, somewhere, who was determined to kill him, if he reckoned right. He knew which direction to take for his ranch and with little else to do he set off, pleased at his lucky escape despite all that had been set against him.

He began walking toward home, aware of the hunger in his belly but at least able to slake his thirst from the streams and small creeks running through the valley. The grass was still quite lush with the fall, and it hid a plethora of wildlife. Suddenly he heard the squawking of a bird he knew well – a prairie chicken. It was similar in taste, texture and looks to the grouse he had known from shoots back in England. Nate prepared himself, clapped his hands and ran wildly toward the sound, and sure enough the birds took off. He palmed the Colt from his waistband and with a sure hand he shot one on the wing, bringing it flapping to the ground. He ran forward, picked it up and squatted down under a large willow that drifted its yellowing fronds across a creek off the trail. Movement attracted the human eye, he knew, and got more people killed than anything else. Now he stayed still, watching and waiting to see if anything moved out in the plains or the foothills behind. There was nothing like a gunshot to draw attention to a man. Nate waited patiently for an hour to see if anyone came to investigate, but all he heard was the silence of the prairie, the occasional cries of animals and the gentle drift of the wind pushing the willow branches to and fro. He risked it, rising to walk to a clump of aspens about half a mile away set inside the sharp turn of the creek. Here he would make a fire, the branches hiding what little smoke the dry wood made. It was risky but better than waiting until dark when the smells would carry and the light of a fire could be seen.

Nate set a small fire and rested, not daring to doze and keeping all his senses alert. He quickly cut the bird with his pocketknife, getting the two breasts spitted over his small fire on a green stick. As soon as it was cooked enough to be edible he pulled it from the fire, killed the blaze and made off with the two breasts on the stick, chewing the meat as he went, not wanting to stay in one place too long, walking off the trail to leave as little evidence of his passing as possible.

He wouldn't make the ranch that day, he knew. He was tired and had lost blood from the head wound and the lacerations to his back, and his body was bruised and battered. As dusk began to draw in, he turned into a small cutting and made a dry camp among some spruce that grew in a sheltered spot. He shivered as the temperature dropped, yet exposed as he was and with just four bullets left in his Colt he dared not light a fire. Nate dozed fitfully on a bed of pine, sheltered from the wind by a break he had woven among the trees that offered small comfort but at least allowed him to keep his body temperature up. At around midnight he heard riders, their horses beating a tattoo upon the trail. A group of ten or so, he estimated, riding at a lope but carefully and all darkly dressed and difficult to see. His first reaction was to call out, but some instinct stopped him from doing so. Men didn't ride in a bunch like that under the cover of darkness unless they were up to no good.

Chapter Thirteen

The false dawn shaded the plains, finding Nate wrapped in a shroud of light sleep. But aware as he was, he did not hear the shadowy figure who crept slowly and carefully toward his dry camp, avoiding the dry twigs and sticks Nate had set out to warn him if anyone approached. The man stood about six feet back and decided not to risk waking him. Instead, he walked back under a tree and started the makings of a small fire, careful to make as little noise as possible, having led his horse quietly to a sheltered spot nearby. With the fire aflame, he set the coffee pot on top and waited for the brew to boil.

He called gently to Nate from a distance, knowing what his first reaction would be. Nate's slumbers fell away, and he became fully awake in an instant, raising the Colt. He had slept with his hand around the gun butt. It was cocked and aligned within a fraction of a second as Jas sat there with his hands raised, stock still. "Easy, Nate, it's only me. Coffee?"

The sheer incongruity of the words stopped Nate dead as he lowered the hammer of the pistol. "You damned injun, sneaking up on a fellow like that. I nearly shot you," he exclaimed in embarrassment.

"Waal, I was going to take your scalp, but it seemed a waste," Jas joked back.

"How did you find me? Damn, but it's good to see you," Nate said.

"I knew you weren't dead, despite what the others said. I guessed you might be trapped, so I trailed around to try to find a way into the canyon – which I did, by the way. That done I rode back again just on a hunch."

Nate knew about the hunches and sixth sense that the Indians possessed. Many white men were scornful, but he knew that some things could be felt, and the Indians set great store by the spirits and what they foretold; they seemed to be attuned to such things.

"You found the entrance?" Nate exclaimed. "Where?"

"Over to the south, so well hidden that you'd never know. I'll tell you more later. Anyways, I trailed you, taking my time 'cause it was getting dark, but you left a pretty clear sign to a man who knows you and how you think. Saw your fire by the creek and worked from there.

"Now what about you? What happened and how'd you git yourself outta there?"

Nate took the steaming brew Jas offered him, sipping at the scalding liquid and feeling a warmth come over him through the coffee and the blanket Jas had given him. The nights were getting colder, and he felt warmer than he had in a while, the coffee seeming to banish the cold from his bones.

He took his time, taking a few more sips before explaining everything that had happened.

"That Jim now, he never did set right with me," Jas said. "Don't know why, but he was like a cross grained mule I once had, never did completely trust either of 'em. You reckon he set the dynamite off?"

"Well, it sure as hell wasn't Montana. Jim was very interested in how the whole shebang worked. I am going to have an interesting talk with Mr. Smith when we get back to the ranch. Talking of which, I saw a bunch of riders careening across the country last night. They were up to no good or I miss my guess. Did you see any sign of them?"

"I did. I reckon they were headin' for the ranch. Funny thing is their tracks were made by shod and unshod hosses. I don't like it at all, Nate. Fact is I think we should get back there as soon as possible, when you're up to it. My horse'll carry double, ain't but a few miles now. You made good time considerin' the shape you were in."

Nate agreed and knocked back the coffee as quickly as he could, keen to be back at his ranch.

They smelled the smoke first, a couple of hours later as they neared the Ranch. Jas put his horse into a trot, and over the next rise they saw a lazy pillar of grey rising upward. Nate saw the devastation before them as they crested the final ridge that led down to his ranch house. He swallowed hard. The bunkhouse was scarred with soot and flame damage but seemed to have been saved from complete desolation, but one of the barns was now a smoldering ruin. His own house, being at the back of the defensive horseshoe of buildings, had apparently suffered the least damage.

Nate swore softly under his breath, then shouted: "Damn their hides to hell! Let's get down there, Jas," he said, slipping off the tired horse and running down the slope to what was left of his home.

Jas's horse was tired, and he too slipped off his back and led him at a run towards the buildings. They were met by an amazed and delighted group of hands and Lily, who burst into tears as she came up to Nate and thumped him on the chest before clutching him and crying into his shoulder.

"Easy now, Lily. My name's not Montana!" he joked, easing the moment and Lily's embarrassment.

"Oh, you stupid limey. When will you ever be serious? I am so pleased you're alive."

"So am I, m'dear, so am I," Nate replied. "But what about all this? Tell me what happened."

Morg came forward to shake his hand. "They hit us in the middle of the night. Injuns, it looked like. Came whooping in, arrows flying, and a few had guns too."

"I know, but it wasn't Indians. Trust me, this was the work of someone very clever. I saw them on the main trail here riding in the middle of the night, and Jas caught sign of shod and unshod horses. Somebody guessed I was dead and decided it was a good time to raid the NC."

"Waal, I went to town and told deputy Macey, an' word would've spread like wildfire after that. Everyone was pretty upset to hear it," Morg admitted. "The preacher was sick so we couldn't hold a service for you."

Nate nodded, an urgent question in his mind. "I don't see Saul or Jim?"

"Saul was killed in the raid, Nate, I'm sorry, we'll miss him. Jim hauled his freight last night. Said he felt bad and wanted to clear out with no job an' all."

"Did he now? Any idea where he was heading?" Nate asked, his voice quiet but with a depth of menace to it.

"Said he was driftin' east. San Antone, mebbe?" Morg ventured.

"All right, that will keep. I am sorry to hear about Saul, he was a good man and I'll miss his humor.

"Lily I'm starving, could you rustle me up some food? Anything will do," he asked.

"Honey, you just go up to the house. They done missed it. I'll get you some grub and I'll clean up that wound on your head. An' while we're at it you can tell me everythin' that happened."

An hour later Nate had a full stomach and a dressed head wound and had told Lily everything that happened.

"Waal, I declare. That Jim fella is slicker than a boiled onion the way he suckered us all in – man's on a first-name basis with the bottom of the deck!" she declared.

"Lily, I'm going to wash and rest for an hour then I'll be back out to help with the clearing and rebuilding."

"You just sit tight, boss man. It'll keep and you need a rest."

"I am dog tired," he admitted before a light came into his eyes. "Did they find my gunbelt in the buckboard out there?" he asked eagerly.

"Morg did, and he was so upset he oiled it and stored it at the house. I'll go fetch it," she said, leaving Nate alone to sit on the couch sipping a cognac from his private stock. When she returned he was lying sideways, fast asleep, the glass still in his hand. She smiled gently, took the glass away, pulled up his legs and placed a blanket and quilt over him, stoking the fire before she left.

* * *

Two days later, Nate rode away from Flat Creek and the Uvalde Valley, looking for answers as to where Jim Smith had gone. Following a cold trail and acting part upon intuition, he was sure that he would have made for the town first, before heading out. Nate did not want the world to know that he was still alive for reasons best known to himself. The prairie telegraph being what it was, he knew that the news of his escape would spread as quickly as the news of his death, so he had warned the hands not to say anything to anyone and quietly slipped out of the ranch and the valley, heading east towards San Antonio in his search for the man known as Jim Smith. A dead man cannot leave tracks he thought, and anonymity was sometimes a useful cloak.

When he had been on the trail for a day on the hundred mile journey to San Antonio, he gave himself pause for thought. He had started later in the day after oversleeping – which was unlike him and showed how much his recent experience had taken out of him. Someone, somewhere, was determined to stir up trouble in the valley, for what purpose he knew not. They also wanted to involve the Indians and cause trouble there as well. The whole thing was unsettling. Added to these thoughts he realized that someone wanted him dead, or at least out of action. But why? What could they gain? These and other questions came into his head. He would send a wire to Paul Tranter once he reached San Antonio, telling him of his misadventures but also informing him that he was still alive so that he did not worry. Paul was the main beneficiary of Nate's will as his silent business partner, along with a permanent place on the ranch for Morg and Lily, but Paul had no way of knowing that and he would never have paid the man he knew as Jim Smith to kill him. So who had? And what connection did they have with the valley, if any? These and other questions needed answering, and the only real lead he had was Jim Smith.

He continued east on the second day, the landscape changing little, with a good covering of grass and clumps of honey mesquite and Texas persimmon scattered away from the main trail.

As the day ended, he had just crossed a ford in the Sabinal River when he spotted a lone rider some distance in front who had stopped his horse and shaded his eyes, trying to make Nate out. The man pulled some field glasses from his saddle that blinked with a reflection from the low hanging sun as he settled them upon the lone horseman he'd seen in the distance, then scanned left and right in search of any deception. *A seasoned man,* Nate thought.

Clearly satisfied, the figure turned, scanned behind him then set his horse at a slow lope in Nate's direction along the trail. Nate in turn put his horse to a faster pace toward the rider. The two men met.

"Howdy. Matt Phelps, scout for the wagon train back there," the man introduced himself.

Nate wasn't sure why, but he used the first half of his double barreled name: "Nathaniel Sinclair, howdy," he replied.

"You come far?" Phelps asked.

"Oh, down the trail a ways," Nate answered, playing the lonesome cowboy. "Had a riding chore over to the other side of Flat Creek and came on this way huntin' a friend of mine who's about two days ahead of me. You see a feller riding past?" he asked.

"Sure, cowboy named Janus, that be him? Few years older'n you, riding a Palomino headin' fer San Antone?"

Nate jolted inside. Janus? He knew of only one man called Janus, an infamous bounty hunter called Janus Shaw. It was said that he would take any job for the right money, and he didn't care how he collected. Rumor had it that he preferred them dead, and he wasn't fussy whether they were facing him or not.

"Sure, sure, that'll be old Janus, good to know that his scalp's not decoratin' some injun's lodge pole," Nate responded.

Phelps smiled. "Well, he stayed with us one night and moved right along. As such we'un's about to halt an' circle for the night any time soon. You pass the Sabinal River recently? 'Cause if you did you're welcome to join us and spend the night."

Despite the fact that it would mean going back a little way, Nate accepted Phelps' invitation, deciding that he might learn a lot this night. He felt a little guilty about the deception he was playing, but these were troubling times and he needed answers that would be freely given. As they waited, the wagon train came into view, upwards of thirty Conestoga wagons lumbering along, pulled by oxen or mules. Outriders rode alongside many of the wagons in ones and twos, tired by their attitude. The canvas coverings, once bright white, were now grey or yellowed to a pale ochre by time and weather of a long trip.

While he waited, he learned from Phelps that they had in part followed the Chisholm Trail from Oklahoma, with many coming from even further back east. As the train closed up he heard the usual mix of languages and accents as the flotsam and jetsam of the world arrived on American soil, all ready for a life in the New World. There were French, Germans, Poles, and even a couple of English accents which made him think again of his parents, though these were the northern vowels of Yorkshire, or he missed his guess.

"Aye lass, thou'd not get owt for nowt. Thee's comin' up short an no mistake," one man called to his wife as she moaned about the hardship before her, of unpacking yet again and toiling against the harsh conditions, tired after a long day's driving.

Nate smiled at the words, which drew him back to one of the grooms on his father's estate, Alfred, who could curse and grumble with the best of them. He was as kind a man to the horses as ever there was and had taught Nate to ride. He was drawn from his reverie by two heavyset fellows with slab-like faces who were driving a large wagon, seemingly heavily laden and flying a flag of red and white horizontal stripes with an intricate banner of a bird that looked to Nate's eyes like an eagle in the center. Every pioneer took a little bit of their home country with them, he mused. They made guttural remarks in a language that Nate did not know. They had slightly slanted Slavic eyes and were hailed by a man who by his dress and demeanor Nate assumed was the wagon master as he rode up when they pushed their wagon out of line.

The rider was erect and military in his bearing. He wore a long coat and a neatly buttoned vest with a wide brimmed hat, shiny boots outside his pants and an Army Colt buckled around his waist. His saddle was more eastern than western, and that was one of the first things Nate noticed after the armament.

"You two, Olech and Beksiński, I've told you many times not to break lines until we're settled."

They ignored him, Nate saw, their flat faces unemotional and arrogant in their ignorance. The one holding the ribbons wheeled the wagon, hauling on the poor mule's mouths as they cut across the lines to get to the far side of the train.

"Damned Poles, either they don't understand or they pretend not to," the rider muttered. "I must apologize for my manners, sir. Martin Bradshaw, wagon master. Phelps told me you are to join us tonight with news of the land ahead. I bid you welcome," he said raising his hat and riding over to shake Nate's hand.

As I suspected, ex-military and a gentleman, Nate thought.

"Howdy, sir, I'm Nathaniel Sinclair, travelin' east as on my way to San Antone." He remembered in time to stay in character. "More'n pleased to spend the night with you good folks, getting' tired of my own comp'ny."

Nate was about to say more when he saw Buck's ears twitch and felt him stiffen under his knees. It was warning enough, he knew, cursing himself for being distracted and assuming there was safety in numbers. He heard the thunder of hooves and whoops of war cries from the trees and low hills to the far side of the wagon train, but his view was blocked by the large Conestoga wagons. Still mounted, Nate pulled his Spencer from its sheath and pushed Buck through the gap in the wagons to face whatever was coming from the other side. Through the dust of the wagon train, he heard cries circling the wagons and knew that it would be too late for the long strung out line to form a defensive circle in time to repel the attackers. Men and women scrambled to pull long guns from the boots at their seats; riders pulled up short trying to reach the safety of the line.

Then Nate realized his foolishness as more cries came from the side he had just left. The defensive grouping of forces had exposed their backs to a secondary attack. They had been pincered in a clever move that was typical of the Comanche, such was their skill at laying an ambush. Two or three wagons had broken ranks under the ribbons of more experienced drivers and were pulling in nose to tail in semi-circles, bringing rifles to bear as soon as they could. More wagons came up to seek safety in mass and numbers, as arrows started to fly, loosed by the greatest horse warriors on the plains. Puffs of powder now rose from the wagons as the pioneers started to return sporadic fire. Nate halted Buck and raised the Spencer, cocking, levering and bringing it to his shoulder before choosing a brave for his target and bringing the man down. He repeated the process of reloading, picking his next target as he did so, the time-worn process performed instinctively.

His rifle spat once more as a brave was about to launch himself onto the seat of the Polish wagon as they were the furthest from the train and most exposed after their foolish maneuver a few moments earlier. He noticed that the two Poles were not firing in defense and seemed to be allowing the Indians to get up on the wagon as two more entered through the rear.

Nate had no more time for curiosity. A woman's scream to his rear caused him to turn toward a new threat. He jacked a new shell from the tube in the stock, bringing the Spencer to full cock in one flowing move, turning Buck with his seat and lower legs. The stallion turned on a dime as Nate saw a Comanche stab a lance through the driver on the bench seat with a familiar war cry as he counted coup and mounted the nearest wagon, his distraught wife trying to cock and aim a pistol as the Indian closed to take her. The Spencer flowed to Nate's shoulder. At less than thirty yards he could hardly miss, and the heavy .56 caliber slug smashed into the Comanche brave's chest, flinging him backwards as it drove him from the wagon bench.

Nate slipped the thong from his Colt, knowing that he would not have time to cock and reload the rifle as another two braves appeared. Flame lanced from the Navy Colt as Nate's shots struck two more braves at a range of only a few feet, one's face turning into a bloody mask, the other caught in the shoulder as he ignored the screaming woman and turned to face the new threat. Another brave was closing from Nate's left as he changed aim, bringing him down in one smooth move, firing on instinct. It was chaos as men fought their own battles, each in a deadly life or death struggle to survive as the thick black powder smoke filled the air with the choking smell of sulfur and saltpeter. It reminded Nate of battles from the Civil War, the stench of death and cries of the dying, the metallic odor of blood and guts.

A woman's cry broke the air behind Nate, and he turned to see a brave with a blonde-haired woman from the train laid across his pony in front of him. He holstered the Colt and cocked and aimed the Spencer, knowing that he was in range and squeezing off a shot that caught the brave in the side of his chest, leaving a bloody exit wound and flinging him sideways, with the captive falling off the racing pony. Booting the Spencer, Nate charged off to save her from capture. Dropping to her side, he saw she was unconscious from the fall. He pulled her up and was about to throw her over the front of the saddle when a brave appeared from his right bearing a lance. Fierce and determined, he had wolf pelts hanging from his waist. *Los Lobos*, Nate thought, his mind standing still. These were the elite of the Comanche: first to attack and last to leave the field. Caring nothing of death, they lived to fight and die.

He made to drop the woman and draw, his hand moving in a blur. The Colt came up, the hammer dropping as soon as it was aligned, and the flame shot out just as the brave made to release the lance. Nate's bullet caught him in the stomach, but despite being gut-shot, the man kept coming, trying to bring home the lance with a final thrust even if it cost him life, his features cast in a mask of hatred for the white man. Catching the Colt on the recoil, Nate fired again, taking him in the throat in a spray of blood. All cries of war stopped as the brave toppled over backwards. Nate flipped the now empty Navy back into the holster and made to draw his Police Colt, then he saw his fate approaching him as another brave raced towards him, rifle leveled, out of range of Nate's weapon. Nate yanked at the booted Spencer, and in his haste the medicine sheath came away with it as he struggled to free the weapon, lever and fully cock it, knowing that he was against time.

The brave saw the sheath held high, and to Nate's amazement he raised his rifle above his head, shouted words Nate could not understand, wheeled his horse and rode back to the other braves. Nate stood in bewilderment, not fully understanding what had happened as the heat of battle ran through him. Then he realized that it was the medicine sheath given him by Raven Wing that had stopped the attack. It had literally saved his life.

It was over as suddenly as it had started. The Indians rode away, and all that remained were the cries of the wounded. Two or three women were crying hysterically over their dead men while others sobbed at their wounds. The wagon master came out from under one of the wagons, rising up, his face streaked black with powder smoke, a pistol still in his hand. He looked around bewildered.

"It's like the war all over again," he croaked, a tremor in his voice.

Nate said nothing. He went to tend to the woman he had rescued, who was now back at one of the wagons. She spluttered as he gently poured water into her mouth, suddenly clawing her hands to scratch and fight. "It's all right, it's all right, steady now," he soothed. "They've gone, you're safe."

She focused on him, then clung to him bursting into

tears, sobs shaking her body. "Where ... where is my husband?" she sobbed.

"I don't know, ma'am. Were you in the last wagon?" She said she was, and Nate left her with another woman so he could go and check, already certain of what he would find.

The sight when he rode up was sickening. The woman's husband had been shot with two arrows and scalped, leaving a bloody mess and the exposed bone of his skull where his hair had been. Nate remounted and rode back to report the man's fate. The pioneers were subdued. Clearly many of them were in shock, having never faced such scenes before. A few had fought in the war and were seasoned veterans, but for them it brought back harsh memories of things they would rather forget.

Later, as the evening dusk fell, the wagons were circled and some sense of normality returned. Nate watched as the dead were buried and supper prepared in that strange mixture of pragmatism and necessity that seemed to control life out here. When he'd eaten, Nate sat down with Martin Bradshaw and the scout, Matt Phelps, sipping a cup of scalding coffee. They had finished cursing the Indians when Matt raised an interesting point.

"You know, the funny thing is they only took one wagon, run by the Poles. They seemed to make straight for it, far as I could tell."

"Where are they, the Poles I mean? Were they killed?" Nate asked.

"Nope, not's far as you'd notice. No bodies is what I mean, they just seemed to have disappeared with the wagon."

"What were they carryin'?" Nate asked.

"I don't know," Bradshaw answered, "but they were mighty close about it. Freight of some sort. Heavy from the look of it."

"Where'd they join you?"

"Not all that far back. Picked 'em up outside Fort Worth. They asked to join the train, signed the papers and paid the fee, so we said yes."

"Uh huh," Nate responded noncommittally. His mind was turning, and he couldn't understand everything that was going on here, but he felt the attack was somehow connected to the happenings of the Uvalde Valley. He turned the conversation to their destination and how the train had started, at which Bradshaw was quite open and honest.

"We met this fella back east. Told us all about this wonderful valley and how there was land there for the taking. New land with Government grants, a chance for a new start. Good land, he said, somewhere a man could make a home for his family." As he spoke, Nate heard the familiar story of the westward migrants seeking the dream of a new life. He felt sorry for them. "Here, see." Bradshaw produced a paper of agreement from a satchel. "All laid out, read it."

"'Fraid I ain't much at readin'. You'll have to read it for me," Nate lied.

"Well now, it says that this land, here." He pointed to the map attached to the deed. "Is land for the taking, and that we can work it under the Homestead Act," he said.

As Nate looked at the two maps, he saw with horror that

some of it covered his own ranch together with Carson Valley and much of the free range. This would cause a range war. What kind of lunatic had proposed this, he wondered?

"Well, what do you think?" Bradshaw asked.

"Waal now," Nate drawled, "I don't know much 'bout land rights and such, and I may be wrong, but I reckon much of this land is already occupied by the local ranches," he said, feigning ignorance.

"Oh, I'm sure we can straighten it out," Bradshaw said. "The lawyer we spoke to said it was all fine and settled."

Nate asked more general questions, but not the one to which he really wanted the answer: what was the name of the man back east who had set all this in motion? It would be an odd question to ask, he told himself, as he was supposedly just a cowpoke after all, and had no reason to want to know – or indeed care. He hoped that someone would let the name slip during the course of the discussion, so he fished some more.

"Waal, I surely hope that this Boston lawyer knows his stuff and ain't just leading you into trouble. I know what these law wranglers can be like, they're an awful slippery bunch," Nate declared expressing the universal western man's mistrust of lawyers.

"Oh, I doubt he'll be comin' out here. His firm is strictly Boston – a good firm by the name of Hoddett & Slattern, they are. But we was put in touch with him by a company advertising and hereabouts in the Uvalde Valley. Nice fella too, very up on all this, and well to do. He said he or one of his men would be here to meet us at the land agent's office."

Boston, Nate thought, and his money was on Timothy

Durrant. He was the only land agent and lawyer in town. But it made no sense. Why would Durrant's son be wrapped up in all this? he asked himself.

Nate changed the subject then, drifting away from the discussion and wanting the matter closed. He had a lot to think about, and he didn't want to raise suspicions about himself.

He left the wagon train the following morning with grateful thanks from the two women whose lives he had saved, although their eyes were still red-rimmed with tears for the death of their husbands. One of them had young children to focus her attention on. It was a hard land, harsh in its judgment with no soft side. You either learned to accept it and bend with it or withered under its brutality.

Chapter Fourteen

Nate rode into San Antonio two days later, the delay with the wagon train having kept him longer than he had anticipated. He was still uncertain as to how the details of what he had learned fitted together, but he felt that the man he now knew as Janus Shaw would have more answers. As always, the livery stable was the font of all knowledge in western towns, and there were two in San Antonio.

Nate called at the first one, asking if his friend had stabled a horse here.

The stable hands shook their heads, so he moved to the next place, Mason's Livery.

"He sure did, if'n it's the same fella. Sorta your build, long face. Tough lookin' hombre, rides that there palomino?" Mason was an old man with grizzled features, and he thumbed a fist over to one of the stalls where Jim's – or rather Janus's – horse stood quietly munching hay.

Nate smiled in gratitude, paid his two bits and asked

Mason to stable his horse and if he could suggest somewhere to stay.

The old timer scratched his chin. "Waal now, that depends," he said. You want somewhere lively and mebbe some company, then I'd go for the Silver Spur Saloon or the Cattlemen's Hotel next door. Reckon your friend was headed to the saloon, myself. If'n you want peace, there's a quiet boarding house on the outskirts of town run by the Morgans. They're nice folks and they keep a good clean house."

"That'll do me well," Nate said. He listened to Mason's directions, took his bedroll and rifle and left the stable to settle down and make a plan as to how he would trap Janus Shaw. He learned from the Morgans that the marshal of the town was another Englishman about the same age as Nate who had also fought for the South during the war. Nate decided he would call upon him.

"Marshal Thompson?" Nate enquired of the man sat behind the desk as he entered. He saw a man in his early twenties, with a long drooping mustache, dark hair parted to the side and eyes that had seen a good deal of life. Ben Thompson was fast making a name for himself as an Indian fighter, lawman and gunman, and rumor had it that he had served down in Mexico after the Civil War as well as fighting for Emperor Maximillian against the revolutionaries. In short, Nate knew he was a skilled gunfighter and a man who would not backwater.

"Yes, I'm Marshal Thomspon, lad. 'Ow can I help?" The Yorkshire vowels were still strong and Nate smiled at such a memory of England.

"My name's Nate Carlton," he replied. "I have a story to tell you and I didn't want to go off half-cocked before I settled what is due. I intend to call out a bounty hunter called Janus Shaw who set me up and tried to kill me. I want to know who paid him and why. It's not your jurisdiction, I realise, but he's here in San Antonio and I felt that you ought to know before I set to."

"Seems I've heard of you, Nate. You used to work for Old Man Randall, from what I've heard. Tell me your story, lad, and 'appen we'll see 'ow I feel."

Nate related the whole incident from start to finish.

"Fair enough, go settle your argument – but don't go killing any innocent citizens in my town. You brace this man Janus – who by the sound of it probably needs killing, any road – you keep it 'tween you two, understood?" Nate nodded, thanked the marshal and made to leave.

"Oh, one more thing, lad." Thompson raised a finger. "Randall's due in today, paying off his crew. I can't help you there, but you'll be buckin' a stacked deck an' no mistake. It's not like in Dodge. Oh, yes, I heard the story and it made me chuckle, I can tell you that much. But here it's a different kettle o'fish. You mind yourself, now."

"Well, Nate, my boy, it never rains but it pours," Nate muttered to himself as he left. "You certainly pick your enemies well." He decided to face Janus sooner rather than later and leave town as soon as he could. He wasn't frightened of Randall, but a face-off with him would be courting trouble he did not need. The saloon was the place to face Shaw, somewhere off the streets where no innocent bystanders or children could be hurt. The anger returned, a white hot rage that had been building in him since he'd been trapped by the explosion in the rocks. This was an eye for an eye, but if Shaw surrendered he would take him back to Flat Creek for trial. He could go in with a gun drawn as others had done, and would do again where famous gunmen were murdered, killing someone out of hand, but it was not his way.

Part of him hated himself for it, acknowledging the Devil on his shoulder that drove him. He wanted Shaw, he wanted revenge and to try himself man to man against him. He wanted to be seen to fight fair, even if he did not know the outcome. Had he become a killer? He did not know, but at this moment neither did he care. This man had tried to bury him under a pile of rock for a killer's bounty, and he would pay or Nate would suffer the ultimate price himself.

Nate strode towards the Silver Spur saloon, slipping off the thong from the Navy. He had already checked the chambers; he was primed and ready and experienced the usual sense of quiet that came over him as the adrenaline faded and the natural ability of a duelist took over. He was focused and it felt like everything was standing still in time. Sounds and smells became more apparent, and he calmed his breathing. He pushed through the batwing doors, stepped to the side and sat down quietly, his face shaded by his Stetson. He was all in shadow as his eyes adjusted to the dimmer light, watching with peripheral vision.

When he was ready he stood tall and turned, walking towards the far side of the room where he had spotted the ever cautious Janus Shaw, who was leaning at the bar where he could look up at the large mirror that gave him a wide-ranging view of the saloon. Nate kept his head shaded with his hat brim tilted forward. After all, he reasoned, Shaw thought he was dead. Only his armament might have given him away to an observant man by the way he carried his guns. He was within twenty feet of the bar, and the more seasoned drinkers had drawn back from him with that sixth sense that something was amiss. He stood upright, his feet slightly apart, relaxed and ready.

"Jim Smith – or should that be Janus Shaw?" he said.

Shaw span around at the words, surprise and fear etched upon his face. As he did so, his right hand dropped and drew with steel rasping on leather, and with the pirouette he drilled downwards, making a smaller target and following the momentum of the move. It was a good move, and one that Nate had often practiced as it seemed to aid the speed of the draw, but it was not enough. As Shaw's gun came clear Nate's Navy Colt spat flame, the .36 slug driving into Shaw's stomach, making him crease forward. He braced himself against the bar as Nate waited, not wanting to kill him. He needed him alive to talk. The change in balance sent Shaw's first bullet wide and downward in trajectory. He made an effort to realign, holding the cocked Colt steady and giving Nate no choice. His second shot smashed into his opponent's upper right chest, the impact driving Shaw backwards, gun arm flailing, his shocked fingers dropping the pistol as blood pooled in a rose of dark red upon his vest and shirt. Nate came forward quickly, kicking away his gun as he made a grab for it. Shaw sat upright, sprawled against the bar, coughing.

"You're supposed to be dead. Knew I was right not to

cross you with a gun. Damn you, Carlton, seems you done shot me to bits." He coughed again, blood seeping from his mouth.

"Who paid you to kill me and why? Tell me and I'll get the doctor to you."

Shaw laughed, and Nate saw the blood staining his teeth. "Ain't no point in doctors. You got me in the lung... I seen it enough times. Whisky'll do me, though." Nate brought the bottle down and Shaw took a slug of it, coughed and spat red. "Warn't one man but two," he said.

"Two?" Nate frowned, a shocked expression on his face.

"Shocked you, huh? Yeah, they got together. Heard about your ruckus in Dodge, I guess, and the man paid a visit to Randall here. Randall wanted you dead anyways, wanted it done after a time had passed so nobody would suspect him. You hurt his pride, Carlton." He coughed again, and Nate saw he was getting weaker. "You made him look small in front of his men ... beat him and set him on his heels. Terrible for man like him, you shoulda knowed ... Worst is, he'll send someone else if'n you don't kill him. That's the joke. You got me ... but there'll be others," Shaw said with a sickly grin.

Nate holstered his Colt and put a hand on Shaw's shoulder, seeing the light start to go out of his eyes. "Who's the other man? Who else?" He shook Shaw as a sickly pallor came over his face.

Shaw gave Nate a final smile. "He's fast, Nate ... real fast, maybe even quicker'n you ... don't trust him when he laughs..."

The light went out of Janus Shaw's eyes and his head lolled back. He was dead.

Nate rose, his mind in turmoil, and at that moment voices broke the silence that had fallen in the bar as the saloon doors opened to admit a group of newcomers and Nate's day became worse. There in the doorway stood Old Man Randall himself, flanked by his foreman, Ted Lineman, and two other hands. One Nate knew from his time working for him. Bob was a tough, gun handy puncher from Nueces who had sworn to fight it out with Nate when next they met.

"Carlton! I heard you were dead!" were Randall's first words.

"Sorry to disappoint you, Randall. Mind, it seems like you had something to do with my supposed demise. Your tame killer there..." Nate jerked a thumb over his shoulder. "Just admitted you hired him to kill me."

Nate was pleased to see that Ted Lineman – who tough as he was would not stoop to such levels – do a double take with his boss. "Say what?"

"Oh yes, Ted, your esteemed employer here paid this bounty hunter to kill me. Damn nearly succeeded, too. Blew me up in a rock face, tried to bury me alive, but I just got lucky and trailed him here. He just confessed before he died."

"You're a liar, Carlton!" spat Randall.

"Well, that's surely not very friendly, Dave," Nate said, baiting him as a plan formed in his head and he decided to fight fire with fire. "Old Janus there said it in front of all these witnesses. I'm not sure they'd all lie for you, even if you are such a big man in these parts. Frankly, I don't care one way or the other, because I know all about your pig headed arrogance and how it eats you up inside. Don't forget I've seen you try to hang an innocent man because he got in your way, so I know about your form of justice. And I also know that when I leave here I'm going to wire my lawyers and leave instructions with them. And this is what they'll do if anything happens to me. If I die in suspicious circumstances, my instructions will be that they are to place an open bounty on your head. Ten thousand dollars, dead!"

There was a gasp from the saloon crowd. No one had ever heard anything like it. "And if anyone tries to kill me and fails, I'll make sure that bounty includes the rest of your family. I'll have you hunted down like the lowlife vermin you are." Nate snarled, walking up to Randall until their faces were but two feet apart. "So you'd better pray, mister, that I live to a ripe old age."

Randall's hands clenched and unclenched at his sides as his face suffused with rage. "You can't do that! It's against the law!" he shouted.

"Says the man who ordered the same thing done to me," Nate mocked. "Well, you should have thought of that before you put that hired killer on my trail."

"Seems to me you done forgot one thing–" The man at Randall's side who Nate did not know started to speak.

"Leave it, Pecos!" Ted ordered.

"Nope, hear me out. Here we got Mister High and Mighty threatening Mister Randall, but I ain't seen him sign no papers or give no instructions yet. So if you die now, legitimately in a gunfight, why Mister Carlton, ain't no one gonna be any the wiser." Pecos smirked.

Bob at his side gave a sneer. "I like that, Pecos. I'm in. I owe you, Carlton, from Dodge. No one makes me backwater and lives to talk about it." At which he slipped the thong off the hammer of his pistol.

"So that's what, four to one? Typical Randall, always having your dirty work done for you. You in on this, Ted?"

"Nope, I'm sick of it, boss, and I don't want nuthin' to do with it." Lineman stepped away and folded his arms.

Randall sneered, taking a pace back. "Nothing to do with me, Carlton. My hands have their own minds. If they want to fight you, it's their business."

The two men opposing Nate stood ready, their hands slightly clawed, tension rising as they waited for the first twitch to trigger them into action that would leave Nate dead and earn the gratitude of their boss. Pecos was first to break. Nate saw the tiny muscles in his face twitch preceding the draw.

The man was fast, a bundle of nervous energy that showed practice, but Nate's hand was a blur of speed as his gun cleared the leather, hammer eared back. Flame blossomed and powder burned as two bullets, the shots sounding as one they were so fast, hit Pecos just beneath the Bull Durham sack, driving him backwards to the floor, all within a quarter of a second.

Nate gave no more thought to him as Bob was getting into action, almost hesitating for a split second at the first concussion. He had seen Nate draw against Gillet on the ranch three years ago, but felt he was better. Practicing every day, he was at his best, but it wasn't enough. Nate's slug caught him in the sternum, sending waves of agony lancing through him, creasing him up as he involuntarily clutched the wound, crying out against the pain with his gun now sideways, both hands to his chest. Nate waited, unwilling to send another bullet home to finish him. The man would be dead in seconds anyway. But in that instant he realized his vulnerability and drew the second Colt with a cavalry twist into his left hand. He only had one more bullet left in the Navy.

Randall had started to move, realizing that he had a chance while Nate was distracted.

"Hold it, Randall!" Nate shouted. "You draw on me and I'll kill you, big augur round here or not. I want you alive; I want you knowing every day that I have you in my sights. I want you regretting the day you waged war on me."

The rancher froze, realizing that his play had failed. At this point, against all odds, Pecos began to raise his Colt, bracing himself on his knees, determined to kill Nate before he died. Nate had no choice and slipped the hammer on the final round in the Navy, the bullet hitting Pecos in the forehead and throwing him backwards in a mist of red.

Nate realigned on Randall instantly. "Now get out, Randall. You're a gutless coward! These men died for you. How many more deaths do you want on your conscience? These men needn't have died, but you just stood back and let them do your dirty work," Nate said, disgust and loathing in his voice.

Ted Lineman broke the brief silence that had descended. "That's it, Mister Randall. I quit, I've had enough of this, go find yourself another foreman!" he said, and made to leave.

Randall went to say something. but he couldn't get the

words out. He appeared suddenly shrunken in the swirl of powder smoke and death.

The saloon doors opened to admit Ben Thompson wearing his customary coaching hat. "Now then, what's 'appened?" he said.

Lineman answered before he left the saloon. "It was a fair shooting, marshal. Nate here did all he could to avoid a killing, but these two pushed him and Randall didn't want it stopped."

With the marshal's appearance, Nate holstered the Police special, broke open the Navy and replaced the cylinder with a second fully loaded one from the loop on his belt, snapping it shut and spinning the cylinder, all the time keeping his eyes on Randall, alert for any more trouble.

"Seems like there's another body at the bar. That'll be Janus Shaw, I'm thinking."

"It is, marshal. He drew first and called the play," Nate answered.

Thompson nodded. "Don't leave town, Nate, I may need a witness statement."

Nate nodded and made to leave the saloon. Three more deaths, and only one man had deserved to die to his mind. Worse, his reputation would spread, the legend would grow. Two gunfights in the space of moments, him the victor of both. He shook his head in dismay. It was not what he wanted, yet he had to take Janus – and the man had been fast, he gave him that. But like a living thing his gun had appeared in his hand, spitting death with a natural talent honed by long practice.

He saw Ted Lineman adjusting the cinch on his horse

and hailed him. “Ted, I appreciate what you said in there and for staying out of it. We used to be friends and I’d have hated to draw on you.”

“My pleasure, Nate. You just made me decide to do what I shoulda done a while ago. The old man’s going sour. As for drawing on you, Nate, all the devils in Hell wouldn’t get me to do that. I swear you’ve got even faster, and I’ve seen some fast men. I want no part of you in a gunfight, believe me,” Lineman said with a sad smile, knowing what his words meant.

Nate said nothing. There was little to add. “I don’t know if I can pay a top hand like you enough, but there will always be a job for you at my ranch,” he offered.

“I ’preciate it, Nate. I don’t know where I’m going to drift to, but if it’s that way I’ll be sure to look you up.”

They shook hands and Ted rode off down the street, heading for Randall’s ranch to fetch his gear. The reaction to the shooting was hitting home now and Nate felt tired of it all. He could not wait to be rid of the town and head home.

Chapter Fifteen

The Hemple Ranch, Uvalde Valley

The night was still, and only the sound of cicadas sounded despite the cooling weather. Around the ranch house other calls could occasionally be heard – the cry of a coyote here and a mountain lion there. The horses in the corrals near the ranch house pricked their ears and moved nervously within the confines of the wooden rails, shuffling, stamping and whinnying.

The last lights were doused inside the bunkhouse, and only Luke Hemple and his daughter Alison remained awake within the main ranch house, the bedroom drapes allowing the light of yellow oil lamps to seep around the edges.

A single lamp was set low at the front door to the main house and the bunkhouse, throwing grey shadows outwards into the night. The nearly full moon bathed everything in a pale bluish tint. Finally, the lights in the bedrooms of the main house were extinguished as the watchers patiently readied themselves for the attack. As one of the largest ranches in the valley, this was a prime target, offering many horses within its remuda, as well as cattle.

An hour later, with infinite patience, the scouts flitted from cover, watched by their mounted brothers in arms as they awaited the signal from the war bonnet chief. They moved like wraiths, slipping from cover to cover in the moonlit night, their targets the corrals of horses that held the ranch remuda. Each carried a horsehair bridle as they slid closer and closer to the corrals, finally slipping through the rails to gently secure a horse each. With innate skill and calm they mounted in turn, riding the horses gently up to the slip rails and releasing them. With this done they herded the rest of the horses through the gap and pushed them as one away from the ranch, driving all before them, whooping now and calling in raised voices.

At the same time, the chief upon the rise raised his lance, looking right then left. He threw his arm forward and the braves surged as one. No sound was made apart from the thump of hooves upon the hard ground as the Comanches sped forward to raid and attack. When they were within a hundred feet of the ranch, one brave balanced on his pony shot out the oil lamp outside the bunkhouse door, spilling oil which immediately ignited to flare brightly against the bone dry timber as hungry flames lapped at the porch.

Inside the bunkhouse, the hands came awake with shouts of alarm and raced to the door. Dressed in no more than long johns with their rifles in their hands, they were illuminated by the flames as they poured forth to be shot by the incoming Comanches. Two men fell back into the doorway, preventing the door from closing, while another made it out, dropping quickly down behind the water trough before realizing his mistake as flames started to eat away at the floor of the porch, getting ever closer to him. If he rose to escape he would be shot as the Indians waited to find any target that moved. If he stayed put he would be burned alive. A bucket stood at the end of the water trough. He reached for it, pulled it close and dropped it into the water, slopping and splashing as he pulled it back.

"Cover me, boys!" he yelled as the rest of the hands poured shots from the two windows at any Indian they saw.

The man withdrew the bucket and threw the water at the timbers nearby, buying himself enough time to repeat the process. A voice sounded from the side of the bunkhouse. "Bill? It's me, Chris, I slipped out the back. I'll cover you. Say when and get yourself back here."

Bill turned, still hidden, then called 'now', rolling over and over, back towards the corner of the bunkhouse as Chris cranked the lever of his Winchester as fast as he could, throwing lead at the shadowy figures who presented themselves as targets. Bill made it to safety and dropped into cover, crouching and able to draw a bead on targets as the two men created a crossfire of their own, backing each other up. The hands in the bunkhouse were still pinned down, with little chance of making it to the ranch house where Hemple and his daughter were fighting off the attack as best they could. But even as they tried to give cover, they saw riders surge around the back, and with a crash of timber breaking they heard screams, and then the two rifles from the house fell silent.

The men in the bunkhouse saw the Indians making off

into the night, a forlorn figure draped across a pony in front of one of the braves as they whooped away.

"They've got Alison!" Bill shouted and ran from cover, trying to shoot the fleeing braves. "No!" he cried, working the lever of his Winchester as fast as he could until it was empty. Silhouetted as he was by the flames, his anger and distress overriding all sense of self preservation, he had no chance. Two separate slugs caught him, bowling him over backwards to lie in a crumpled heap.

Chris called to him but it was too late. The main house was now on fire and the ranch hands were emerging from their own bunkhouse from the rear door, ducking and diving between cover as they tried to make it to the boss's house.

As quickly as they had come, the Indians disappeared, fading off into the night, the darkness their friend. They left burning chaos and death behind them. Realizing this, the hands of the Flying H ran to see if their boss was still alive and put out the fire that was starting to engulf the main house.

They ran in and dragged the wounded Hemple out of the blazing house, gagging and coughing with the smoke. They made a chain, throwing water onto the flames that had yet to engulf the house, while others put out the smoking bunkhouse. The rancher was barely alive and was drifting in and out of consciousness.

"We need to get him to a doctor," one of the hands stated.

The foreman, Phil Cauldwell, answered. "Only horses left are those in the barn stalls. Get 'em hitched to a buckboard and we'll set off for town. Only ridin' horses are the boss's and Alison's," he choked, thinking of her fate at the hands of the Comanche, wondering if they would ever see her again.

Within minutes the hands had hitched up the team, set the buckboard with blankets and a pillow in the back and carefully laid their boss out while one man took the ribbons, the other kept guard and a third in the back kept watch over Hemple.

Nate was two days ride out of San Antonio and well on the way back to Flat Creek. His mind had been turning over the events of the days he had spent there. It was time enough for him to send off various messages by telegraph to Boston. One had confirmed that the lawyers mentioned by the wagon master, Hoddett and Slattern, existed in Boston. But it was the second wire that had sparked his interest. His original message had asked who dealt with matters on land, in particular relating to Government Land in Texas. That partner had been robbed and killed in the street when walking home a week ago. Nate had probed further, and it transpired that his office had also been broken into and papers stolen.

He also wired Susannah, enquiring if she was well, and was surprised to receive a reply from her. He learned that she was safely home and that her aunt was on her way back to Boston for the winter, thinking the opulent new ranch house 'cold and uncomfortable'. Nate was surprised at the candor of Susannah's reply, but she made no mention of leaving the drive, as if she were naturally entitled to do so. He engaged lawyers to employ an enquiry agent on his payroll to look into Susannah and her family and to send a summary of the report by wire, then by post to Flat Creek. It would take a while, he knew, but it was important to confirm or dispel his suspicions.

Nate finally made it home to his ranch as evening drew in on the following day, tired and in need of a bath and food. The hands were pleased to see him, and told him about the raid on the Flying H. They begged details of what happened and whether he had found Jim Smith. Nate explained and skated thinly over the details of the shooting, not mentioning Randall or the second gunfight, and the crew were very interested to hear about the wagon train. As he explained what happened, Lily listened from the kitchen. She had seen Nate in action in Langtonville and liked none of what she heard. When the crew had gone from the ranch house and Lily was tidying, Morg came back in.

"What are you going to do, Nate? I know that look on your face. It means trouble for someone."

Nate gave a tight and humorless smile. "Yes, you know me well, Montana. My thoughts are with Alison Hemple and those two Gilmore girls. I hate to think of them taken like that and what they must be going through. I'm heading out tomorrow to see if I can find the Comanche camp and try to get them free, though she'll have been gone a week now. Is Hemple still alive?"

"He is – or he was last thing I heard when I went to town a day ago. But there's somethin' else you should know. Now bear in mind that we did as you asked and no one knows you're alive." Nate nodded in agreement, although he had almost forgotten that part of his plan. "Waal, when I was in town I bumped into that young son of Durrant's, you know from the land office, the lawyer?"

"Go on," Nate encouraged.

"This might surprise you, but he said that with you dead he assumed the ranch would be sold. Said he'd be willing to offer for it if no one wants to work it, and he knowed that you had paid the six month fee to the government and owned it outright. Same thing with the Carson place, he said, as you haven't been on it for the six months to pay the acreage fee, or so he reckoned. Which I figured all ties in very neatly for his ends."

Nate looked into the distance as things started to become clearer. "It's a mighty smooth move there on young Tim's behalf," he said. "He's certainly an ambitious young man. I think I'll have to pay him a visit and see how he feels about negotiating with a ghost.

"But for now I need a night's rest, then I'll ride out tomorrow. Is Jas back?"

"Should be tomorrow, if not later tonight. He's been out scoutin' all over the place since the raid on the Flying H. He looks more Indian and wilder'n ever."

"If he gets back soon, ask him to track me west of Carson Valley. He'll know where I'm going easily enough, but there's another valley where the Comanche were camped the last time I saw them. There was a small herd of buffalo nearby and it looked like good range even for their hundreds of horses."

"Do you want any company?" Morg asked.

"Kind of you, but no. It'll take either a company of cavalry or just one man to do this job. And the less threatening the better. Jas will know what to do, and my guess is he will stay out of sight until needed."

The next morning saw Nate well on his way to the old Comanche camp. He had risen before dawn and set off with Buck and Patch, riding relay and making good time, wanting to reach the old camp as quickly as possible. He broke the rise where the camp had been weeks ago, and as suspected the Comanche were long gone. The grazing was stripped off, but not to the roots, and even to his basic tracking skills the passage of the tribe was easy to see and follow. They were heading northwest, deeper into Comancheria, which stretched all the way from the Rio Grande in the south, east almost to the Gulf of Mexico, up to Bent's Fort and then west to Albuquerque and the White River area to the northwest.

This was an area that the tribe had carved out, ousting other tribes and forcing the white man to respect their line, though from what he had read even this vast tract of plains had shrunk with the white man's intrusion. By the end of the day, following the tracks and the creek in a northwest direction by the line of the pale sun, he had circled in a wide loop using Flat Creek as the center. He was about eleven o'clock from the town, but further away on a wider radius. When he saw the two horses twitch their ears, he halted. He patted Patch's neck and murmured: "I know, boys, I sense them too."

He could see nothing, but the hairs at the back of his

neck were rising like when he was out scouting in the army and he'd know somehow that combat was close. The Cherokee scouts had taught him well until it became an inbuilt instinct, useful for man who lives on the edge in a wild place, where a feeling can mean the difference between life and death.

He reached down and slipped the knot holding the medicine sheath to his saddle, bringing the Spencer, still sheathed, to lie across his legs as he rode. He kept it visible to any watchers, and hoped and prayed that it would be enough as he rode deep into the heart of Comanche territory.

Chapter Sixteen

Nate rode onwards, twisting and turning with the trail, ever watchful, knowing all the time that somebody was out there. Before him he saw a rough stone arch about thirty feet wide and twenty high. The rock face soared upwards on either side, guarding the trail and forming a gateway carved by nature that opened onto a vista of a new valley beyond. As Nate rode under the arch he felt a presence behind him and turned to see four mounted warriors, lances balanced on the tops of their feet, shields on their arms, their brown faces impassive as they moved to hedge him in, pushing him beneath the shadow of the arch, their wordless intention clear. The only thing keeping him safe right now was the medicine sheath upon his rifle.

He rode forward and looking up he saw more Indians staring down at him from the upper ledges of the rock face, arrows notched in their bowstrings. He continued to ride forward, completely ignoring their presence. When he was past the rock face and into the new valley, other riders emerged from either side of the trail to flank him, drawing closer and testing his resolve and courage to see if he would break or run. He did neither, but continued to look forward, ignoring their presence, smelling the rank body odor and antelope grease mixed with the sweet tang of hot, sweaty horse.

For another mile they trailed him, sometimes crying in Comanche and riding up fast to his side, trying to goad him into a fatal action. Then, passing a lip of rock the ground dropped away and the trail weaved its way down into a valley full of aspen and flowing grass as the mighty Pecos River meandered its way south through the valley. Nate saw thousands of horses before him, moving out from the vast line of tipis that lined the riverbanks like some gigantic snake of buckskin, painted and marked with each man's sign. Fires smoked into the air and children ran and played the games that had been taught for generations, each leading to a skill they could use in manhood, where hide and seek would become a way of life that their existence would eventually depend upon.

As he rode forward, Nate made out one of the larger wikiups which opened to reveal Raven Wing, who stood proudly in calf length moccasins and a doe skin dress, her hair braided and a soft leather band around her head.

As he approached, Nate gave the sign for friend and peace, which Eagle Feather answered in the same manner, standing impassively and looking as magnificent as he had the last time Nate had seen him. Behind him to one side stood the tribal elders and a medicine man garbed in the skin of a buffalo with the horns about his neck.

"How," Nate said, raising his hand.

"How, Nate-With-Fast-Hands," Eagle Feather replied, his face friendlier but still not breaking into a smile. "You are welcome to our camp, and you are brave to come here."

Nate flicked his right leg over the horn of his saddle and slid gracefully down from Patch's back, keeping his rifle in its sheath in one hand and the reins to both horses in the other. He offered a smile and thanked Eagle Feather in the few words of Comanche that he had picked up from his last visit. He was good with languages generally but found the hard guttural sounds difficult to pronounce and find a framework of grammar upon which to build. He continued as best he could, hoping that he got it right: "I come in peace and to trade."

The chief nodded, as all Comanches liked to trade and barter since they had fought to open trade routes south from Mexico, east to Kentucky and north to the far tip of Comancheria. Indeed, many of the warriors wore as much white man's clothing as Indian in a disparate mix of styles and colors.

Nate was invited to sit around the fire, and food was brought. As they sat cross-legged, they were surrounded once more by the chief warriors and elders of the tribe, with Raven Wing looking as beautiful as ever by Eagle Feather's side, ready to translate once the two men had used up their knowledge of each other's language.

"You come to us again, Nate-With-Fast-Hands. You must be very brave or in great need to have done this. You took a great risk by coming here. No other white man would be allowed to enter – and no other white man would be permitted to leave here alive," Raven Wing said, her head held high and proud in that manner he remembered well, her raw beauty a living memory in his mind.

"I know, and I thank you for your gift, for it has great medicine and saved my life upon the trail this week past."

She frowned. "How so?"

Nate explained about the raid upon the wagon train, and Raven Wing translated to the rest of the tribe. Eagle Feather nodded as if understanding something.

"Eagle Feather says he has heard of the fight, and one was praised who fought well and counted coup many times, shooting with great skill. He now knows who they meant.

"Is this why you come, to talk about the wagon train?"

Nate hesitated, not sure how to begin on uncertain ground. He sighed and then carefully began explaining the reason for his visit. He explained about the two young Gilmore girls and Alison Hemple and said that he hoped that he may be able to trade for their safe return.

A long discussion ensued, far too fast for Nate to catch any meaning, yet there was clearly disagreement around the fire. Finally, the discussion ended and as Eagle Feather nodded in Nate's direction, two warriors stood and left the fire, mounting their ponies and riding off.

"You must understand, before I tell you all." Raven Wing paused, considering how to phrase the words. "The *Numunuu* are not like the white man. No one man speaks for all, but when white men make demands they think that a chief can speak for everyone. It is not so. Different bands break away and go their own way, still part of the *Numunuu* – yet not..." She struggled to find the correct word. "Responsible to the original band. Do you understand?"

"I do, I have read of such matters in white man's books," Nate replied.

"Good, then you will understand this. A group of young warriors has broken away not just from the Penateka but also from the Quahadi to fight and raid by themselves. What they do we cannot say. They have found guns, repeater rifles, and have become very powerful with big medicine. As they win each raid they draw others to the band. It is this band who made the raids and has the white women that you seek. If you approach their camp, they will take you prisoner, torture you and kill you, and even the medicine boot will not save you."

Nate nodded, uncertain of what to say as Raven Wing continued. "If you still wish to meet Quanah Parker, who is the chief of this band, and speak with him to ask for a trade to release the captives, Eagle Feather will take you. But there is a condition, which is that you must be blindfolded. If you know where they camp they will not let you live. If you do this, Eagle Feather says that this is the last thing that he will do for you.

"Do you accept?" she asked, lifting her head.

Nate thought briefly, fear forming a knot in his stomach, knowing that a terrible death by torture awaited him if things went wrong. But he had no choice. Three white women depended on him and him alone to save them from a terrible fate.

"I agree," he said quietly.

Raven Wing nodded in response and turned to tell Eagle

Feather all that she had said. At a nod from him, she faced Nated once more.

"You are Nate-With-Fast-Hands. You must know that the chief of this band is half white, like yourself. His mother was a white captive taken on a raid many summers ago. Quanah Parker has powerful medicine, and the prophecy is that he will one day rule the Comanche Nation. Do you still wish to go to him?"

Nate swallowed, finding his mouth dry. He had heard the name of Quanah Parker and knew the stories that were told about him. Yet still his honor drove him on. "I do," he said.

Eagle Feather nodded. "Then we go, for their camp lies a good ride from here. But we shall be there before sundown, which is good."

Nate mounted Buck and was surprised to learn he was not to be blindfolded until the last part of the journey. They headed north northwest by his reckoning, passing into wild country that no white man had seen and lived to tell of. To the far north would be El Paso, but this country on the edge of Comancheria was uncharted. It was beautiful, full of game, tall mesas, and buffalo. Wild grasses blew and weaved in the breeze. It was good country, and Nate admitted that the Comanche had chosen it well and would fight hard to keep it, having taken it from weaker tribes before them. They halted on stony ground, leaving few signs of their passing that only a skilled tracker would be able to follow.

"Here we bind your eyes, white man," Eagle Feather said.

A warrior came forward and tied a cloth around Nate's eyes, securing it tightly in place. They rode on for another half an hour, with Nate locked in his dark world and trusting the Comanche to lead him safely to the Parker's camp.

After what felt to Nate like half a mile of being led at the mercy of the Comanches, the party stopped. He heard guttural voices speaking the Comanche tongue and felt a perceptible sense of animosity welling up around him. He recognized Eagle Feather's voice, and there was a second stronger voice which he assumed belonged to Quanah Parker.

With a sudden movement his blindfold was removed, and he blinked in the strong late afternoon sunlight. As his eyes became accustomed to the brighter light, he saw that the gathering before him was much smaller than Eagle Feather's camp. There would be maybe one hundred to a hundred and fifty warriors present, a smaller amount of wikiups and even fewer squaws. This was a new group of young men proving themselves as warriors, keen to make a name for themselves by gaining more horses through raiding, and with it greater wealth.

Comanches were not by their nature large people, compared to tribes like the Apache, who were generally much stockier and better muscled. It was only when a Comanche mounted his horse that his true ability and majesty became apparent.

Yet the leader of this war band looked impressive in any company. Well-dressed in the traditional manner, he had a doe skin cloak draped and tied over his broad shoulders, and a porcupine breast plate covered his strong chest. Yet to Nate's eyes his face was more memorable than his unusually impressive physique. At first glance the man was pure

Comanche, with the typical straight, almost aquiline nose, high cheekbones and slitted dark eyes set in a square and rugged face that was seemingly cast from granite.

But looking more closely, Nate discerned the influence of his mother and her race. From the chin and the balance of his forehead he could see the duality of his lineage.

One arm was relaxed while the other was bent, and in the crook was a brand new 1866 Yellow Boy Winchester, the gleaming brass of the side metal plates of the breech housing as yet untarnished or scratched. Looking around Nate saw that many of the braves were similarly armed.

Nate dismounted, sliding off Buck's back to stand before one of the most feared and respected of all the Comanche chiefs. Trying to look beyond the creased brown face to establish his age, Nate saw a man of around the same age as himself, with great charisma and the arrogance of a born leader.

"White man known as Nate-With-Fast-Hands, why do you come to our camp?"

Nate realized that Parker already knew the answer and was testing him, and the likelihood was that his English was good. "Great chief, I come in peace as a friend of Eagle Feather who brought me here," Nate replied. "I come to trade and to leave in peace once we have traded."

"These are good words if they are true. Come to my fire that I may know you better and understand what you wish to trade for."

Taking this as a good sign despite the hostile glances from the surrounding braves, Nate nodded and followed

Quanah Parker to the campfire, where he sat cross-legged to speak with a living legend in the making.

"Chief Parker," Nate began when they had all sat down, "I come to your camp in peace and to seek trade with you for captives taken during your raids on the ranches in the Uvalde Valley." He watched carefully to see how his request was received, always aware that his life was balanced on a knife-edge.

"Who do you want for trade?"

"Two young white girls from the Gilmore ranch and an older woman, full grown, Alison Hemple."

"Why do you seek them?" Parker asked.

"They are of my people – of my tribe," he began, trying to get inside the mind of the Comanche as much as he could, trying to think as they would if the circumstances were reversed. "Their families wish for their return."

As he spoke, Raven Wing, who had accompanied Eagle Feather, translated for the rest of the tribe. The discussion went to and fro and then the bargaining began.

"What will you offer for these captives?" Parker asked.

"Cattle and horses," Nate offered, knowing that the Comanche valued horses above all else, particularly stallions to create better blood lines. They were virtually the only plains Indians apart from the Nez Perce who really understood breeding horses and singling out bad blood lines as geldings, leaving only good mares and stallions to create pure stock.

Then the bartering began, as Nate joined in with one of the Comanches' favorite pastimes. A warrior at Quanah Parker's side was interested in the proceedings and kept raising fingers, but he did not look happy as Nate settled on thirty horses in return for the three captives.

"This is Running Bear," Parker explained. "He owns the captives and has taken the one you call Alison as his woman. We have few squaws, and they are valuable. He says that he is willing to trade for the two younger girls but not for the woman Alison." Chief Quanah pronounced the word strangely, stressing all the syllables as Al-li-son before continuing. "She is another matter."

Nate looked at the strong wiry figure by Chief Parker's side. He was all sinew and muscle, not as well built as Parker but no doubt a deadly warrior. Silence hung in the air as Nate looked at him.

What the hell does he want? Nate wondered. He kept calm, suspecting what was coming. "What does he want in addition to the horses?" he finally asked.

Running Bear spoke quickly, nodding towards Nate. Quanah Parker looked implacable as he pronounced: "He says he will fight you for her. If you win, he lets her go and he gets the horses you promised."

"And if I lose?"

"Then you will die, white man, for he wishes to count coup over you. You have great medicine, for he has heard of your skill with a gun and wants to see it. He does not believe a man could perform such feats."

Nate grasped at a chance. "So if I am being challenged do I get to choose the weapons?"

Something of a smile came over Chief Parker's face. "No, Nate-With-Fast-Hands, you will fight the traditional way, with knives. But first he would see your skill to know what medicine he is to face. He wishes to see you draw and shoot."

Nate knew that the Comanche and the Mexicans were some of the best knife fighters in the world, learning and training from an early age to kill as efficiently as possible. He himself possessed little beyond a rudimentary skill that most westerners gained. He had a long Bowie knife in a sheath in his saddlebags, but he had never fought with it. Yet the lives and a terrible future hung in the balance for the three captives, and he had not come all this way to go home empty handed. Maybe if he impressed Running Bear enough he would forgo the challenge – especially if he was skeptical of Nate's skill with a gun. Nate did not like to boast of his skills, but he knew one trick that he still practiced that might impress the Indian enough. But first he wanted to know that the captives were alive and safe.

"Before I decide, I need to see the captives to make sure they are the right people," Nate said. It was as far as he dared go without calling Running Bear or Quanah Parker a liar.

Running Bear spat on the ground and called for Nate to follow him once Chief Parker translated. Surrounded by other braves, Nate went with the warrior to his tipi, and there outside it were the two blonde Gilmore girls, working on preparing food. Their names were Sheila and Ginny, he recalled, and as he spoke their names they stopped beating the maize and chewing the meat to tenderize it for a moment and looked up with sad, dead eyes as though they were in a trance. Running Bear spoke and they rose, standing with downcast eyes. Yet if Nate was surprised at how they had changed, he was shocked by what happened next. A group of three squaws came into the camp carrying firewood, laden down by its weight. Two had dark black hair, while the third, staggering under her load, had her sun bleached brown hair in two plaits running down from her neck. Her skin was paler than the other two women, and she wore an Indian dress of skins. Her face was bruised, her hands and arms red and raw from work. Nate barely recognized the vibrant, pretty girl he had last seen at the barn dance on the Durrant ranch weeks before. Lines were now etched around her eyes, aging her, and her skin was marked with dirt and grease.

"Alison?" Nate asked.

She slowly raised her head, looking first to Running Bear, who then shouted what seemed like a command. Alison nodded, her eyes not meeting Nate's.

"Alison, it's Nate Carlton. We danced at the Durrant's ranch, do you remember?" He was shocked to see that she already appeared broken in body and spirit. She would die here, worked to death at a comparatively young age or in childbirth. She would provide new blood for the tribe, serve Running Bear and the camp and that would be her lot until the end of her days.

She finally found her voice, low and timorous: "Go back, Nate, go away. I am lost now." All the hope seemed to have been taken from her body and mind.

"Alison, I'm here to take you and the Gilmore girls back. Your father is still alive, he wants you back," Nate gambled, thinking that it may give her some hope, although his own life was hanging by a thread. Her head shot up at this, her eyes briefly alive with hope. She made to speak before Running Bear shut her down with harsh words of command.

I am beginning not to like this man, Nate realized, and based on such an irrational thought he decided to accept the challenge. He could not let Alison, or the two other girls, stay here to face their certain fate.

Nate scowled at Running Bear and told Quanah Parker that he accepted the challenge and would first give a demonstration to show his skill. He walked away, giving a backward glance to Alison and winking at her. She made no response, but a slight twinkle in her eyes told him that a tiny feeling of hope had been kindled within her. But as he looked at her, Nate was forced to do a double take, for there, further down the line of tipis under the shade of some wild oak was a Conestoga wagon from which still fluttered the red and white flag with the eagle emblem. He turned back then flicked his head around again, as he did so he saw a furtive figure jump from sight. He could have sworn it was one of the slab faced Poles from the wagon train. He carried on walking and said nothing.

The band had gathered to witness Nate's demonstration of his gun skills. He stood in a clear area, and with Raven Wing's help organized what he needed, as two braves stood, each with a pinecone in their hand, thirty or so feet from Nate and twenty feet apart to make a loose triangle. Satisfied that the eyes of the whole tribe were upon him – especially Running Bear who stood to one side, his eyes mere slits, unsure of what he was to witness – Nate made a final adjustment to his holster. He tied the pigging cord tightly to his leg and slipped the thong off the hammer, easing the Navy Colt in the holster to make sure it was free. He then turned his back on the two puzzled braves who were holding the cones.

Nate forced himself to relax, breathing slowly, a calm coming over him as always. He told himself that this was not showing off as it could save his life. "Now, Raven Wing, when you call it, they throw straight up as I said, upon your command."

"You do not face them?" she asked, puzzled.

"No," he responded calmly.

She explained briefly to the two braves, who nodded, and asked, "Are you ready?"

"Do it," Nate commanded.

She raised her arm and shouted: "Go!"

At the command, Nate span around, his hand a blur, drawing the Navy and bringing it up as he turned in a crouch, his left hand out for balance. Hand-to-eye coordination was everything. Nate saw the right-hand cone start to fall first. He aimed and it exploded in a burst of fragments, then he made a final alteration to his stance and the left cone, easier to target after the turn was complete, shattered a fraction of a second later. Two shots, two cones in under half a second. The looks on the Indian's faces said it all.

Quanah Parker nodded. "Aieee! Well are you named, Nate-With-Fast-Hands."

Nate looked to Running Bear as he ejected the spent caps from his Navy to be reloaded later. He could not tell what the brave thought, but as if in answer to Nate's skills he pulled the knife from his belt, flicked it into the air, caught it by the tip and flicked again, this time catching it by the handle.

He said something in Comanche, and Quanah Parker translated. "He says it will be big medicine for him to take the spirit of such a warrior as yourself."

Nate looked skywards, seeing the light begin to fade. *It had been worth a try*, he thought. He went to Buck and reached into his saddle bag as the horse stood patiently. He patted him and removed the Bowie knife, drawing the blade from its sheath. It was razor sharp, but that would do him no good if he did not make contact with Running Bear. A loose circle formed as Nate removed his gun belt and hat, hooking both over the pommel horn of his saddle, then he stripped off his leather vest and started to stretch his legs. He knew that he had only one way out of this in a contest with a man who was his superior in knife fighting, and that was surprise. Comanches always eschewed the white man's fixation for fist fighting. They wrestled and used the moves to trip and then kill an opponent with a weapon once he was down. They would certainly not be aware of Savate or the devastating kicks that were part of the art. In many ways the angles and distances were the same as fighting with a knife, and Nate just needed to stay alive long enough to land a blow.

The Comanches formed a large ring with the campfire at its center. Each fighter's knife was taken to one side and pushed into the ground. Nate's mouth was dry; he was unsure of how to fight this Indian who was clearly a master of the knife. He had a plan to start with but after that, all depended on Running Bear's style and how he fought.

On a shouted command, both men dived for their knives. Instead of squatting down or folding, Nate dived forward, grabbing the hilt of his Bowie and rolling forward just as Running Bear drove down to where he had been a second before. If he had chosen a more orthodox approach he would now be dead or at least badly wounded. In an instant the Comanche was up, crouched in a classic knife stance in perfect balance on the balls of his feet, his knife held with the blade pointing downwards, Indian style. He came in confidently, feinting with his left hand, and then the blade flew across Nate's face as Running Bear turned his wrist deceptively, raking the blade outwards. The sharp point passed within a hairsbreadth of Nate's chin, but Running Bear was not done. He reversed the stroke, coming back just as quickly and catching Nate on his left forearm which he had thrown up in defense and to balance himself as he stepped backwards. Nate kept retreating. He flicked out with his knife clumsily, which Running Bear easily avoided and leapt into the void of Nate's open guard, not fearing Nate's left hand. It was a mistake, and Nate punched hard with a short hook, catching his opponent on the side of the temple. Running Bear lost his balance and staggered, bringing his knife to bear with anger in his eyes. The man had not expected a fist in a knife fight, and the wicked blow had made him briefly see stars. He snarled under his breath, now wary of the left hook, giving Nate a little more time.

Yet even as he recovered from Nate's blow, Running Bear renewed the intensity of the attack, his knife held at eye level, weaving and darting like a snake's tongue. Twice he faked a downward strike and caught Nate off guard with the speed of his strikes. Nate was now feeling tired. He was bleeding from three cuts and with every minute he was losing more blood and getting weaker. He forced himself to concentrate and follow through with his plan. His right arm flew out, the wicked point of the Bowie licking outward seeking flesh. Fractionally slower, he launched an overhand left as Running Bear's head dropped to avoid the fist, and to the Indian it seemed he had the advantage and the greater range as he stepped outside of the punch.

Nate sought the exact angle as the distance was greater. He stepped slightly to the right, leaning his torso away from Running Bear. Staying well out of his range, he lashed out with his left foot in a classic *Chassé Bas*, driving the hard heel of his boot into the shin. Nate knew that what made the kick so effective was that it was effectively a stamping action driving forward in a side kick. Nate struck as Running Bear's right foot had just landed to follow Nate with his knife, the deadly blade driving downwards. Such was the force of the kick, with all Nate's weight and skill behind it, that Running Bear's leg was driven backwards, forcing the knee to collapse by driving it in a direction that it was not intended to go.

To the onlookers it seemed odd as Running Bear's leg bent backwards at an unnatural angle. But Nate was not finished. He chambered the left foot again and in a lightning move lashed straight at the falling Indian's jaw, breaking it with a sickening crack as the unconscious figure fell to the ground. Nate stood, his chest heaving, bleeding profusely from the three cuts he had received.

Quanah Parker spoke: "Finish it, white man. To the

death, for if you do not, he will come for you and seek to kill you in revenge."

Nate shook his head, panting with exertion, holding one arm above his head to try to stem the bleeding. "Let him come," he shouted to the crowd. "I will not kill a defenseless man for any reason," he said.

Chapter Seventeen

Nate left Quanah Parker's camp in the dark, accompanied by Eagle Feather and his warriors. On the ride back he had thrown up from his wounds and the fight, and he now felt weak from loss of blood and an empty stomach. An agreement had been reached that he would bring the thirty horses and ten cattle to Eagle Feather's camp, and Quanah Parker's followers would be there in a week to fetch the trade price.

The most difficult part had been to persuade them to release the women so that they could ride back with Nate and the Penateka. It was agreed that they would stay with Eagle Feather in his winter camp until Nate returned with the horses and cattle. It had not been easy, with mistrust on both sides, but it had finally been settled. The Comanche had been lied to so many times by the white men that Nate had some sympathy for their view, but he pledged his honor, and as he pointed out they knew where his ranch was situated and could always raid it in retribution. It had been a brave thing to say, according to Raven Wing, especially as

Running Bear would be out for revenge as soon as he was physically able. The warrior was in terrible pain, and Nate doubted if he would ever walk properly again. The cold, damp winters would always remind him of his encounter with Nate, even if the leg healed straight, which he doubted. His broken jaw was bound, and he had stared with terrible hatred at Nate as the party left, unable to rant and curse at his opponent. His pride was hurt as much as anything, as Chief Parker had predicted.

Alison Hemple clung to Nate's back as they rode double on Buck, her bony frame fixed to his like a limpet as she finally dared to believe she might be free of the nightmare. There had been tears of fear and anger as she had refused to go at first, screaming curses and eventually collapsing in a bedraggled heap. Nate had picked her up and placed her on Buck's back, where she clung on wordlessly for dear life.

When they finally reached the Penateka camp, Nate dismounted and weakly helped Alison down. He then went to the two Gilmore girls, who had not said a word since they left the camp and stood mutely clinging to each other, not understanding what was happening, all sense of reason seemingly lost to them. He brought Alison to them and asked her to look after them. Strangely, now that he was back in Eagle Feather's territory, Nate felt a curious sense of relief wash over him, even though he was still far from home and absolute safety. Yet compared to the animosity and anger he had seen at Parker's camp it was a massive relief. He knew that here at least he would not be attacked during what was left of the night and could relax as much as he dared.

Raven Wing came to him as he stood in the darkness

looking at Alison and the two girls. "Is the one called Alison your woman?" she asked.

"No. I danced with her a couple of times at a local dance, that's all. I know her father and for what it is worth I don't like him. Nor he me."

"Then you are either very brave or very stupid. Why did you fight for her and sacrifice all?"

Nate paused before answering. He had acted instinctively, knowing it was the right thing to do. "Because it had to be done and I was the only one who could do it," he said eventually. "In the words of the South, I was raised up right, and I felt obligated to act the way I did. Also, I took three lives recently and maybe these three will atone for them." He shrugged.

"You are very strange, white man, and there is a difference between our people such that we will never understand one another."

Nate nodded, feeling too tired to argue and wanting to rest as he did not feel well.

The following morning, he woke after a fitful sleep dominated by memories of the knife fight and the brown faces in the firelight that would stay with him for a long time. But as he woke he realized that all was not well. He was bathed in sweat, his clothes soaked within the suggan, and when he felt his forehead his hand came away wet. He felt awful when he made to rise. He had no energy, and his head was spinning. His wounds had been bandaged and poulticed by one of the older squaws, but even in his semi-delirious state he knew that he had an infection and was using all his energy to fight it. Raven Wing came in to see him as the older squaw was wetting the poultices and bringing a gourd of water to his lips, from which he drank copiously.

"You are with fever. Bad spirits are about you, Nate-With-Fast-Hands. Here is a broth I have prepared for you. You must finish it and gain your strength to fight the evil that seeks to take your body," she urged him.

He barely nodded, his vision blurring in and out of focus as he shivered with cold inside the warm wikiup. Raven Wing fed him as the older medicine woman covered him in more blankets.

"He is bad," the old woman said. "The evil enters his body. He will shiver then burn later this day, and the night will tell us whether he sees tomorrow or not. The spirits hover above him. I see them," she added, nodding and looking through the scented smoke that she wafted towards Nate.

Nate slipped in and out of consciousness for two days. Alison came to visit him bringing the broth that Raven Wing made. She was petrified that Nate would succumb to his fever and die, leaving her stranded with no one to take back the terms of the trade. Nate's death would mean victory for Running Bear, and she would be returned to him to face a terrible fate. As the evening of the second day arrived, Nate changed from being constantly cold and shivering and began to burn up. The heat radiating from his body could be felt all around the wikiup. The medicine woman spoke to Raven Wing, issuing commands. More women came inside, carrying a form of stretcher made from a thick blanket borne between two poles. They placed Nate upon it and made their way down to the river, as he ranted and raved, tossing and turning in his feverish state and running a high temperature.

The shallows gave into small inlets covered with shale down from the banks, and small rocks provided sheltered, shallow pools. Alison came and watched in horror thinking that he would die, or that they were about to drown him in some strange ritual.

"Stay here and do not interfere. Walks Far knows what she does, she has much skill and heals all," Raven Wing said, holding Alison by the arm to stop her moving as they lowered Nate, still on the stretcher, into the cold water of the river. He thrashed in his fever as they pushed him down to keep all but his neck and head submerged, making ripples in the still pool. Then Walks Far began chanting above him in the tongue of her people, rising up and down in cadence to invoke spirits that none save her could see.

For half an hour they left Nate in the cold water, then the fever left him, and his temperature dropped. Finally, he shook and shivered, his shoulders trying to hunch and rise.

"It is done," Walks Far commanded. "Now lift him and bear him back to camp."

The old Comanche women stripped him of his clothes, seeing the scars of many battles about his body and nodding in approval. It was a warrior's body, and it was right that he should be so marked. They dried him thoroughly and laid him upon a thick buffalo robe as his body shivered and shuddered at the recent assault from the cold waters.

"Now *Al-li-sun*, now is your time to help him, for he is

of your people. Lie with him, hold him and give your warmth to his body," Raven Wing commanded.

Alison Hemple looked down at Nate and back at Raven Wing, still unsure, damaged by her experiences with Running Bear and his brutality. She moved forward hesitantly towards the naked form before her, more embarrassed that he was a white man, which somehow made a difference to her sensibilities.

"Hurry, for he must now have warmth if he is to live," Raven Wing's final words spurred her on, and she dropped her skin dress and lay beside Nate's shivering body, snuggling close to him and wrapping an arm about his chest, raising her other around his head, pulling his body to hers, willing him to live. The squaws then laid blankets and another buffalo robe over the supine pair before finally stoking the fire within the wikiup to stifling levels.

Alison held him tightly through his dreams and fever. Nate's body shivered, then began to relax, as finally his breathing returned to a normal rhythm. He entered into a deep and peaceful sleep as the air, filled with the smoke of cleansing herbs, helped his recovery.

With her job done, and to prevent any embarrassment to herself or Nate, Alison eased herself out from under the blankets in the early hours of the morning, dressed and went to fetch broth and put more wood on the dying fire that swiftly flared back to life.

Later that morning, as she knelt before him, Alison watched Nate's eyes flicker open, blinking in the light of the fire.

"Alison?" he croaked. "Where am I? I dreamt of another place, somewhere with green meadows, sunlight...and water flowing over me."

"You are safe," she answered.

"So thirsty. Water please," he muttered.

She brought a gourd to his lips, and he swallowed in great gulps, then coughed, raising himself upwards in a surprising show of strength for one who had been so weak with fever hours before. As he took more water, Alison explained what had happened, leaving out the part where she had kept him warm.

With the broth eaten along with small pieces of tender meat and pemmican, Nate managed to dress himself, finding his gun belt with his clothes, taking comfort from its reassuring weight as he strapped it around his waist. He flipped open the Colt, removing the cylinder and replacing it with a fully loaded one from his belt loop, checking the chambers as he gently rotated the new cylinder.

Alison watched him as he asked, "How long was I under for?"

"Three nights," she answered quietly.

"Then I must move. Time is running short," he murmured, still feeling weak from the fever. He knew he must act quickly to meet the deadline, offering Running Bear no excuse to claim that he had reneged on the terms of the trade.

He pushed open the flaps of the wikiup and went to find Buck and Patch, who were hobbled and grazing nearby. They whickered as Nate approached. He saddled Patch and checked that the Remmington Beals was still there in the saddle bag and loaded. The effort made him realize how weak he still was, and Nate knew he must husband what strength he had or his endurance and stamina would suffer. He led the horses to the wikiup where Walks Far waited with Raven Wing and Eagle Feather.

He thanked them for their help and promised to return with the horses and cattle. Then he turned to Walks Far, the medicine woman, and thanked her for saving him. She nodded impassively and handed him wrapped poultices, which through Raven Wing's translation, must be kept damp and changed regularly. Then as he mounted, Walks Far came to his side, the deep dark eyes looked seemingly into his soul and surprisingly spoke to him in his own tongue: "Take care, Nate-With-Fast-Hands, there are those who seek your death. Watch your trail." She turned without another word and walked away.

He felt a shadow fall over him and looked for Alison to say goodbye and assure her that he would return, but she was not there. All he saw was the pathetic vison of the two Gilmore children, still clinging to each other in silence, their faces blank and expressionless.

The weak sun was lower in the fall sky as he rode out of the camp, accompanied by a party of braves who escorted him to the stone archway. Once there, he was motioned by the leader with his lance to ride away. Nate nodded his thanks and rode on without turning back to look, his shoulders prickling with suspicions as he left the Comanche camp. After an hour he felt in need of a rest, if only for a cup of coffee and to eat some of the pemmican he had been given.

He was hungry, his battered body desperate to recoup lost energy.

He stopped by the river in an oxbow near some willows that were now losing their yellowed silvery leaves as fall came in with vigor. A small outcrop of rocks gave shelter from a lazy north wind that had started to get up as the day waned. He built a fire within a circle of stones and set his coffee pot on to brew. He chewed on the pemmican as he began to clean and reload the half empty cylinder, finally setting new nipple caps on each load.

All the time he rested the Remington Beals revolver on his lap and kept his Spencer by his side, half-cocked and ready. It was not a time, he reflected, to be scrabbling for a weapon if he was attacked, and he would not feel safe until he was back at his ranch. The coffee pot started to burble away, then Nate stiffened, hearing the low crack of a twig and the scrape of a boot on rock. Behind him, one or more people were closing in on him. His left arm was still stiff from his wounds and he was weak, but he was damned if he would not go down fighting. He cocked the Remington, holding the Navy in his left hand as though checking it.

A figure appeared, no more than a shadow to his right. Nate simply fell over sideways to his left, and while in motion he squeezed the trigger of the Remington, the explosion happening at exactly the same time as his attacker fired his own handgun. It was a distance of around thirty feet, and with the movement Nate's aim was slightly off, even as a bullet whistled through the air where his head had been a second before, whining as it hit the rock behind and ricocheting off in fragments. He thumbed and fired three shots as fast as he could, the first taking his attacker in the shoulder, the second at the top of the thigh and the third in the chest as he settled back, finally in balance. The body crumpled and collapsed, dropping onto one knee still trying to raise his pistol. Nate had no choice. He fired a fourth round into the man's head that emerged from the back leaving an exit wound like a smashed watermelon.

He now had one shot left in the weapon because of the conversion to metallic cartridges, which meant it could only fire five shots. He cocked it ready upon the recoil, waiting, then another shot crashed out across the camp. He span round to face it knowing he would be too late, wondering why he had not been hit. A dry cough sounded from some fifty feet away followed by a thud as a second body hit the ground.

A familiar voice floated out from the direction of the stream, masked by the willows and longish grass. "Nate, you OK?"

"Sure, Jas, thanks to you."

A shadow unrolled itself from a different position than Nate thought, concealed in small scrub that he would not have thought could give cover to a jackrabbit, let alone a man. His Winchester laid across his arm, Jas came forward, relaxed but watching the slumped figure upon the ground, not happy until he levelled with him, kicking away the rifle that lay partly in the grip of his right hand.

The downed man coughed and started to speak as Nate approached. The words came but neither man understood them because they were all in Polish. It was one of the two waggoneers whom Nate had seen in the wagon train and again in Quanah Parker's Comanche camp. The man spluttered some more and died there in front of them cursing away in his own language. Nate was angry. He wanted answers and never seemed to be able to get them.

"Nate, for one man you sure do have a heap of talent for makin' enemies. Was you to try, I reckon you could start a war all by yourself," Jas joked, shaking his head. "I saw you with that Running Bear, now, he warn't much pleased with you, neither. But it were a brave thing you did – and man, that trick shootin', I ain't never seen the like. I was fixin' to let him have it if'n he looked to be beatin' you and to hell with the consequences. I thought you was finished at one point, but you rallied, you surely did."

"Jas, you old coon hound, you were there?"

"Yup, I tracked you early on then stayed back some, and nigh on scared myself to death bein' that close to all them damn Comanches," he said laconically, as though he were talking about a ride into town.

"You dammed injun, well I'll be. Where were you hidden?"

"Up in the mesa to the west, a good distance away but still within rifle shot. Damn near got found once but tuckered on down and hid myself tighter'n a pack rat. Had to leave my horse aways away and go the last bit on foot. That Quanah Parker now, he sure is something. Word is he's gonna be the big chief of the whole Comanche someday."

"That's what they say. He has a certain presence, I'll give him that. Jas, we need to get moving. I only had a week from leaving Parker's camp and lost three days of it to fever."

"Yeah, I thought as much from what I could tell. What is

the trade for? There must be one for you to take on like you did."

"Thirty horses and ten cattle on the hoof."

"Waal now, Gilmore's dead, but he was all right and I reckon there'll be those who will rally round to get the girls back sure enough. Let's get goin' and you can tell me 'bout it on the trail."

Chapter Eighteen

Nate left Jas to head back to his ranch, but broke off to visit Buck Durrant's Rocking D on the way to see if he could rustle up some cattle and horses so he could get back to the Comanche camp more quickly. He rode up to the imposing ranch house exhausted, and staggered as he stepped down from the saddle, dropping Buck and Patch's reins. Nate had forgotten that he was supposed to be dead and was surprised at the consternation his sudden appearance caused. The hands ran up and crowded round as Rick came up to help him up to the house.

"The old man's inside," he said. "Man, we sure are shocked to see you. What the hell happened to you?"

"Long story, Ricky, I'll tell your father and you can listen in," Nate answered with a weak smile. "That way I'll only have to say it once."

Nate was led through to Buck Durrant's study, where he gave an abbreviated account of much that had happened, leaving out certain matters that he wished to keep to himself.

The old man listened with interest, asking questions as he went, but when Nate got to the wagon train, Buck raised a hand to stop him.

“What you say tallies, as a wagon train of new folks are camped outside of Flat Creek. They moved on to the free range a few days ago,” he said. “I tell you it don’t sit well, and there’s been voices raised against it already. Newcomers are sayin’ they got a right and you can guess how that’s goin’ down.” He raised an eyebrow, his face stern and his meaning clear.

“I know only too well,” Nate replied. “I was less than honest with them on the trail about who I was and what I owned, so I learned a great deal – none of it good. Someone has encouraged them to come here with the promise of good grazing on Government Grants – and the sad thing is they’re not wrong and there is nothing illegal going on. But like you say, it’ll only end one way and that’s with war in the valley. With the Indian problem we have going on, it gives me great cause for concern.”

At this, Nate continued his story and told them all that had happened at the Comanche camp.

“The hell you say. You went to Quanah Parker’s camp and traded for the captives? Nate, you’re either a very brave man or a fool, and I ain’t sure which,” Rick said, impressed at what Nate had done.

“Amen to that,” Buck added, looking hard at Nate. “You’ve had a bad time of it, boy. I didn’t realize the extent of it when you turned up just now. Seems if we’re to get those women back we need to move fast. What do you need, Nate?”

"I am glad you said that, sir, and I'm more than happy to chip in. But time's against us. I need thirty horses and ten head of cattle. We have barely four days now to get them to Eagle Feather's camp and retrieve the girls."

"Waal don't you worry 'bout that. I'm sure others will come round when they hear about it. Those poor girls – and Alison, dear Lord what she must have gone through." Buck shook his head. "I like Alison, and Gilmore was all right. Always chirpy even in the bad times, and up against it too, running that small spread of his the way he did. Luke, now, he's a grumpy old so-and-so, but he thinks the world of his girl and if he lives, he'll see me right. We'll make sure he builds it all back up. Got hit pretty hard in the raid, I hear." Nate could see Buck squaring his shoulders as his natural ability to command returned. "Rick, shake out some of the boys and round up thirty horses. Mixed stock, you know what I mean. Cut out ten head of cattle and start 'em moving straight away. If we get 'em on the trail we may be lucky and get 'em there in two days, three at most. Either way, we'll be in time."

"I'll ride ahead and tell them we're coming," Nate added. "But most likely they'll know the minute we get on the trail. There's no flies on those Comanches. Sir, I really appreciate this, and I will see that you don't go short."

Buck waved a big beefy hand in dismissal. "I know you will," he said, rubbing his shoulder. "I still get rheumatism in bad weather from an arrow I took here back in the old days. Good days too in some ways, they were. The Comanche are good men; brave and fearless. Just they're so different to us it's hard to read 'em and know which way they're gonna turn. They have their own values, and they stick to them. After all you've done – and you've done enough already – but what drives you, Nate?" he asked, as Rick left to give the orders.

Nate shook his head sipping his second cup of coffee. "I don't really know, sir. It's what my father would have done, and I guess his teaching stays with me. He was man of principle, and he gave everything for his values, even sacrificing his place in English society. I knew I could do it, or at least I thought I could, and there were innocent lives at stake, women and children, so it had to be done. Simple as that, really."

Buck looked hard at him and nodded, appreciating his words. "Go on, son," he said. "Get yourself on home and we'll see you on the trail."

"Sure. I'll send Jas out. He'll guide you and I'll catch up once I've changed and eaten."

"That's fine, Nate, you'll find us soon enough as we'll be slowed down by the cattle 'n ' horses."

Nate gave rough instructions for the trail they should follow and how it would come to a fork where they were to take the left track. By then he reckoned that he, or certainly Jas, would have caught them up.

Reaching his ranch, he was not surprised to see everyone waiting for him. Jas had been to the Hemple ranch, alerting the hands to the news of Alison being found and hopefully returned to them in a few days. Nate sent Morg to town on a hunch to warn Macey what had happened and to tell Luke Hemple his daughter had been found. Nate then had an afterthought: "Montana, one more thing before you go.

Warn Macey that the town is to be on the alert. It may be nothing, but everyone's concerned about their ranches, and folks will be focusing on getting the girls back. The town will be distracted. Towns have been attacked before, and it usually happens when it's least expected. Tell Janet to be on the lookout and to keep a gun handy."

"You think it might get that bad?" Morg asked.

"I don't know, but if I didn't warn Janet, Lily would never forgive me, and I'd never forgive myself. A few men up on the roof with rifles for the next few days wouldn't do any harm. Macey's all right as far as it goes, but he's green and too trusting. Also find out for me on the quiet if Tim Durrant's around. I want to know what he's up to."

"Sure thing, Nate. You go easy too. You've taken a beating of late."

Nate nodded and went to get a bath and a change of clothes, which immediately made him feel better.

He slept well that night and set off at dawn the next day. Dancer was young and eager to go and seemed as fresh as ever as he covered the ground at a mile-eating lope.

He caught up with the herd towards the end of the day. They had made good time, and just before he joined them he skirted around and scouted ahead, looking for any sign of Indians. At the far side of the herd, he saw Jas keeping a wary eye around and rode to join him.

"How're you feeling?" Jas greeted him.

"Better than I did, thank you. How's it going?"

"All right. Can't see 'em but that don't mean they ain't here. I know they're around, watching, checking on us. My guess is that they won't let us near the camp, like you figured. They'll likely bring the captives out tomorrow, when we're about a day's ride from the stone arch where they stopped you last time. One thing's certain, old Running Bear won't be there after you messed him up, and he'll be fit to bust when he learns that you killed his two Poles."

"I know. I'll have to face him at some time, but I've got enough to worry about just now."

Jas nodded and they rode down to the small drive, where Nate saw a few of the Flying H hands were helping. One was driving a buggy ready for Alison and the two Gilmore children. He nodded to them as Clint Straw, the Flying H foreman, rode up to him.

"Nate, we surely do 'preciate what you did. It took guts and we are grateful. Specially as the old man and you don't see eye to eye all the time," he said, shaking Nate's hand.

Nate was embarrassed by the effusive thanks and shrugged it off. "Least I could do, Clint."

"How is she ... Alison. I mean was she ... you know," he stumbled, embarrassed and ashamed to ask such a thing. "Aw hell, Nate, you know what I mean. We all love her, and we care ... well, you know..."

Nate's voice took on a flinty air: "I'll say this for your ears only, Clint. Running Bear took her as his woman. She's been shaken by the whole thing and badly treated. She won't be quite as you remember her, so be ready for it and give her time."

Clint looked sad, tears welling in his eyes that burned with anger. He gave a knowing nod, understanding all that Nate had said. "If only we'd been able to stop it."

"Don't go there, Clint. You did all you could. She'll be all right, and she's still alive. Just give her time."

The foreman looked dejected as he nodded, turned his horse and rode back to the herd. Nate shook his head sadly. *Whoever had started all this needed to pay*, he thought. So many lives had been lost or ruined.

The mixed herd was pushed along, and by Nate's reckoning they were about a day's drive from the stone arch he had passed under just a week earlier. It seemed like a whole world away.

"Don't look now," Jas said at his side, "but we got ourselves some company."

Nate nodded calmly. "I'll pass the word along. I don't want any trigger-happy yahoo starting to pull a gun – especially Clint, he's taken it hard, Chris, too, by the looks of things. I think he was sweet on Alison and from what I can gather he feels responsible for Bill's death and for Alison being taken."

"Yeah, we need to keep a lid on it, that's for sure," Jas muttered as he rode off quietly to pass the word to the other hands on his side of the drive.

Nate sidled up alongside Rick. "Ricky, there are Comanches on either side of us," he said. "No, don't look. Keep calm and don't let any hotheads get spooked and start shooting. I'm going to move on to the Flying H boys and make sure they stay calm."

Nate was ready for Chris's reaction. The fool reached for his gun, forgetting that the loop was still on the hammer. Nate grasped his wrist in an iron grip borne of hard work and constant practice with his pistols. "Leave it, you damned fool, do you want to get us all killed? Or have Alison taken back? Because if you do, you're going the right way about it," he snapped.

The young cowhand looked upset but nodded in agreement, apologizing for his action.

"Good, now keep a lid on your temper or you'll be the death of us all," Nate said as he rode off to the next hand.

The Indians appeared, seeming to metamorphose out of the rock, blocking the trail and rising up on the ridges on either side. Nate shouted ahead: "Ricky, hold 'em steady. Nobody move or do anything stupid. That's Quanah Parker up there and he understands English and he'd just as soon take your scalps as look at you." Nate pushed Dancer into a lope, skirting the herd and coming to the front, where Jas, Buck and Rick sat like statues leaving Nate to do the talking.

Suddenly whoops of war were heard as two bands from either side flew down the rock slopes onto the talus that spread out before them, riding like centaurs, seemingly at one with their horses. Buck, mindful of their ways, sat implacably, knowing that they were being tested. He knew that where some of the Comanche were visible, others were sure to be hidden.

The screaming warriors came on, pulling up at the last second, sliding their ponies to a halt and crowding the white men at the head of the herd. Without saying a word, they moved in and skillfully cut the horses and cattle out from the cowhands, with Nate shouting, "Let them do it. Do *NOT* try to stop them!"

Chris started to object.

"Clint, shut him down or we're all dead and Alison will never see her father again!"

He did not turn his head and heard nothing more except a thud that sounded a lot like a man falling off a horse. With the horses and cattle taken, Quanah Parker nudged his horse forward, coming down from the higher ground. He was splendid in his magnificence, his skin shining with antelope grease, his dark features harsh and unyielding. He rode directly in front of Nate, majestic and seemingly omnipotent, at one with his surroundings, flanked by two warriors with wolf pelts hanging from their belts, each holding a new Winchester Yellow Boy, eyes dark and unreadable, arrogant in their self-belief.

"You came, Nate-With-Fast-Hands. You are a true warrior, and you honor your people by keeping your word."

"As it should be between our peoples, Chief Parker," Nate answered. "There must be trust or we shall never have peace."

"Just so, yet that time may be far off." At which he raised his hand and more warriors appeared, two leading horses bearing the Gilmore children on one and Alison Hemple on the other. She looked to Nate's eyes as ravaged as ever by her experiences, her eyes frightened and her skin drawn tightly across her cheekbones. The braves rode down and motioned for the white women to dismount. They obeyed fearfully and stood in silence, awaiting orders.

"It is done, Nate-With-Fast-Hands, we have both honored our word," Chief Parker said, "and to honor this I pledge you as blood brother." He pulled out his sheath knife, which made Nate flinch. He had had enough of Indians with knives, but he forced himself to hold firm as Parker rode to his side, pricked his own palm and did the same to Nate, grasping his wrist in a calloused hand. Nate knew what was expected and offered his palm, which Parker took in a firm grip. "We are now blood brothers and will not make war upon each other."

Nate nodded, not sure what to say. He decided that Indians, like women, were mighty unpredictable. The chief spoke words in Comanche, sheathed his knife, wheeled his horse and joined the others, speeding away up the hill and whooping until they disappeared out of sight.

"Waal, Nate, if that don't beat all," Jas said, amazed at what he had just witnessed. "There's somethin' to tell your children and grandchildren about one day, how you became blood brothers to the great chief of the Comanche Quanah Parker."

Nate looked around in a daze, finding it just as hard to believe what had just happened. Then he shook himself, before sliding off his horse and going to the three white women, where Alison collapsed in his arms sobbing in relief. He gently pushed her away and holding her by the hand he moved to the two Gilmore girls, pulling them to him until they all stood wordless in his embrace.

Chapter Nineteen

Nate returned to his ranch after leaving Alison and the two girls in the care of the Rocking H hands, having escorted them back to the ranch house on the buggy. It had been a difficult time, and Nate felt drained and tired as the events of the past few days caught up with him. His wounds seemed to be healing well and the skin was no longer red and angry, just stiff as the scabs formed and his body healed itself.

Two days later he sat on the porch, cleaning his guns with a cloth on a table before him, thinking over recent events and wondering to himself how it was all going to end. He still had many questions that remained unanswered as to what was going on in the valley, but the picture he was building in his mind was not a pleasant one and he hoped that he was wrong.

He saw a lone rider cresting the ridge to the front of the ranch, and by the way he rode he recognized the figure as Deputy Sheriff Macey. He was coming at a fair pace, and

Nate knew that it did not bode well. Macey's horse was lathered with sweat even in the cool of the early morning. Macey sat deeply into the saddle, thrusting his legs forward, and the horse broke back to a walk as he came within a few feet of the hitching rail before the porch. The animal came to a sliding halt, blowing hard from the exertion of the ride.

Nate stood waiting for him, unconsciously rubbing his arm as the healing cuts itched beneath his shirt sleeve. "Howdy, Macey, step down. Looks like you've come hard and fast. Is everything alright?" he asked.

"Mornin', Nate. I have, and no it ain't. By the way, I'm right glad to see you alive and well, after all we heard."

"Sit down and tell me what's amiss. It'll be better after a coffee," Nate offered, walking back to fetch a pot and second cup from the house.

Macey thanked him. He dismounted, easing off the cinch and allowing the horse to blow out as he led him to the trough for a small drink. Finally, he sat down, pushing back his Stetson to the back of his head and wiping his brow, which was wet with sweat. He gulped at the sweet, black brew that Nate handed to him, winced as it scalded his mouth, sighed and then said: "There's hell to pay, Nate, and I need help, what with Paul dead an' all. Jackobsen's place was hit by Comanches the night you met them. They didn't come for the town like you figured, they hit another ranch instead. That whole damn valley is laid to waste now, from Gilmore's place right along to the free range." Macey spat in disgust. "Jackobsen and his wife barely made it out alive. He had a cellar with a back exit into brush, an' they got out and played doggo until he could get away. Was found by one of Buck's hands and came into town to tell all. They razed the whole place to the ground, burned him out.

"Hemple's barely alive, but better since his daughter came back – though poor Alison ain't the same and she sure is getting a rough time of it. Then there's all those wagon train folk camped out on the free range, looking to stake their claims and the local ranches up in arms saying it can't be used 'cos they cut their winter hay from it. I got me a war on one side between the incomers and ranchers and a war on the other with the Comanches. I'm damned if I know which way to turn.

"I'm out of my depth, Nate, and I know that you held down a badge up to Langtonville, so I was wonderin' if you could help – especially as some of the range they claim is part of yours up to the Carson Valley and the new valley you found where you was nearly killed. Talkin' of which, how the hell did you get out? Then you go and track down old Janus Shaw and hand him his needings. Man, what a story that made," Macey said, shaking his head in disbelief.

"I'm sorry to hear about the Jackobsens," Nate said, ignoring the comments about his gunfight with Shaw. "Are they all right – I mean apart from being burnt from house and home?"

"They are, but they're planning to leave. They've still got another year or so until it becomes theirs under the Homestead Act, but there ain't no way they can pay the fee now. Another farm'll go empty as folks are driven out."

"Macey, I don't see what good I can do. I held a badge

for just a few weeks and that was in a wide open town where I didn't have to fight Indians and settle land disputes. But I'll do all I can to back you and help out," Nate offered. "Though I will say that someone is pulling the strings in this valley, and I saw all those Comanches had new Winchesters. Now what you need to ask yourself is where did they get them and who would give them brand new rifles?"

"Do you have any idea?" Macey asked, aghast at the fact that only a fool would arm the Comanches for no apparent reason.

"I do," Nate said hesitantly, "but I have no proof to back up my opinion." And then a thought occurred to him. "Say, is the stage due in today? I've lost all track of time."

"It sure is, should be here by noon. Why? You expecting someone?"

"Not someone, some important mail that I was hoping might be arriving soon. Look, I'll tell you what, I'll ride back with you and on the way we'll call into the free range and speak with the wagon train boss, Martin Bradshaw. I met him on the trail, and he seemed like a reasonable sort of chap. I'd also like to learn a little more from him about who set up this land deal and organised the train from the east. With you along it makes it more official asking questions that I couldn't ask otherwise."

"Now you're talking. See? I knew you'd find a way. But you sure do cover a lot of territory. How'd you know Bradshaw?" the marshal asked.

"I'll tell you on the way. Let me saddle a horse and I'll be right with you."

They entered the western valley that began with the free range two hours later, and there circled before them was the wagon train that Nate had encountered seemingly an age ago on the trail to San Antonio. Further along was a dust cloud that showed cattle being moved towards them.

"Looks like we got here just in time," Macey said, pushing his horse at a faster pace towards the circled wagons. A group of wagon train people stood on the western side of the circle, including Martin Bradshaw, rifles in their hands ready to shoot to defend the train against the oncoming cattle. Nate and Macey rode past them to place themselves between the wagons and the herd about a hundred yards west of the train on the main trail through the grasslands.

Nate saw Rick Durrant at the fore riding point. He hailed him from a distance, and seeing Nate he pushed forward to meet the two men, flanked by his brothers. The herd slowed as they arrived, clearly under orders to await their return.

"Nate, Macey." He nodded as they closed the distance, sliding to a halt. "Didn't expect to see you up and around here, 'specially sidin' with them nesters and such," Rick said bitterly.

"Ricky, I'm not siding with anybody. I just don't want to see bloodshed happening over a misunderstanding," Nate said, seeing a bandage on Dan's head and a bloodstain on Benny's arm that showed through his shirt sleeve.

"Little late for that. We got hit last night by the damned Comanches. Killed some stock, stole some horses and rode off. Two hands dead and us shot up some. Your blood brother," he said with a sneer, "was busy enough, but he left you alone, I see."

"I'm sorry to hear that, Ricky, but it was not on me. I have no deals going with Quanah Parker, and are you sure it was Comanches?" Nate asked, keeping his temper in check.

"Waal, they was shooting arrows at us and whooping, and they sure weren't dressed in their best go-to-town clothes, if that's what you mean." Rick snarled.

"Where's Buck? Is he alright?"

"Yeah, he went off to San Antone to send some cables east looking for answers," he said. "Anyways, I figured to settle matters here, seein' as we're being attacked on all fronts. Thought I'd make a little war of my own and clear this land of squatters," he said, jerking his hand at the wagons.

"Ricky, it don't have to be like that," Macey said, trying to calm matters. "We're here to talk to them and find out exactly what they've been told about the land and grants and such. Just come and see what they have to say, will you? I don't want trouble and I can see you're upset about all that's going on, just like we all are. All I'm askin' is that you come and talk to them," he pleaded.

Rick shook his head in disgust, motioned for the herd to be halted and circled and then sent Benny back with his orders, while Dan rode with him towards the wagons. The four horsemen approached the wagons, where Martin Bradshaw stood at their head.

"Nathaniel Sinclair, this is a surprise. I thought you were headed for San Antonio to meet up with your friend Janus Shaw?" he said, clearly puzzled and slightly suspicious.

"Howdy, Martin. In part I was, although I will admit to not being entirely honest with you."

The others looked on, as interested as Martin Bradshaw was about the circumstances of Nate meeting up with the wagon boss.

"Hmm, you sound a little different, too," Bradshaw commented, as the scout Matt Phelps nodded in agreement and looked on with interest, his rifle lodged in the crook of his arm, everyone aware of the tension in the air.

"Well, that was part of the subterfuge, I'm afraid. I'll explain all to you now, then maybe you'll understand a little more clearly what has been happening in this valley and why tensions are running so high," Nate said.

The riders were invited to step down and were offered a cup of coffee as they were ushered into the center of the wagons circled against possible attack from either whites or Indians. Nate received smiles from the two women that he had saved, and went over and exchanged a few words with them, asking after their families and how they were faring. This went some way towards reminding all present on the train of the debt they owed him for his intervention and action that day.

He went on to explain about Janus Shaw and the mystery man who had arranged for a bounty to be put on his head, the raids by whites as well as Indians that were intended to stir up trouble, and the fact that the lawyer who had arranged the train's passage was now dead and his offices ransacked. He finished by telling them about the Poles who had miraculously escaped the attack and who turned up in the Comanche camp before being sent to kill him.

Ricky and Dan had already been aware of much of what Nate said, but even they were amazed at some of the revelations that came out as he told Martin Bradshaw everything that had happened both within the valley and outside it that all had a bearing on matters.

"You say that this lawyer dude was from Boston? This being where you all started out from originally, Mister Bradshaw?" Ricky asked, slightly puzzled.

"Make it Martin, please, and yes, that's correct. It all seemed so perfect in the beginning: time for a new start and opportunities. We were all so excited. But it seems that nothing is as we thought."

Ricky continued not liking where this was heading. "And you, Nate, from what you've said these here two Polacks were shipping guns out here to sell to the Indians. They joined the train later at Fort Worth, then they let 'em loose to turn on us and raid the valley. That right?"

"Yes, that's pretty much what I think. All the Indians in Quanah Parker's band had brand new Winchesters, and some came in soon after the mule train hit the forts. I reckon some guns came that way and around via Pecos."

"Pecos? Why Pecos?" Ricky asked.

"Because its northwest of here, you can get there easily and it's where Parker's band live for a lot of the time. And think about it; the raids that started before the guns arrived and out on the trail when we were herding cattle to Fort Stockton, it was all made to look like Indians to stir up trouble. So was the raid on my own ranch. Now where did those white men come from? The local ranches weren't involved, or not directly at least. No, someone is – or was – coordinating all this, and that someone needs a group of men that can be kept and hired from somewhere not in the valley. My guess is – and this is why Marshal Walker was killed – that they are hiding out at the old Carson spread or somewhere nearby, maybe the Gilmore place or what's left of it. No one's been near there, especially not me, but I bet if we did we'd find evidence that someone has been living there and with tracks of horses going to and fro. This has been well organized from the start, and someone with brains is behind it."

"You know who it is, don't you, Nate?" Rick asked tentatively, his own mind working in a way that he did not like and refusing to accept the answers it gave him.

Nate nodded somberly. "I think I do, but as yet I have no firm proof, and I need that before I call them on it."

"Waal come on, Nate, spill the beans. Who hell is the son of a bitch?" Macey demanded, more surprised than any at all these revelations that were suddenly being put together for him because of his youth and lack of experience. He was far from stupid, yet he had never encountered such a devious situation before.

"Too soon to say, Macey, until I am certain. All I do know is that Hoddett and Slattern, the law firm you mentioned before, have lost their partner. But what I haven't told you is that I wired them and also put an enquiry agent on the case. I've asked a number of pertinent questions, and when I get their report with the answers, I will have my proof – or as much as I need to confront the person I think is responsible." Then turning to Rick Durrant, he said: "Ricky, can you hold off until the old man gets back and I get some answers to my questions? It won't be very long. It might just save more killing and unnecessary upset."

"Oh, what the hell, sure, Nate. I guess we owe you that much after all you've been through and done for the valley. Say, did you really make Old Man Randall back-pedal and call him a liar and a backshooter to his face, and then threaten to put a bounty on him?" he asked, amazed.

Nate nodded and answered quietly: "I did. He had it coming."

"Waal I'll be. He and Pa have known each other for a while. They go back a long ways and came to this country 'bout the same time, still calls by from time to time. Man, I'd dearly liked to have seen that."

"Two more went down that day, way I heard it," Macey interjected, "Pecos and Bob Turner."

Nate's heart sank; the story was already spreading.

"You took out Pecos and Bob Turner?" Ricky exclaimed. "Pecos was reckoned to be right handy with a gun. What did Ted Lineman do? Was he there?"

Nate shrugged, saddened by the whole affair. "He was, and he wanted no part of it. Ricky, can we drop it? I don't want a reputation as a gunfighter."

Rick nodded, his face a picture of awe and surprise. He had never seen Nate shoot or even draw a gun, yet this was something to be reckoned with and he wanted the whole story. Someone would know, he thought. Someone in San Antonio would have seen it all. He gathered his horse's reins then turned back. "Mister Bradshaw, I'll be seeing you. Thanks for the coffee," Rick finished curtly, motioned to Dan, and the two men mounted and returned to the herd.

"What's eating him?" Bradshaw asked, knowing that if a man still called you mister in Texas after being introduced and friendly, it meant that all was not well.

"A good deal. From his way of life to who he thinks is responsible for threatening it, and he isn't very happy about it. Now, Macey, gentlemen, I am heading into town to see if my report has arrived on the stage."

Chapter Twenty

Martin Bradshaw decided to accompany Nate and Sheriff Macey into town. It transpired that Bradshaw had not yet met the land agent promised them by Hoddett and Slattern, and he was anxious to resolve all the problems peacefully and not sour the hopes and dreams of all those on the wagon train, for whom he felt responsible. He asked Nate more questions on the ride into town and was surprised at some of the answers, unaware of the upset and the capture of the white women by the Comanche, who had been stirred up to raid and kill.

"What do you expect this report and answers to your questions to say, Nate?" Bradshaw asked.

"I'm not sure, and I'd rather not speculate until I have all the information to hand," Nate answered, indicating that the subject was closed for now.

They reached the outskirts of the town and headed down Main Street, getting quite a few gasps and surprised looks, as it was the first time that Nate had been into town since his death had been reported. People pointed at him, Lazarus-like in his reincarnation, and Nate was disappointed to see just how many people recognized him. They pulled up in front of the sheriff's office and tied their horses to the rail, Nate slackening off Patch's cinch to allow him a drink from the horse trough. Nate headed for the Wells Fargo office to see if the stage had arrived, and upon learning that it had, he walked across to the post office. He was pleased to find the report had come through in record time, carried by rail to San Antonio then onward by stage to Flat Creek. He slipped out unnoticed and went to the café run by Lily's mother for a quiet cup of tea that Janet had learned to brew just the way he liked it. This, along with her bear sign, was the perfect antidote to the day's events.

"Nate, it's good to see you up and around. We were so worried about you." She greeted him, squeezing him in an affectionate hug. "Still getting yourself into mischief, I hear," she admonished, wagging a matronly finger at him, her plump chin wobbling as she did so.

"Now, Janet, it's not me, it's all the other fellas," Nate replied.

"Oh, sure. So what'll it be, the usual for the afternoon?" she asked kindly, seeing that he was troubled and wanted to be left alone. He agreed and found a quiet table at the rear of the café, partly obscured from sight by a wooden partition that offered some privacy for customers.

He undid his holster cord, sat down, removed his Stetson and slit open the envelope that was addressed to him using the knife from the table. Before he could begin reading, his tea was delivered by a shy girl that he barely recognized: it was

Ginny Gilmore. She said nothing, but placed the tray of tea things and bear sign upon the table and looked at him, raising a small hand to squeeze his calloused paw. Nate smiled and thanked her, and she turned quickly, scooting back to the kitchen where Janet stood, arms folded watching over her protectively. Nate felt tears rise in his eyes and shook his head and nodded to Janet, who smiled in return. It was good of her to take them in, he thought. There were good people in this town, and they deserved better than to have their lives ruined by one man's greed. Nate forced himself to concentrate, pulling out the report to find that it was written in neat, copperplate script and covered three sheets of paper.

At times Nate read and reread parts, looking up and staring into the distance as he absorbed and considered what he had just read. "Damn it all, this is a mess and no mistake," he muttered.

Nate barely heard the bell tinkle above the door in the fading light to admit Martin Bradshaw. The wagon master glanced around the café, his gaze passing over the customers seated and chatting amiably over a coffee or food until he located Nate in the corner. He walked over and took a seat.

"Just been to try and find that lawyer and land agent. Young fella by the name of Timothy Durrant. I take it he's related to the cowpuncher Rick who we met on the trail today?"

"He's his half-brother. Did you find him?"

"No, seems he lit out earlier today. No one knows where he's gone. Say, is that the report that you were expecting? I thought that you said you couldn't read and write, or was that all part of the subterfuge, too?"

"It is, and it doesn't make for good reading. And yes. I'm afraid I misled you to keep in character because I wanted to hear what you had to say. I didn't want to go off half-cocked until I knew the whole story – which now sadly I do. I don't want to repeat myself, so is Macey coming over?"

"No, he's at the jail."

"Right let's go see him."

Nate paid and the two men left.

Seated in the jailhouse with Macey, Nate began to explain what the report had said. "I asked about Susannah's family history and the finances for both sides of the family – including Timothy's mother, Anthea Durrant. Their position was suspicious, and I felt the whole answer to this riddle of the valley and its problems lay at their door. Turns out I was right.

"Around the time that Buck headed up to Boston and met Anthea, the fortunes of her family took a turn for the worse. They were old Boston bluebloods and had lots of interest in mining and stocks, but when these failed all they were left with was all the society but no money to back it up. Susannah's family was equally impoverished, and reading between the lines I suspected that one of the things Anthea asked of Buck was to bail out Susannah's parents as part of the marriage settlement, such as it was. Anyway, long story short, old Buck did so, married Anthea and kept both families afloat.

"So much for background, but how does that all tie in with what's been going on here?" Macey asked impatiently.

Nate nodded. "It has everything to do with it. You ever watch Tim with his three half-brothers? They steal the limelight and treat him with contempt as a weak eastern dude. He's half their size and he's soft. His mother pampers him – or has done from what I can tell – and he's different. Even old Buck is patronizing at times, although he's clearly proud of his new family. Tim feels he has no respect here, he's just the clever lawyer making his way on his Pa's coat tails. He's a mummy's boy. He and Susannah are cut from the same cloth. She's a Boston socialite with no money who's become dependent on a coarse – at least to her eyes – western rancher. She's bitter at the turn of events that's made her poor in the eyes of her friends. And on lesser circumstances wars have been fought," he finished.

"But I still don't get it. You mean nice little Tim Durrant is behind all this trouble?" Macey asked, amazed.

"And there you go. See how you view him? Not all bad men are six feet tall, bristling with guns and built like Goliath. Sometimes it's the quiet, brainy ones you have to watch. Something had been puzzling me, but the gap was filled in on the range earlier today. Ricky said that David Randall called at the ranch from time to time, where he would have met Tim. Knowing what I now know about Randall, I reckon he marked him for the future. And I'm the wild card here. I came late to the valley, and I've been making inroads, buying up where I can. I guess that sticks in some peoples' craw, but especially an ambitious man like Tim. He wanted me out, and he set me up for trouble. But in case that didn't work out, he set up an insurance policy with Randall, having heard about the trouble I had with him up north. He put a bounty on me and hired Janus Shaw to kill me and make it look like an accident. He tried to frame me for rustling first, because I think he was behind all of that, stealing from his own family. Randall became little more than a pawn in his game."

"But the injun attacks, what about them?" Macey asked.

"Oh, he armed them after stirring up trouble while he waited for the Winchesters to arrive. He was clever, he brought them in in two loads: one from the north and one in your train, Martin. It would all have worked too, if I hadn't happened upon the Apaches trying to take Eagle Feather's bride that day and then gone on to get the girls back. When I was injured and presumed dead, he raided my ranch with his party of mixed gunmen and a few bad hat Indians. I saw them riding across the range the night I escaped from the rock fall.

"Tim wanted your train to take the land. He'd make a lot of money and cause a range war where he would clean up – maybe even killing his own father and taking the ranch for his own or mopping up the smaller ranches to build a spread that would give him independence and the reputation he so desperately craved. He'd snap up the land for a song after a range war, and he'd make a killing in more ways than one.

"Anyway, that's how I see it. Some of it is supposition, but the facts fall into place, even getting Susannah to go on the drive to find out where I was heading. I also got a telegram from San Antonio and the sheriff up in Pecos. He confirmed that some hired gunmen had been taken on and were hanging around up there, disappearing and coming back at odd times. I guess they're hiding out either at Carson's old place or camping near Gilmore's partly burned out house. There's still a barn standing from what I can gather, and while everyone else is hunkered down and wary of Comanche attacks – which suits Tim well – they're not going to attack the men who supplied them with guns."

"Something you just said now struck a chord, Nate," Bradshaw began, taking up his theme. "When we met with Mister Forbes from Hoddett and Slattern, the firm of lawyers, it wasn't just him. He had a land agent with him, or so he said, the guy was his junior, it seemed. Anyways, he was in business with him or associated in some way. Glaston, or something?"

"Glascock?" Nate offered.

"Yes! Why that's it."

"That was Anthea's maiden name, before she married Buck."

"Waal, this young fella was about five eight, five nine. Blond hair, slim build, well-spoken and well educated."

"That sounds a lot like Timothy Durrant."

"Waal I'll be. Didn't occur to me until now," Bradshaw said.

Macey had been taking it all in, trying to formulate a plan as to what he should do next. "So what do we do now, Nate?" he asked. "Go after Tim Durrant? We have no proof of any of this, just circumstantial evidence. All that killing, Comanches on the loose, ranchers killed, families destroyed, all for land and greed. It don't seem possible."

Nate considered for a moment. "I'll stay at the hotel in town tonight, get some supper and ride out to Gilmore's place tomorrow, maybe Carson's old place on the way round and back if I have no luck," he said finally. "My guess is that Tim will stay out of sight or maybe try to contact you,

Martin, outside of town to keep things moving along. He needs to get the Comanches to attack again if he is to succeed. He may get them to attack the town and cause chaos. But he won't know I am alive yet. From the reaction of all those in the town today I was a ghost come back to haunt them. He'll still think he can get my ranch and that part of the valley, and with his father away, he'll try to cause more trouble between the train and the ranches.

"The only fly in the ointment is if he meets up with Quanah Parker and he puts two and two together with the story of me getting the girls back."

"Won't you be afraid of attack yourself?" Bradshaw asked.

"Not from the Indians. I'm a friend of Eagle Feather and now a blood brother to Quanah Parker, I also carry a rifle sheath that's big medicine in their eyes. It doesn't get much safer." Nate offered his companions a wry grin.

"That's a story I'd like to hear some time," Bradshaw said with awe in his voice.

"Macey, best thing you can do is ride out to the Rocking D tomorrow. Alert them and see if you can roust out some boys and get them to meet me over at the Gilmore's place or failing that on the trail near the old Carson ranch. I think Ricky already has an inkling things aren't right with Tim, so he won't be hard to persuade. In the meantime, I don't want to tell you your job, but I'd put the town on alert, keep some men on the roofs with rifles for a few nights, wagons across the street at night. Better safe than sorry."

Macey nodded, and they all agreed to split up and get some food and rest. Before going to his hotel, Nate made his way to the doctor's house where he had heard that Luke Hemple was still being tended.

He found Alison Hemple at her father's bedside. She turned at the sound of his knock and rose upon seeing him there diffident, hat in hand, uncertain of what to say or do.

"Miss Alison, good evening. I just came by to see how you and your father were doing."

"Oh, Nate," she exclaimed. "I thought I'd never see you again – well, not like this, anyway."

He was puzzled. "What do you mean?"

"You know with what happened to me," she replied, her gaze fixed on the floorboards. "The townsfolk seem upset by it and they're avoiding me, apart from Jenny, who's renting me a room above the café. She's taken the two Gilmore girls under her wing, too," she said quietly.

"I know. I called at the café to get a cup of tea. But what do you mean about avoiding you? Who would do a thing like that?" he asked, his ire rising.

Alison clasped her hands in front of her. She shrugged her shoulders, raising one hand in a gesture of despair. "Oh, you know, I'm a 'squaw woman' now, and they think ... they think I'm soiled goods, and that they'll catch something from me, tainted by association, I guess."

The words were wrung from her, and tears welled in her eyes as sobs shook her body.

Nate was moved by her state and opened his arms to hug her, smoothing her hair as she cried on his shoulder.

"Thank you, Nate," she said, drying her eyes in embarrassment. "That's the first human contact I've had in a while. I miss being held."

Nate was upset on her behalf. He freed her from his embrace and held her by the shoulders at arm's length. "Now just you hush, Alison, and wait until the next dance. We'll show them a thing or two and I'll beg the first two with you, so keep your card clear."

She smiled at this despite herself, nodding in agreement as she led Nate to her father's bedside, his head a swathe of bandages and a sickly pallor upon his face in the lamplight.

Chapter Twenty-One

The following morning Nate rose with the light, washed and made his way down to breakfast. He had not shaved, having left his razor behind at the ranch, and wore a day's shadow on his face, riding off before the barber's shop opened. He had not slept well, his mind turning over the events of the previous day and his fraught meeting with Alison Hemple. He had not really known what to expect, but the damaged woman who had stood before him made Nate sad and angry.

Nate thought of all the people who had been needlessly killed and whose lives had been damaged by one man's greed – especially the women who had lost husbands on the wagon train and the poor Gilmore girls, and finally Alison, who was hurting mentally as well as physically. Like most western men, he had a deep-seated respect for the women who braved this harsh life and would defend them to the hilt against any who sought to harm them. He felt an anger burning within him as he rode. Until now he had never actively sought conflict, yet Tim Durrant had sent Janus Shaw after him and was now responsible for this ride to hell – whether in search of justice or revenge, he could not tell. He had not felt such anger since the war, when he had lost his senses in the heat of battle, just wanting to kill and keep killing as his friends and comrades died beside him.

With Patch rested and cornfed overnight he was keen to run, and they made good time. It was good country, offering shallow valleys well fed by streams and small pinewoods populating the undulating landscape, clinging to the hills that lined the valleys. It would have been hard work farming and ranching this land, and his heart went out to Gilmore and his family, who had struggled as many small steadings did.

He had ridden this way maybe twice before and started to see familiar signs of cultivation. A haystack built against the oncoming winter stood forlorn in a cut meadow as a last memorial to the Gilmores' dreams of a new life.

He crested a rise and smelled the smoke of a campfire drifting in the air, and Patch's ears twitched as his nostrils flared to whinny a greeting to other horses that he had scented. Nate was aware that he was being watched, sensing rather than seeing the watchers, but he rode on carelessly, not wanting to act suspiciously. The dull report of a rifle shot echoed around the valley and a puff of powder smoke showed the shooter's position. Patch sidled and skittered as the round ricocheted off the scree in front of him, and Nate brought his legs to bear, steadying the stallion. A voice floated out from some pines to the right, followed by the ratcheting sound of a rifle being levered. "Hold it right there, mister."

Nate looked up towards the smoke making no sudden movements. He had been expecting it, but he said nothing and did not react.

"Who are you, and whaddya want?" the harsh voice demanded.

"New hire, boss sent me over," Nate responded, sounding curt and Texan in his speech.

"Come on up slow, we got you covered," the unseen shooter responded.

At least two of them, so where was the other one? Nate asked himself, then he saw a flash of light on metal about twenty yards off to the right, still in the trees. Unseen, he casually slipped the thong off his Police Special in a nonchalant move with his hand still on the reins. As he approached, the two men appeared, each carrying rifles.

"Easy now, fellas, no need to go shootin' me. Like I say, the boss has been hirin' and told me to come and join you at the Gilmore place. This it?" Nate asked in an easy drawl.

"Where you from?" the shooter asked, a tall lanky man with the hard stare of a gunman. His Adam's apple bobbed as he talked, his voice higher than expected.

"Here and there, but right now I'm down from Pecos, where the boss picked me up. Now quit this jawin'. I'm tired and hungry, you got any grub down there?" He nodded, his voice taking on a hard edge.

The two men saw an unshaven man with two guns in rumpled and trail stained clothes, riding a horse that looked as though it had traveled a few miles. Yet still they were unsure. They had been given no notice of any new gun hands and were puzzled by his explanation.

"Boss ain't been to Pecos in a week or so, how'd he find you?" the gangly man asked. The Winchester was still balanced in his hands, though the barrel was off target now, dropping slightly. "And you're comin' from the wrong direction. All the other boys've gone to the Carson place first."

Nate sighed as if irritated, stepped up to stretch his legs, and settled back down again easing his seemingly tired back. His right hand dropped the reins in a continuation of the move and the Colt Police Special flashed outward in a blur of movement, flying in a fast cross draw. It was what Nate always used the smaller pistol for when he would be hindered by sitting astride a horse as he was now, just as Sam had shown him, the right to left movement aiding his aim, shooting first the gangly man, taking him in the chest and neck in a double shot that was so fast it sounded as one. At under twenty feet he could not miss.

The reaction time of the second gunman was slow, lulled by the talk and the cover of his partner's Winchester. By the time he brought his Spencer to bear across his body, Nate's third slug hit him in the shoulder, spinning the man around. Nate let fly twice more, fearing the large Spencer slug at close range which would kill him instantly if he was hit. The bullets drove though the gunman's side, smashing ribs and ripping inwards shredding his chest, killing him instantly and dropping him to the ground.

Nate dismounted and checked that both men were dead, then walked quickly to the edge of the ridge to look down onto what was left of the Gilmore ranch. As he had been told, the barn was still intact and all that remained of the house was the stone chimney and part of the end wall, from which a lean-to had been rigged from the few remaining roof timbers that were charred at the ends. It was from here that the smoke was emerging, and someone was clearly cooking on the fire in the hearth. He also saw two newly dug graves some way to the right of the house.

Keeping back from view he lay down creating hardly any profile and saw a figure emerge from the barn, shielding his eyes against the low sun to look up to the ridge where Nate was hiding. “Pete, Ike? you all right?” the man hollered up the valley.

Nate slipped back and ran to the dead man, pulling off his hat and peeling off his vest. Keeping his head low, he grabbed the Winchester and went back to the ridge, coming into view from the waist up and waving the rifle left to right, signaling he was all right. “Just a trespasser, he’s done for,” he shouted back, hoping his ruse would work. The lone figure below waved and turned to the smoking chimney, seemingly satisfied.

Just one man to contend with, Nate thought. He found the two dead men’s horses tethered in the shade, dumped their bodies across the saddles, tying them to the stirrups and riding out north in a large circle to come upon the barn from the closed end where the barn doors were shut. He cut the two dead men free of their horses in a small copse and left the bodies where they would not easily be found by anyone riding in. Nate gathered the reins and led the two horses off Patch, coming at a quiet walk to the rear of the barn. Here he dismounted, hitched Patch and walked the two remaining horses down the side, hidden from the ruined house. Then, satisfied he could get no closer undetected, he mounted one and led the other. Spurring them forward, he started yelling and fired the dead gunny's rifle into the air. He dropped down in a diving roll just as the startled figure appeared from around the ruined wall, his eyes drawn to the two running horses that flew before him, pistol in hand, tracking their progress and putting his back to Nate, who had risen and stood against the wall ready. He was but ten feet from the stranger and directly behind him. The sound of a hammer coming to full cock was unmistakable. "Drop it, mister. I can't miss from this range!" Nate ordered. The man started to move by instinct, but then Nate's words bit home. "Drop it!" Nate repeated. "I won't ask again."

The pistol hit the ground with a dull thud, and the man raised his hands high. "Knock your hat off and walk three paces forward, slowly," Nate ordered.

The man complied.

"Turn around, keep your hands raised high above your head."

The gunman turned as ordered.

"Unbuckle your gun belt with your left hand and walk to your right, now sit."

The puzzled gunman looked up at him. He was dark skinned, tanned by the sun, and wore a sweat-stained shirt and vest that smelled of wood smoke and cooking.

"Now sit on your hands."

The man sighed, raised his eyebrows and did as he was told. "You sure don't take no chances," he rasped. "What's with the hat?"

"I know that some men in your line of work keep a hideout gun like a Derringer in their hat."

The gunman nodded. "Waal, you ain't no greenhorn, that's for sure, and I can't believe I fell for a trick like that with the horses. Who are you?"

"Nate Carlton."

"Waal I'll be. Your supposed to be dead, old Janus Shaw hisself took care of you, so Tim said."

"Don't believe all you hear. I'm alive and Shaw is dead."

"Mister, you must be hell on wheels if you took Shaw in a fair fight. He was damn fast, all respect to you."

"It was a fair fight. Now who the hell are you and where is Tim Durrant?"

"I'm Dutch Manning, but I don't know no Tim Durrant, only Tim Glasscock. Blond dude about five nine, educated?"

"That'll be him. Where is he?"

"Over at the Carson place, I guess. Don't know when he'll be back," Manning answered blandly.

Nate didn't believe a word he said. Something in his eyes gave him away, the answer was too pat and glib. Which meant just one thing to Nate's mind. Durrant would be here – and soon.

"Say can I get up? My hands are going numb," Manning whined.

Nate came closer, Winchester ready. "Twist and lie on your front."

As Manning sighed and went to do as he was told Nate brought the stock of the rifle down, knocking him cold. When he came to he was outside, trussed up at the back of the barn, ankles to wrists with a loop around his neck that cut tighter every time he tried to wriggle free and a gag in his mouth secured in place by his own dirty bandana.

Nate had rounded up the dead men's horses and taken them to the copse behind the barn. He had given feed and water to Patch, then stabled him in the dark of the cool barn while he ate before moving him to the copse near the other horses. He sat in the shade of the ruined house, drank coffee, ate the stew that was bubbling on the iron stove and waited for what he was sure would come next.

He did not have long to wait. By early afternoon he heard hoofbeats along the plain of the stream from the south as a lone rider appeared through a cutting in the valley side. Nate looked through one of the ruined windows backing up enough to see and not be seen. It was Tim Durrant riding his palomino gelding. Nate slipped back through the rear of the damaged farmhouse, hiding behind the partially burned rear wall as Tim's shadow fell across the house.

"Dutch? Pete? Where are you, boys?" he called out, easing his Smith and Wesson Russian from its holster. He turned his horse, seeing no sign of life except the smoke and the simmering stew, and walked his horse over to the barn, looking around him, wary of any movement. He dismounted at the entrance to the barn, leaving his gelding hitched to the rail outside, every instinct warning him all was not well. By this time the knot around Dutch's neck meant that he could make no movement. His muscles were cramped, and he was semi-conscious.

Tim Durrant moved further inside the barn, his eyes widening in the gloom, seeing nothing but still shadows and checking the stall to find Dutch's horse still there and happily stabled. *Where the hell is everybody?* he wondered, holstering the Russian.

He left the barn walking softly, still not sure what exactly was wrong, blinking as he re-entered the light.

"Howdy, Tim. You're a long way from home," Nate said quietly standing relaxed in the soft afternoon sun some thirty yards from the entrance, balanced easily, one leg slightly forward, hands hanging negligently by his side. He could be wrong about all this, he knew, yet he was taking no chances, filled in by the admission from Dutch Manning that the boss's name was Glasscock.

Tim Durrant almost jumped at the words, and he stopped the reflex action of moving his hand towards his holster.

"Nate, why you're alive! Damn it's good to see you. We thought you were buried in that terrible accident over at Carson Valley." He made to move forward a few paces to shake his hand.

"That's far enough, Tim," Nate said, putting his left hand forward, palm out.

Tim opened his hands. "What do you mean, Nate? What's the matter?" he pleaded innocently.

"Enough, Tim. I know all about it. You arming the Comanches; the raids on the ranches and hiring Janus Shaw to kill me in cahoots with Old Man Randall. Shaw's dead by the way, he told me everything before he died. The game's over."

"You killed Shaw?" Tim asked incredulously.

"I did."

"And Randall?"

"No, he's alive, but he admitted your part in all this," Nate said, continuing his bluff. "But why, Tim? Because of the money, is that what this is all about? The innocent lives lost and ruined just so you could get a ranch of your own? Stirring up trouble at the dance trying to draw me in. It was you that night in the dark with Bull, wasn't it?"

The innocent face before him changed into an expression of twisted hatred and evil: "You have no idea, Carlton, do you? No idea what it's like to be patronized and patted on the head. 'Poor little Timothy, just good for book learning'! My mother nothing more than a high-class whore, selling herself to that man for the price of a decent life back home to keep her place in society. Do you know what it's like to lose everything but your name and be treated like a poor relation? Well Susannah and I do. We hated it and I hated to see my mother act like a kept woman," he spat.

"Actually, I do know what it's like to lose everything," Nate replied. "But I didn't arrange to have families massacred and traded to the Comanches, farms burned and a decent lawman killed. The trouble in the valley, the rustling from your own father. All that, just to fulfill your twisted ambition. How do you sleep at night?"

"Yeah, the great Nate Carlton, forging his career as a trail boss and cattleman. You pious little fool. I nearly broke you, but each time you came back." Durrant shook his head in disgust, hands falling to his sides, opening from clenched fists. Then he changed, shaking his head as he started to laugh, the sound rising to a giggle that was almost manic. "There's the irony, I tried to break you and here you are breaking me!"

Watch him when he laughs, he's fast, Nate, maybe faster than you...

The words came back to Nate and as he started to move, pushing off slightly with his right foot, heading left so that Tim would have to move against the wrist outwards. Nate took his step drawing smoothly in the fluid, effortless motion of a true top gun.

Tim had started to draw as he shouted '*me*', the Russian coming up fast, the hand a blur, clearing the leather in blinding speed, flame blossoming from the shortened 5 inch barrel sounding at the same time as Nate's own .36 Navy. Nate felt a tug at his shoulder but no pain, his own two bullets sounding as one as they took Tim in the chest and stomach and drove him backward, ruining the aim of the second .44 slug that spat wide. Tim gasped and collapsed, dropping to his knees and holding his stomach in agony.

"You're good, damn your eyes, Carlton," he muttered through the pain. "Never going to be taken. I thought I could beat you, no one would believe ... believe I could do it, just a harmless ... dude," Tim croaked.

Nate kicked the Smith & Wesson away and went to Tim's horse. Fetching a water canteen from his saddle and unstopping it, he raised the dying man up to drink, placing the rim at his lips to allow him gentle sips.

Tim coughed, spluttering. "Too late for that. Done for, thank God, never going to jail ... Tell my .... my mother ... tell her I died well ... and tell my father I said to go to Hell ..."

With that he stiffened slightly in pain, pushing back on Nate's supporting arm as the life left his eyes to stare sightlessly up into the sky. Nate closed them with a finger and thumb and laid his head gently back. He looked down at the Smith & Wesson, and he knew that the instinctive alignment wasn't as good as the Colt. He fingered his own Navy with the reassuring grip that fitted naturally into a man's hand, allowing it to point like a finger.

Could I have taken him alive? Nate wondered if he were becoming a cold-blooded killer like so many others. Like Tim Durrant and Janus Shaw. Was the gunman's ego driving him to pit himself against another man's speed? Tim had been fast – too fast for comfort. Durrant and Shaw. Two men he had actively gone to seek out, now both dead. But was it justice or revenge, he questioned himself.

He buried the two dead gunmen in the copse, draped Tim's body over his horse, tied Dutch to his own animal and headed off southeast to the Durrant ranch and an unenviable meeting with Rick and the others.

Chapter Twenty-Two

Halfway there Nate saw a posse of riders cutting across the trail from where the Carson place was located, and as they got closer to him, he saw some were wounded, evidence of the fight they must have had with the hired gunmen at the Carson hideout. Buck himself was at their head with Rick, Benny and Dan riding at his side. Nate was not looking forward to this encounter – even with Macey there to uphold the law.

They pulled up, and Dutch Manning looked wary, clearly frightened for once in his life, wetting his dry lips, knowing what he had helped to do to these people and knowing that they would hang him on the nearest tree given half a chance. As they met, the horses halting and blowing, a tension filled the air. No one knew quite what to say, and it was Macey who filled the void, everyone recognizing Tim Durrant's distinctive Palomino horse.

"Nate, you have trouble?" he asked.

"I did, and it's not good news," Nate answered.

"Tell it," Buck snapped. "'Cause that looks like my boy there draped over his saddle," he said, his voice hoarse.

"It is, Buck, and I'm very sorry. I had no choice. He drew on me as we were talking. He was fast, Buck, unbelievably fast," Nate said, trying to give Buck Durrant something to hang on to by telling him that his son had gone out like a man.

"Who, Tim?" Rick said, surprised. "Fast with a gun?"

"Your father taught him, Ricky, and he went on from there," Nate said calmly. "He said last time we spoke that he was aiming to get better, and he did. If I hadn't been forewarned he'd have had me. But I knew his tell and the gun he was using."

The others looked on puzzled, and he explained until Buck interrupted: "Did he say anything?"

"Yes. He admitted it all, said that he wanted more in so many words and felt ... well he felt as though he didn't fit, like he wanted to prove himself."

"Anything else? His final words, anything?"

Nate hesitated: "He said he was sorry and hoped that you and his mother would forgive him," Nate lied.

Buck Durrant said nothing, but sat astride his horse, his shoulders slumped. Eventually he dismounted and walked over to his son's body, gently ruffling the lank blond hair that hung downwards, tears forming in his eyes. Buck seemed to shrink before them, a broken man.

Nate offered his apologies again and made to move off, leaving Dutch Manning in Sheriff Macey's care. He wanted no more of it and needed the peace of his ranch and the solace that he hoped to find there.

* * *

Three days later Nate had recovered, but dreams of the war and Tim Durrant's face as he died still interrupted his fitful sleep. He rode into town and stopped at Janet's café, then hired a buggy to take Alison out for a picnic. The gesture caused stares and no doubt gossip from some of the busybodies in town, yet he did not care and was determined to make everything as well as he could for the brave rancher's daughter. Others would catch on – especially Clint Straw from the Rocking H who had been to town that day and would no doubt go back and tell the others, hopefully inciting a bit of jealousy and giving Chris the nudge to ask Alison out.

It was a pleasant late fall day and they had sat huddled under blankets by a good fire, talking amiably and endlessly about all and everything. They both felt better when they got back. She told him that her father would make a good recovery but would still carry some of the pain from his wounds. He had been asking after Nate and wanted to see him, but Nate could not yet bring himself to visit the old man. There was still too much pain, too much emotion. He wanted time to heal wounds, both inside and out.

The following day Nate saddled Buck, tying his rod and line onto his saddle. He told the hands and Lily that he was going off fishing for a couple of days. His father had taught him to fly fish in England and it reminded him of those peaceful, treasured times. He rode off to the secret valley that Jas had found, where from different points both men had spotted a wide stream, unspoiled and hopefully full of fish, where he could be at peace and away from the world for a few days. He told them that if he was not back in two days to send out a search party, but as he rode he kept looking backwards, feeling that someone was trailing him after the first two hours. No one seemed to be there, but he could not shake the feeling. Ignoring his instincts, he put it down to imagination and the delayed reaction from the events of the last few days.

Eventually Nate found the secluded entrance that Jas had shown him on his growing map of the ranch, and seeing an overhang he followed the tracks of cattle and wild horses that led to a red rock wall which narrowed to a trail about fifteen feet wide, sheer on both sides. It would not have been easy to find if Jas had not given him directions. He shivered, thinking about the last time he had been nearly buried alive in such a fissure, but pressed on and came out unscathed in the lush valley beyond.

He rode forward, seeing undisturbed pasture verdant in hue. Wild cattle moved on at the strange intrusion and the smell of man, many never having encountered a biped in their lives. Wild horses thundered away, wary of one of their own bringing this strange being to their land. Finding a good spot at a bend in the waterway, Nate rode under tall cedar elms, rising upwards in their majesty to seventy five feet in places on the banks of the broad stream, offering shade against the late fall sun and shadow to entice the fish. Nate unsaddled Buck, lightly hobbled him and set to building a camp as he had done so many times before. With a good fire going, bounded by a hearth of stones and rock, he made up his line and planned nothing more than to laze for the rest of the day in the quiet wooded area with nothing to disturb him. His hat pulled down across his eyes and his saddle for a pillow, he dozed.

But no man ever truly relaxes in the wild with no one to look out for him, and Nate caught Buck's warning, a low nicker and a stamp of his foot that pulled him out of his stupor. He eased the Colt Police Special from its holster, tensed and relaxed his muscles in readiness, showing no outward effort. He exploded into movement, rolling onto his knees, gun arm forward, ready to face whatever was there and take whatever action was necessary. He saw him then, thirty feet away, and it took Nate a couple of seconds to recognize him as the would-be gun hand from the saloon, seemingly so long ago, the boy who wanted to try and outgun Nate. Jimmy, his name was, Nate remembered.

"You young backshooter, trying to sneak up on me and bushwack me!" Nate spat. "I ought to just shoot you now and bury you out here."

"No, Carlton, I never intended to bushwack you." A look of horror came to his face to be thought of as such a man. "I came to challenge you. You're a hard man to track down. I bin waitin' for my time and now you done rode out here I figured it was right. You got some reputation, you know. What with Janus Shaw an' everythin'. Yet I still figure I'm faster than y'all."

Nate released the hammer on the Colt slowly as the young puncher stood empty handed, holding his arms above his head. "You're a stupid young fool. I might have killed you and I've had enough of killing to last me a long time," Nate snapped back at him. Then a thought occurred. "But if you're determined to kill me and prove how fast you are, let's at least have a Last Supper."

"Say what?" Jimmy asked, completely thrown by the invitation.

"Never mind. I've caught some fish and was just about to cook them. You like pan fried trout?"

"Sure do, and I'm damned hungry after trailin' you. But don't you go thinking it's gonna change a thing. We ain't never gonna be amigos," Jimmy said.

"Never crossed my mind," Nate said, deliberately turning his back upon the young puncher, his senses alert for the whisper of steel on leather. He walked back to the fire and set about cooking the trout. As they sat back and ate, picking at the final scraps around the bones of the tasty fish, Nate began probing as to what drove Jimmy.

"Kinda figured I'm right handy with my Colt," he said, self-consciously patting his side. "Reckon I'm faster'n you," he bragged.

Nate took it head on. "You might be. But there's more to it than that. Tell me, did you ever kill a man? I don't mean an Indian or a bad man attacking you, I mean standing in the street, mere feet away, with your mouth going dry, watching his face, looking in his eyes and knowing it's him or you and that only one of you will walk away. Knowing that it could be you as much as him as the Devil drives you, feeling the shakes start, your muscles turning to lead. You ever feel that?

"Because most bad men, most so-called gunfighters were forced into it, often by the war. Killing a man isn't easy, especially when you're feet away, your rifle empty and him charging you, a saber raised or pistol cocked in your face, knowing that you have a split second to live or die, and your pistol goes off. You're lucky this time and you watch the light go out of his eyes, and then there's another man to be killed, and so it goes on until you become sick to your stomach. Because for everyone you kill a little bit of you dies with him. And it stays with you and you can never pass it back. And I've just said more to you than I've said to any other man since the war, so listen to me.

"That's how most gunfighters are made. Oh sure, they find they have a good natural skill, and they practice, they hone that skill until it becomes second nature. Then one day it comes on them again, that split second to live or die, and because they've killed before, it comes easily and gets easier. Is that what you want?"

Jimmy was dumbfounded. He had never been spoken to like this before; he had figured it would be all glory and dueling like knights of old. Now he was faced with the harsh reality. He fell back upon bravado. "I still reckon I'm faster'n you."

"And like I said, you could be. But to stand there and give no tell, few can do that even in poker. To stand and draw, shoot and kill; fewer still can do that and most that can are hardened by war, circumstances or some kind of evil that drives them. I don't think you're evil, Jimmy, just misguided. You're just a cowpuncher who is good with a gun, you're no evil killer of men." Nate deliberately turned away once more to clean the pan and plate. Washing them in the stream, he stood and laid them to dry, his back to Jimmy. He knew it was coming, sensed it build in the younger man by dint of experience.

"Carlton!" Jimmy shouted, but Nate was already dropping and turning, as he had with the fir cones. Less than quarter of a second later his Navy was out, hammer back and lined on Jimmy, whose gun had just cleared the leather. Time froze for the young puncher, knowing that if he raised his Colt one fraction of an inch higher he was dead. He waited for the report that he would hear just before the lead ripped into his body.

"Go on, kill me, I deserve it," he said.

"No you don't. Put it back in the holster."

Jimmy did as he was told. "How did you know? I've never seen anything so fast."

"Like I said, there's more to it than being fast on the draw. Now go back to whatever ranch you work for, leave off your gun, and never call out another man again."

Jimmy nodded, saddled his horse and started to ride out, then paused and turned in the saddle. "Mister Carlton, thanks."

Nate tipped his hat and smiled as Jimmy rode away, pinwheeling the Navy as was his habit before slipping it smoothly back into his holster.

Not a cold-blooded killer, Nate, my boy, not a killer, and that's just what your father would have done, he thought.

Afterword

I know that you have over a million choices of books to read. I can't tell you how much it means to me that you choose time to read one of my books.

I really hope that you enjoyed it and that you found it entertaining. If you did, I would appreciate a few more minutes of your time, if I may humbly ask for you to leave a review for other readers who may be trying to select their next reading material.

If for any reason you weren't satisfied with this book please do let me know by emailing me at simon@simonfairfax.com The satisfaction of my readers and feedback are important to me.

Best wishes,
Simon.

About the Author

Simon Fairfax writes in three different genres: International financial thrillers, medieval fiction and classic westerns

He is a former Chartered Surveyor, Editor of an online polo magazine (having played polo for a number of years) and has practiced martial arts, fencing and shooting. He now restores old classic sports cars for fun.

As a lover of crime thrillers and espionage, Simon turned what is seen by others as a dull 9 – 5 job into something that is exciting, and as close to real life as possible, with Rupert Brett, his unwilling hero.

His latest medieval series now has 6 books released in the full series. The first, A Knight and a Spy 1410, is set in a tumultuous time at the English court. It tells the story of Jamie de Grispere, squire in training and his two companions as they fight the French to save Calais, Welsh treason and Scottish revolts.

Details of all his books can be found at www.simonfairfax.com or email him at

simonfairfaxauthor@gmail.com

A Knight and a Spy 1410

A Knight and a Spy 1410

Sir James de Grispere, squire in training, is thrown into a world of treachery, the Hundred Years' War, revolts, battles, the wool trade, piracy and pivotal events.

Medieval history is brought to life in this story of fifteenth century England and thefight for the crown.

Click here to read

A Deadly Deal

A Deadly Deal

The trading floor should be counted in deals not bodies, yet they are mounting in number. Can a dealer trade on his wits and manage to stay alive?

Set in the 80s flowing from London to Italy it features Rupert Brett, a new kind of hero, an ordinary man thrown into extraordinary situations.

Buy A Deadly Deal today to see if Rupert can leverage his only commodity and survive the brutal game of winner takes all?

Click to here to read

Acknowledgments

First of all my great thanks to my editor Perry Iles who helped so much in making my book come alive, my proof reader Charlotte Gledson.

The books I would recommend are:-

Empire of the Summer Moon - S C Gwynn
The Comanche Empire - Pekka Hamalainen

Made in the USA
Middletown, DE
04 March 2026